Bookworm

BY

COOKIE O'GORMAN

BOOKWORM

Copyright © 2023 by Airianna Tauanuu writing as Cookie O'Gorman.

All rights reserved. This book is a work of fiction and any resemblance to any person, living or dead, any place, events or occurrences, is purely coincidental. The characters and story lines are created from the author's imagination or are used fictitiously.

No part of this book may be reproduced, transmitted, downloaded, distributed, stored in or introduced into any information storage and retrieval system, in any form or by any means, whether electronic or mechanical, without express permission of the author, except by a reviewer who may quote brief passages for review purposes.

Cover Design © Cookie O'Gorman. All rights reserved.
Book Formatting by Derek Murphy @CreativeIndie

Ordering Information:
For details on quantity orders for educational or business purposes, please visit the author's website at http://cookieogorman.com.

Bookworm / Cookie O'Gorman. -- 1st ed.
ISBN 978-1-960547-00-2

*To all the book lovers, flower boys,
awesome librarians & hopeless romantics.*

&

To Mom, Pat, and Colleen.

1

Happiness is a choice.

I was pretty sure I read that somewhere on a fortune cookie.

The cookie was both right and wrong. Sometimes it was a choice, but happiness could also be a person or a place or even a book.

That last one was where I most often found my happy.

To me, books were these little pieces of magic created by author-magicians for the purpose of making the world a better place. They created these worlds we could escape to when things got rough, places of refuge, safe spaces to breathe, feel, and imagine. I firmly believed there was a perfect book for everyone.

Even the morose child standing in front of me.

"Hi, I'm Charlotte," I said with a smile.

"Welcome to the Chariot Public Library. What do you like to read?"

The girl rolled her eyes. "Nothing. I hate reading."

"You do?"

"Yes, and I hate you."

"Can I ask why?" I said. "We just met."

She shrugged. "You smile too much."

"Sorry, I can try and tone it down. Is this better?"

"Ugh, it's worse, and this is a total waste of time." She turned her eyes up to her mother. "I'm going back out to the car."

"But Darlene—"

"It's Darkling," the girl cut in. "I've told you that a thousand times, Evelyn."

Her mom winced but gave a forced smile. "I know you don't like your name, honey. But I told you before. I am not calling you that. And it's 'Mom', not Evelyn."

The girl sighed, her gaze moving back to her phone.

Her mom glanced over to me and spoke, the plea clear in her voice. "Can you please recommend something? I just don't understand it," she said. "At her age, I loved reading. I could devour a book a day. I'm not expecting it to go that far, but I have got to get her off that phone."

The young girl continued typing away.

"Sure, can you tell me a little about her likes and dislikes?" I asked then shot her daughter a wink. "Besides me, of course."

I had to give her credit. The girl had one heck

of an eyeroll.

Her mom laid it out for me quickly:

Darlene (AKA Darkling)

12 years old (going on 20)

Favorite color: black; favorite TV show: anything with action, mystery, and/or a supernatural element; favorite book: none; favorite pastime: texting; least favorite pastime: reading (obviously).

Okay, so it wasn't a lot to go on. But I also gathered a few things from observation. As the girl texted, every now and then she'd get a little smile on her face, which meant she might have a crush. I also noticed the stars painted on top of her black nail polish, and the little sticker on her shirt that said "Being normal sucks. I'd rather be a mutant."

I tilted my head and said to her, "You know, I used to hate reading too."

The girl's fingers didn't pause.

"I preferred movies, and besides, there were so many other fun things to do. Plus, the books they required us to read in school sucked."

She finally looked up and crossed her arms.

"Like really sucked," I said. "Depression-inducing tales by men who were either too out of touch to write for normal people or too stuck up to even try."

Her mother frowned, but the girl chuckled.

"Sounds about right," she said. Then she gestured to me, "But then how'd you end up working at a library?"

I grinned. "Well, when I was about your age, I started making my own reading choices. Turns out

I have better taste than the board of education."

"Books are so boring though."

"Not all of them."

"They're depressing like you said."

"Not always," I replied. "Some books can bring you to whole new worlds where there are awesome characters with superpowers and epic battle scenes and even a little romance—if you're into that kind of thing. YA fantasy has some great choices."

After a beat, she shrugged. "That doesn't sound so bad."

"I can give you a couple recommendations if you like," I said. "There's just one catch."

"What?"

"If you love it, you have to come back and tell me."

"And if I hate it?" she said with an arched brow.

I shrugged. "Then I guess you can tell me that too—but you won't hate it. Matching books with readers who will love them is my superpower. It's a librarian's assistant thing."

The girl rolled her eyes again, but I wrote down the book recs for her and her mother, pointed them in the right direction, and a few minutes later, they checked out both books (as well as a few others in the series). As they were leaving Darlene/Darkling was already nose-deep in book one, and her mom turned back to mouth "Thank you" before they left.

"I still don't get how you do it," Casey said in awe.

"Do what?" I said.

"That girl was two seconds away from burning the whole library down, and you converted her in under five minutes."

"Oh that." I smiled and stretched. "What can I say? It's a gift."

Natalia walked over then, pushing the book cart back into place. "We've really got to figure out a better system. Some of those books are heavy," she said, pushing the glasses back onto her face and wiping her brow. "What did I miss?"

"A mysterious stranger walked in," I said with a smile.

Casey nodded. "He was tall, dark, and handsome."

"Oh yes," Natalia said.

"But not too handsome," I put in.

Casey put her hands on her hips with a pout. "Why not?"

"Yeah Lottie," Natalia said, "you never want them to be gorgeous. Why is that again?"

I nearly laughed at their petulant expressions. "Because as everyone knows, if they're too pretty, they usually can't be trusted."

My friends sighed in unison.

"And," I added, "not every one of our imaginary library visitors can be TDH. It's just not believable."

Casey nodded. "True...but this one is. And he has eyes that shine like stars."

"And he can cook," Natalia added.

"And he's a football star."

I laughed. "You and your jocks."

"And," Casey went on undeterred, "he just won the championship."

"So he came here because he wanted...a good book?" Natalia said.

I shook my head, joining in on the fun. "That was his excuse," I said, picturing our mystery visitor in my head. "But he really came to escape the footsteps he heard following him, and—

"—and to celebrate with a quick make-out session in the stacks," Casey said.

"Or a long one," Natalia added, following it up with a suggestive waggle of her brows.

Shaking my head, I said, "You know no one really does that right? Comes here to make out? We would've caught them by now."

Casey and Natalia exchanged a look.

"What?" I asked.

Casey held up a hand. "I've seen several couples playing tonsil hockey in the stacks. Sometimes doing more than that, but they never noticed me. Too preoccupied."

My jaw dropped.

"Same," Natalia said, and my eyes shot to hers in surprise. "It's actually a pretty common occurrence."

"You're joking," I said.

"Nope," Casey said. "Happens all the time—especially in the ancient history section."

With a nod, Natalia added, "Oh yeah, those books may be old, but they see a lot of play, if you know what I mean."

I was both horrified and incredibly curious.

"Why didn't you guys tell me about this?" I asked.

"It's kind of a rite of passage," Natalia said.

Casey nodded. "You can't really consider yourself a true employee—"

"—volunteer," I cut in.

"—until you've walked in on your first bookish hook-up."

Honestly, I was still kinda shocked. There were people, *real* people, who came to the library of all places to have illicit trysts among the shelves? Where all the books could see? If what my friends were saying was true, the library was a prime hook-up spot. Who knew?

But they were acting like it was no big deal, so I just said, "Oh cool. What do you do when it happens? Do you just step in there and say, 'Hey, you kids. No kissing on my watch'?"

Casey grinned. "I usually just sit back and enjoy the show."

When I gasped, she chuckled.

"Don't look so surprised, Lottie." She giggled again at my scandalized expression. "I bet you'd do the same. I mean, how awkward would it be to interrupt?"

She had a point, but...

"Yeah," Natalia said, "plus, it's kind of romantic. Don't you think?"

Our eyes shifted to her, and a blush stole up her cheeks.

"The library is a romantic place," I agreed, "and I'm all for romance. I'm just surprised people are good with that level of PDA. And around all the books?"

Natalia sighed, and Casey lifted a brow as if to say, *That's kind of the point.*

Okay, okay, so I could definitely see how it might be fun...terribly romantic even...I was already secretly imagining my first kiss happening in a library setting, the ultimate haven for books and book lovers alike—though the ancient history section was a no-go. Give me fiction, preferably romance with plenty of swoony bits.

"I think she's seeing the upside," Casey commented.

"Who wouldn't?" Natalia gave another dreamy sigh then said, "Don't worry, Lottie. It's only a matter of time."

Not sure if she was referring to me catching people hooking up or my current un-kissed state, I shook myself out of it and made a non-committal noise in the back of my throat.

"Why ancient history?" I asked.

The question had been rolling around in my head.

Natalia thought it over. "It's probably because that section is out of the way. Kinda dark back there too."

"Or maybe they have some weird fetish about hooking up near kings and queens who all died gruesome deaths," Casey replied. "Maybe we should get that Darkling girl back and ask her."

I couldn't help but laugh at that. "She was a cool kid. Bet she's going to love the books."

Casey scoffed.

"Hey, that was the highlight of my day," I said.

"The girl told you she hates you because you smile too much," she said back.

I'd opened my mouth, a reply on the tip of my tongue, when the bell above the door trilled, announcing a new visitor. I smiled as I would for any new customer. Unfortunately, it was someone who really did hate me. And he never tried to hide it.

Ugh, why did he always have to come in?

This was the absolute worst part of my day.

"And here comes the best part of my day," Casey murmured, eyes bright and her lips pulling up in a beatific smile.

"You have a boyfriend," I reminded her under my breath.

"That doesn't mean I'm blind," she murmured back. "And I'm looking for you."

"Bo Stryker?" I scoffed softly. "Yeah, right. We're different as night and day—I'm day, obviously."

"And he could be your knight in a tight, fitted t-shirt."

"Nice wordplay, but not in a million years," I said, staring at Bo beneath my lashes. The guy *was* gorgeous. I could admit that despite our history. The broad shoulders, the pretty-yet-stern face (which somehow made him even more attractive, ugh), the deep voice...life was so unfair. My grumpy next-door-neighbor hadn't looked our way yet, thank goodness. I wouldn't give him the satisfaction of seeing me ogle him. "It's the muscles isn't it?" I said.

"Or the hard chiseled jaw," Natalia said.

"He *is* pretty, like a member of a K-Pop band."

"Or Batman," she said.

I bit back a grin because I could totally see it.

"Those dark, intense eyes, that sexy frown..."

"Can frowns be sexy?" I asked.

"It's everything," Casey said back then called out,

"How's it going, Bo? Wasn't sure we'd see you."

I shook my head as he changed trajectory, walking toward us with that slow, confident gait.

Bo Stryker stopped at the counter, and I could feel his piercing stare on the top of my head, though I hadn't looked up yet.

"Hey Bo," Natalia said, and out of the corner of my eye, I saw her twinkle her fingers in a wave.

"Hey," he said back, his voice deep and rolling, like thunder. "What were you girls talking about?"

Casey grinned. "Nothing much. I was just reminding Lottie about the tween who came in. This girl said she hated Lottie 'cause she smiles too much. Do you believe that?"

There was no response.

I could still feel that stare though, so after a moment, I pasted on a bright expression and looked up—right into the severe, unsmiling face of Chariot High School's #1 soccer player and grump. Bo studied me a second longer then said...

"Yeah, I can see that."

It took all my willpower, but I forced my smile to stay put and made my voice extra cheery.

"Ha ha," I said. "You're so funny, Stryker."

His frown didn't budge. "Wasn't trying to be funny, Kent."

Why, oh why, did he have to be so serious all the time?

"Does your face hurt at the end of the day?"

"Does yours?" I snapped back, and his eyes gleamed. If I didn't know better, I'd say he was amused. But that couldn't be right. Bo always kept his emotions on lockdown. Recomposing myself as my friends laughed softly, I said, "Do you need something? We got a brand new batch of books in if you wanted to check something out."

Bo cocked his head. "What do you recommend?"

I answered with a bright grin. "Well, I—"

"On second thought, I'll choose my own," he said. "I know what I want."

"Oh?"

"Yeah," he said, pushing a sheet of paper across the desk, a slight grin appearing on his lips. That little tilt made me nervous. "Can you show me where to find Liv Lamoreaux's books?"

"Liv Lamoreaux," I repeated.

"Yeah."

"You know she writes romance, right?"

He shrugged those big shoulders then crossed his arms. "What's with the judgy tone?"

"Oh," I said, holding up a hand, "no judgment at all. I love romance."

"Figures," he grumbled.

Unable to help my blush, I added, "I'm just surprised you do. There's a lot of heat in those books, you know."

A grunt was his only response.

But it was true. Lamoreaux wrote steamy, passion-filled romantic stories. I'd enjoyed more than a few of them myself. And maybe it was a bit judgy, but I just couldn't picture the icy, no-laughs-ever Bo reading romcoms about sexy cowboys/billionaires/bad boys and the fierce women who bring them to their knees.

When Bo first started coming in with his little

lists of steamy books, I thought he was doing it just to fluster me. I still kind of thought that, but...it had been months, and he really did check out a lot of romance—especially for a teenage boy.

"You gonna show me where the books are or what?" he said in that deep voice.

I closed my eyes on a sigh. "We've discussed this, Bo. You know where the fiction section is."

"I'm not sure I remember," Bo said.

I narrowed my eyes at him. "You're enjoying this way too much."

"Am I?"

"If you want someone to show you where these specific books are, I'm sure one of my colleagues would be more than willing to help," I said.

Natalia was just beginning to nod when Bo shook his head.

"Or you know, you could go there by yourself," I suggested.

"I want you, Kent."

Those words did strange things to me, made my stomach flutter and heart flip, as did his lips which were once again turned down at the corners.

Well.

That answered that question.

Frowns could indeed be sexy.

Such was the case with Bo Stryker.

His frown was sexy and so were his words—even if I knew I was taking them completely out of context.

But I had to resist at all costs. Because again, the guy was my enemy. Always had been. Always would be. Hence the stern frown and merciless teasing.

"It's a big library," he added. "I might get lost."

Bo lifted a brow, giving me his patented glare.

"Isn't it your job to help people?"

"Fine," I said. With a sigh, still smiling for all I was worth, I moved around the counter. "But we both know you know your way around. You never check out anything except romance and horticulture anyway. The fact that you work at the flower shop across the street is honestly adorable."

His jaw ticked in what looked like a mix of annoyance and amusement.

"Nice of you to notice," he said. "I didn't know you paid attention to my reading habits."

"I don't—"

"Good to know you care, Kent." He lifted a brow. "And that you think I'm adorable."

Gah, he was annoying.

Before I could say anything back, the bell above the door announced another visitor. This time it was Addison DuPont, a girl from our senior class, one I was pretty sure had the hots for Bo.

"Bo baby, I've been looking all over for you," she said and took his hand. "Come on, we need to have an important chat."

Bo grumbled something but allowed her to pull him along. Either that or she was packing superhuman strength. As I watched them walk away, a real smile ate up my face—thank you, Addison—until I turned to my friends. The conspiratorial looks on their faces couldn't mean anything good.

"What?" I said.

Casey gestured to where the couple had just retreated.

As I followed her gaze, I realized they'd gone to...the ancient history section.

Oh no.

"Looks like you'll get your chance to break up a make-out session after all," Casey said with a grin. "Or watch."

"Can't one of you just—"

"Nope," Casey intoned, cutting me off. "This is your time, Lottie. Embrace your destiny."

I went to protest again, but Natalia gave me a somber salute. "Good luck, my friend. May his kissing skills be as glorious as they are in my head."

Forcing a laugh, I turned and began walking toward the stacks.

As if I cared about his kissing skills.

Bo Stryker was seriously the worst.

2

I didn't know what I expected.

I'd already decided there would be no watching. I wasn't some kind of voyeur despite what Casey said—and if I'd occasionally ogled Bo and found that little scar on his jaw distracting, that didn't mean I wanted to make the transition into full-on stalker.

As a hopeless romantic, I was also against interrupting any form of romantic interaction. My plan was to just check things out, make sure no books were injured in the course of...whatever...and then leave.

But as I drew closer, Addison's words surprised me.

"Why are you being like this?" she said.

"Like what?" Bo replied.

"This," she said, and when I caught sight of

them, they weren't locked at the lips or doing anything else risqué. There was a huge gap between their bodies. Addison stood facing Bo, the two of them as far apart as the library aisle would allow. I stopped one aisle away and could only see the back of Addison's head and Bo's face.

Predictably, he was frowning.

"You act like we barely know each other," Addison said.

"That's because it's true," Bo said back.

"But that's what I'm saying. We totally could," she said, stepping toward him. "You'd like me, Bo. Everybody does—well, everybody with good taste."

Addison put her hand against his chest and tilted her head back.

"Don't you want to get to know me?"

She leaned up, but Bo turned his head.

Addison laughed it off. "Can't you just kiss me like a normal guy?"

Bo sniffed.

"And would it kill you to smile once in a while?"

"It might," he said.

I nearly gave myself away by laughing but smothered the sound just in time. Addison groaned in exasperation, not getting the joke, but Bo's head jerked my way as if he'd heard. I prayed he wouldn't see me peering through the gap in books—but Addison put her fingers on his chin, turning his head and attention back to her.

"You know, Bo, I don't get it," she said. "You're so cold and unfeeling. You're like a freaking robot."

Bo stared at her impassively.

"You're also selfish. All you seem to care about is soccer and working at that dumb flower shop."

"It's not dumb," he muttered.

Addison simply shook her head, sighed, and then took a step back. "We could've had a good time, you and me."

Bo said nothing as she took another step back.

"Just so you know, there's an ongoing bet at school to see who can get you to break that icy façade," she said and tossed her hair back. "It's the only reason I'm here. I wanted to win so bad, rub it in the other girls' faces. But no one's that hot."

Addison waited a beat then delivered her last parting shot.

"You're a heartless jerk, Bo Stryker. I doubt any girl will ever want you for real."

Oof, I thought. Even I felt that one, but Bo didn't flinch.

With a huff, Addison walked away, passing my hiding spot without ever noticing me. Bo was still standing there when I looked back. He was looking to where Addison had just disappeared. I was about to go when suddenly there was movement.

Bo's face changed. The iciness melted away, cracks appearing, brow drooping until he just looked tired...and hurt.

I couldn't believe what I was seeing.

A deep sigh escaped his lips. He lifted a hand to rub at the back of his neck as he shook his head, tilted it back, and closed his eyes.

It was a very vulnerable position.

A captivating moment.

I must've leaned forward, drawn to this show of real emotion, because somehow, I dislodged a book with my hip.

As it thudded against the floor, Bo's eyes opened.

And landed right on me.

My own eyes widened, heart thumping wildly in my chest, as our gazes caught and held. I was so busted. Fight or flight kicked in, and I did the only thing I could.

I ran.

Hiding in the staff room probably wasn't the most mature way to handle the situation. But it saved me from having to face Bo again right after witnessing his moment of weakness. A moment I had no business being a part of. I should've left. I shouldn't have listened to his and Addison's conversation. Jeez, what was wrong with me? So what if now I knew the iceman had feelings. It was wrong, and I knew it. I didn't come out until the girls assured me he was gone.

But if I thought that would be the end of it, I was wrong.

So wrong.

#

"You enjoy spying on people, Kent?"

I nearly jumped at the sound of his voice.

Taking a deep breath, I slowly closed my locker door—and looked up into the eyes of Bo Stryker.

I hadn't even heard him approach. He was obviously light on his feet—which was saying something because Bo was a big guy. I'd been avoiding him all day. Literally, this morning when I was leaving the house, I pretended not to hear him call my name from next door and sped out before he could flag me down. I could've been listening to earbuds, right? Then at school, I'd surreptitiously checked around corners before walking the halls, hoping to avoid exactly this. But now, Bo was standing with one shoulder pressed against the locker beside mine, his brow furrowed.

"Why are you smiling?" he asked.

"A smile is an excellent way to improve an awkward situation," I said. "Or at least, that's what I read once."

Bo's jaw ticked.

Gripping my books to my chest, I added, "It may also be a defense mechanism. I laugh at inappropriate times, smile when I'm nervous. That kind of thing."

"I make you nervous," he said.

"One hundred percent," I said back. There was no use lying. My cheeks were starting to hurt I was smiling so hard.

Bo, on the other hand, looked like he was gritting his teeth. Then he asked, "So, you ever going to answer my first question?"

I looked up, feigning thought. "What was it again? As I age, I find that I'm super forgetful, so..."

"You, spying on me at the library," Bo said.

"Ah that," I murmured. "I can explain."

He waited.

"There's a really good reason for what happened. I'm sure you'll find it hilarious."

"Stop stalling, Kent."

Alright then.

"I was checking to make sure you and Addison weren't up to any shenanigans," I said. At his look of confusion, I cleared my throat. "By shenanigans, of course I mean, making out, hooking up, having relations, or as they say in Britain, snogging."

Bo's lips twitched. "I see. So, you wanted to see me snogging?"

"No, absolutely not." I gave my head a vehement shake. "As a library volunteer, we have certain duties. One of them, apparently, is making sure no one's getting busy in the stacks. In my defense, I only recently discovered this was a thing. I had every intention of leaving once I assessed the situation."

"And how long did you stand there?" he asked.

"Not long," I said quickly.

Bo's brows lifted. "Your voice just went up a notch."

"It did?"

"Hmmm," he said. "I call B.S."

Jeez, was he a human lie detector or something?

Putting a hand on my hip, I said, "Okay, I heard some stuff. Only enough to get the gist of the situation. And I've got to say Addison was harsh. I mean, sure you're a little frosty and closed off—"

Bo's lips pinched, and I hurried on.

"—but you're not a robot. That's just absurd."

I shook my head.

"If anything, you're more like a disgruntled koala bear."

His glare only grew.

"And the flower shop is awesome," I went on. "I know I've never been inside, but the outside is so lovely, vibrant, and whimsical. I'm sure the interior is just as fantastic."

"Sounds like you heard a lot," he said.

"Not really"—I held up a hand—"though I confess, I knew nothing about the bet. Me, being a senior, I felt a little left out. But gossip makes me uncomfortable, so I avoid it at all costs." I tried but was unable to stop my last words. "Ooh, and obviously, she was wrong about no one wanting you.

Everyone has a soulmate. Even you, Stryker."

"Even me," he repeated.

I gave him a reassuring nod.

"Are you training to be a detective?" he asked.

The question caught me by surprise.

"No," I said slowly.

"Good," he said, "because you'd suck at it."

I laughed lightly. "Yeah right, I'd be awesome. I've read all the Nancy Drew novels, seen every episode of *Murder She Wrote*, and can figure out the ending of any movie mystery or NCIS episode within the first five minutes. I'm basically Sherlock Holmes in female form."

I tilted my head.

"Lottie Holmes has a nice ring to it."

Bo's frown deepened. "Am I supposed to be impressed?"

I shrugged. "Maybe."

"*Maybe* I would be if you hadn't revealed yourself by dropping a book and then running away."

"I didn't run," I huffed.

"You stomped around like a hippopotamus in the dark."

"Again, I didn't run—and if I had, it would've been softly, like a dainty owl."

"You ran." Bo straightened from his position and crossed his arms. "But I guess I can understand why."

I sighed in relief, thinking I'd gotten through to him. "You do?"

"Yeah. I've had girls stalk me before, Kent. But this is taking it to a whole other level."

My jaw dropped as I sputtered.

Without another word, Bo started walking down the hall, tossing his bookbag over his shoulder. His long legs ate up the distance—at six-foot-something, the guy had at least a good foot on me—but I tried to keep up with him.

"I wasn't stalking you," I hissed.

"You sure?"

"Yes."

"Let's look at the facts, Kent," he said, still walking at that quick pace, his stupid long legs forcing me to jog to keep up. "You followed to see if I was making out with someone" he said.

"Yeah, but—"

"You clearly saw there were no shenanigans between Addison and me."

"Can you slow down?"

"And yet you stood there, being nosy, listening to our entire conversation—"

"Well—"

"—like it was one of your romcoms."

"I wouldn't say—"

As we got to the school exit, Bo stopped suddenly and turned to face me. Startled, I came to a halt too, glad for the reprieve.

"I guess I should be flattered," he said, "that a girl like you would stalk me."

"No," I said, trying to lighten the mood, "if anything, Stryker, you should be flattered about that bet. Must be cool knowing so many people desire you and want to be the one who finally breaks through. In books, that kind of thing always leads to happily-ever-after."

Bo just shook his head.

"This is my life," he said. "Not a book."

"I know," I said. "And seriously, I'm sorry. I'm sorry for following you and invading your privacy. I really am—but you didn't even give me a chance to get to the apology part."

His next words were anything but flattering.

"Apology accepted," Bo said, "but maybe you should stop reading romance. Go out there and find your own."

I swallowed thickly.

"Just a suggestion, Kent."

"Maybe I will," I retorted.

His eyes gleamed in challenge, and I tried to match it—though I suspected we both knew it was a lie.

As I watched Bo leave, I had the strongest sensation to call him back, to tell him I was a freaking catch. I was Charlotte Louisa Kent, bookworm extraordinaire, mediocre violinist, lover of helping people, hater of being cold, and hopeless-yet-hopeful romantic. Any guy or girl would be lucky to have me stalk them (though I definitely wasn't doing that). Unfortunately, though, I did end up trailing behind his black truck on the way home. My sister Scarlett had something after school, so I was riding solo. Turning off the main road, I tried taking the long way at one point, but Bo and I somehow ended up pulling into our driveways at the same time. Our car doors even slammed in unison upon our exits. I winced at the sound.

Being next-door-neighbors with someone you wanted to avoid sucked.

Bo did something then that he never did.

"Hey Kent," he called just as I got to my door.

"Yeah?" I said in surprise and turned to face him.

Bo was still standing beside his truck.

"I know you're dying to see me make out with someone, but we discussed this. You gotta stop following me."

Though his voice was serious, I saw the twitch at the corner of his mouth.

It made my own lips turn up.

"Maybe you're the one following me," I said with a flip of my hair. "See you around, Stryker."

Though hopefully not anytime soon, I thought.

There was a lot for me to unpack. Walking into the house, our conversation played out again in my head. Bo's words rang through me.

Maybe you should stop reading romance. Go out

COOKIE O'GORMAN

there and find your own.

3

Okay, so I was never going to stop reading romance altogether.

That was just ridiculous.

But as much as I hated to admit it, what Bo said had some merit.

Maybe I should begin actively looking for my HEA.

I'd been putting it off for a while, waiting for something to happen, a meet-cute that gave new meaning to the word swoon, but there were a few problems with that.

1) Anxiety.

I got anxious and tongue-tied around guys, especially ones I found attractive—well, except my grumpy-yet-hot next-door-neighbor, who I couldn't seem to shut up around. I'd have to examine that later. Maybe it was because Bo annoyed me so much I forgot to be nervous.

2) Fear of the unknown.

It may have sounded like the title of a Tom Clancy novel. But seriously, I was afraid of what I didn't know—which was basically everything. First base, second base, all the bases were an as-yet-unlived mystery to me. My cluelessness plus the guy-induced anxiety made every interaction feel like a minefield.

3) Readerly expectations.

This one went without saying. All romance readers had high expectations based on fictional worlds, and I was no different. I had imagined how my first kiss would go a million different ways. All of them were amazing—even though I knew from the girls at work, typically, first kisses were awkward. Still, romance novels had set the bar higher than high. I knew it could never be Julie Anne Long-novel good, but maybe my first kiss could at least be memorable?

4) Fate.

Waiting on fate to make a move was how I ended up here: 17, about to graduate, and never been kissed. Hmmm...maybe fate wasn't my biggest fan—or maybe she was just waiting for me to be ready.

5) Mixed feelings.

Honestly, I wasn't sure if I *was* ready—or if I ever would be. Books really gave me all the romance I could ever need. Love in real life was too complicated. In books, you always got a guaranteed HEA. In life, I knew that rule didn't apply. My mother didn't teach me much before she left, but she had taught me that. Was I willing to risk it? Risk my heart?

I'd already made a list of possible love interests.

Whether or not I would approach any of them was still in question.

I chewed on the Twizzler in my mouth, debating.

I'd just swallowed the last of the red sugary goodness when movement outside my window drew my eye.

Bo.

I checked my watch, and yep. He was right on time.

The fact that I couldn't look away grated on my nerves—as did the fact that I knew his routine at all. Ugh. But it never changed. He appeared like clockwork, every day, 24/7. I reached for another Twizzler.

The guy did all his exercises in the driveway.

Which was in public.

And also just happened to be directly across from my bedroom window.

I knew I shouldn't look—but gah, it was impossible to ignore.

First came the warm-up.

He'd roll his shoulders, crack his neck from side to side, jog a bit, then he'd move onto the soccer ball. It traveled effortlessly between his feet, changing directions as if it were a part of him. He'd do this for a good five minutes.

Then he did some high knees.

Running in place was never my thing. Actually, running in general wasn't either, but Bo must've enjoyed it.

Next up, punches (four of them) and a kick, multiple reps.

And then, the grand finale.

My favorite exercise: Pushups.

Bo made those look easy too. He'd get down into position, holding himself up with those strong arms and hands. Then he'd lower his body to the ground...and come up again...then down...and up...and down...

"Man, he's strong," I murmured.

"Lotte, are you watching Bo Stryker again?"

I nearly fell out of my chair, choking on my Twizzler when it went down the wrong pipe.

My sister Scarlett rolled her eyes as she watched me struggle.

"Seriously, you've got to stop doing that," she said.

"Seriously," I said once I could speak, "you've got to learn to knock."

She shrugged. "The door was open."

"You could've at least tried to help, Scar, jeez. Ever heard of the Heimlich? I could've died."

"Death by Twizzler," she said drily, walking farther into the room and crossing her arms, "what a tragic way to go."

I laughed, couldn't help it, and took in her perfectly coordinated ensemble and gorgeous hair. Scarlett was the perfectionist of the family, always put together, always prepared, never caught unawares by anything. Like me, she didn't have much romantic experience. Unlike me, it was because she thought romance was overrated and preferred to stay focused on her 4.0 GPA, college admissions, and her five-year plan.

"You're supposed to take me to school early today," she said, running a hand down her already smooth mahogany hair. "I'm meeting with the counselor to discuss scholarship opportunities and my mentoring program."

Oh yes, and she also had a heart of gold.

I might just hate her if I didn't love her more than life itself.

"No worries, Scar," I said. "I didn't forget. I was just about to come get you."

"But then you got distracted by tall, dark, and broody."

Frowning, I shook my head. "You know I'm more into nice guys who are soft and cuddly."

Scarlett sighed then looked past me with a grin.

"He is sorta nice to look at though."

Following her gaze, I watched as Bo completed one last pushup and jumped to his feet. "That may be true, baby sister. But he's also sorta rude, and he hates me, so..."

"I don't think he hates you," she said.

But of course, she didn't know about our talk the other day—the one where Bo called me out for eavesdropping on him and a lady friend. If he didn't hate me before, he definitely did now.

Pushing any leftover guilt aside, I stood and gathered my things. I went to grab my list, but my sister got there first.

"What's this?" she asked, picking up and skimming the paper.

"A list of possible suitors," I said.

"How very efficient of you, Charlotte. I thought lists were my thing."

Laughing, I gently pushed her toward the door, snagging my bag on the way. "I guess you're rubbing off on me."

Scarlett and I walked into the kitchen where we found our dad doing a crossword. His job as a software developer allowed him to telework most days, so he was still in his pajama pants and tee shirt. Dad looked up and smiled.

"There are my girls," he said. "What do you have planned for today?"

"The usual," I said with a grin. "Going to try and

be the rainbow in someone's cloud."

"You're always that for me, Charlotte," Dad said then switched his gaze to my sister. "And you, Scarlett?"

"Nothing much," she said while grabbing an apple. "Lotte made a list of suitors, so I was thinking I might try and help her with that."

I cut my eyes at her. "You're officially my least favorite ever. Congratulations, Scar. That slot used to be reserved for the devil."

"Hey now," Dad chuckled, stepping in between us, "let's leave the fire and brimstone out of this, and maybe count to ten. I'm fine with my offspring finding suitors—"

Scarlett and I exchanged a look.

"—so long as I get to meet them first," he finished.

"Okay, we're going to be late," I said, moving to the door.

"We'll also need to have the talk, of course."

"What talk?" Scarlett asked, and I sighed.

"I'm glad you asked, Scarlett. We haven't actually needed to discuss this since you've never shown an interest in dating."

"Romance is a distraction," she said. "Who needs love when you've got goals?"

Dad nodded like that was the smartest thing ever. "You should listen to your sister, Charlotte."

"I try," I said sweetly, "but it's so hard to hear

past the betrayal."

"Ugh," Scarlett said. "You're so dramatic."

"Just wait. You haven't heard 'the talk' yet," I warned. To Dad, I added, "And hey, I never expressed an interest in dating either."

"Until now," Scarlett said.

I gaped at her, unsure whether to laugh or strangle her.

"Charlotte, come on," Dad said. "You may have never said anything. But this whole house is full of your romance novels, and on movie nights, you always pick a chick flick. Far as dating goes, I knew it was only a matter of time."

"So, what's the talk?" Scarlett asked.

"Ah, yes." Dad's smile turned menacing as he cracked his knuckles. "I was referring to the talk about how if anyone ever hurts one of my girls, they'll end up six feet under. I'd enlist your uncles' help. The Kent Brothers made a pact long ago. They'd never find the body."

"That's...terrible, Dad," Scarlett said.

"Oh don't worry, sweetheart," he said. "That's the beauty of having the talk beforehand. If the boy's smart, we won't have any issues."

Ushering my surprised sister out the door, I shook my head.

"Thanks for the pep talk, Dad," I called back. "Love you!"

"You're welcome," he said, waving to us. "I'll fine

tune the talk before meeting any of your suitors, Charlotte."

"Love you, Dad," Scarlett said then looked to me. "He sounded serious."

"Pretty sure he was," I said.

We both laughed it off. Dad was acting like a diabolical villain, but he was a softie at heart. There were five Kent Brothers—Dad being the oldest—but I couldn't imagine them making some weird pact. 'The talk' was just Dad's way of dealing with us, his two girls, growing up.

Once we'd parked in the Chariot High lot, Scarlett passed back my list.

"So what?" she said. "You're just going to talk to these guys and see what happens?"

"I will also be attempting to flirt," I said. "Though it'll probably end in disaster."

"Hmmm, not necessarily."

"There's a good 93.5 percent chance."

"Ah, I give you at least 70-30 odds."

She was being kind, but it was appreciated. Getting out, I met Scarlett at the front of the hood.

"Kind of a short list," she said.

I shrugged. "Quality over quantity, right?"

"Those are some good names."

"Thanks," I said back. "Glad to have your approval."

"Hope you don't mind," she said, "but I added one."

My eyes trailed to the bottom of the list...and I shook my head.

"You forgot a very important suitor," Scarlett said, smiling as she left me standing beside the car.

"Scar, why would you do that?" I said.

"Don't pretend. Neighbor or not, even if you wanted to, you never would've added his name. So, I did it for you."

"How thoughtful," I said.

Scarlett turned back for a moment and met my eyes. "Seriously, good luck, sis."

"Thanks, I'll need it."

Especially if Bo Stryker was suddenly on my list.

#

As the school day progressed, I realized a few things.

First, Bo really was the subject of some bet.

Either that or he'd suddenly become Chariot High's Most Eligible Bachelor overnight. I'd noticed people hitting on him all day. The funny thing was he didn't look pleased about it. Go figure.

Second, as predicted, my flirting skills were non-existent.

And third, there was a problem with my list.

Well, *problems*, as in more than one. A plurality of flaws that I hadn't seen coming. But this was what happened when bookworms tried to bring about their own HEA.

Total chaos.

Number one on my list was my first crush from back in elementary school, Trevor Delonega.

I remembered him as being the smartest kid in our first grade class. He'd always been soft-spoken and willing to share his crayons. He was also pretty cute in a nerdy way—which seemed perfect for me.

Seemed being the important word there.

Here's how everything went down.

It happened between first and second period. After a deep breath, I approached Trevor at his locker and tapped him on the shoulder. He'd turned to me in surprise.

"Hi, Trevor," I said.

"Hi," he said slowly. "Do you need something, Charlotte?"

"Um well..."

"I've gotta run to make it to physics."

"Ooh, I'm sorry."

"For what?"

I shook my head. "I just meant...physics. Yuck, ugh, kill me now. Am I right?"

As I chuckled, he looked at me like I was crazy, and I suddenly remembered that back in the day Trevor was a member of the science club. Heck for all I knew, he still was. He was probably the club president. Awesome start, Charlotte. Insult the subject the guy you're hitting on loves most. Blech.

"Not that physics is the worst thing ever," I hurried on. "I can definitely think of at least...seven other things I dislike more."

"Me too," Trevor said, shutting his locker and turning to face me. "Like a million other things, including small talk, social situations, and parties."

I smiled thinking it was a joke.

By the serious look on Trevor's face, it wasn't.

"So, what's up? Like I said, I should get going."

"Oh it's nothing," I said, attempting not to fidget. *Just ask him if he wants to hang out.* "Again sorry about the physics thing. It just isn't my best subject, so—"

Trevor sighed. "Listen, if you need a tutor, I might be able to work you into my schedule."

"That's not what—"

"No promises though," he cut in. "Like you, a lot of students have trouble with science and math. Girls mostly, which is typical."

"I'm actually awesome at math and every other science besides physics," I said, but he wasn't listening.

"My time is valuable," Trevor went on, looking down at his watch. "I'm on track to be valedictorian. Because of my intellectual prowess, I'm in very high demand."

"I'm sure you are," I murmured.

"You can find my rates online." As the bell rang, he handed me a business card and said, "Gotta go. See you around, Charlotte."

"Bye," I said to his retreating form. He was long gone, but of course that was when I finally found my voice. "I don't like parties much either, and I'm sure I couldn't afford you even if I did need a tutor. Also, the comment about girls being bad at math and science? Completely false and a tad misogynistic."

With a sigh, I crossed him off the list.

Oh well, I thought, shaking it off. That was only my first attempt. It was bound to get better, right?

Onto the next.

4

Number two on my suitor list was Chester Copperfield.

He'd always been so stylish, open, and cool. Much more approachable than Trevor, that's for sure. When I walked up to him between classes, the guy's eyes lit up.

"Lottie Lotte," he said, pulling me into a hug. "I feel like I haven't seen you in forever. Where've you been hiding, girl?"

"Nowhere," I said with a nervous chuckle. "Well, the library mostly."

"I knew it." He pointed at me. "You always loved that place. Hey, thanks again for all your help last year. I definitely wouldn't have passed Algebra 2 without you."

"Yes, you would've," I said—though I had helped

him a lot.

Free of charge.

Take that Trevor.

"This is an interesting ensemble." Chester's eyes swept me from head to toe, taking me in. "Nerd Girl Chic. I dig it."

"Thanks," I said, trying to imagine how I looked in his eyes. My black and pink "Readers Gonna Read" t-shirt was one of my favorites; the zip up hoodie I had wrapped around my waist was for if I got cold; my jeans were fitted yet comfortable; and my shoes were tennies with colorful little books on them.

My hair was pulled up in a messy bun, silver earbobs shining in my ears, and I'd put on light makeup in an effort to look more fresh-faced. It was my version of pulled together.

Chester, on the other hand, looked like he'd stepped straight from the pages of *Vogue*.

Perfectly tousled hair, button-up shirt, plaid vest, fitted slacks, and wing-tipped shoes.

The guy was rocking his look from top to bottom.

"I love your shoes," I said.

"Oh, these old things," he said, pointing a toe. "I got them on sale last summer in Paris."

"Wow," I said then gestured to him. "Actually, I love your whole outfit."

Chester was beaming.

"You always look so nice," I added.

"You're a sweetheart, Lottie. Thanks," he said. "Did you want something?"

I nodded, working up my courage. "Yes," I said. "I wanted to...well, to see if you'd...maybe like to hang out sometime?"

His brow furrowed. "Hang out?" he repeated. "Like outside of a school setting?"

I blushed. "Yes..."

"Was there a specific 'out' you had in mind?" he said.

"Not really," I mumbled.

"Sorry, Lottie, I'm just not really understanding what you're asking me here."

"Oh no, I'm just doing a terrible job of it," I said on a laugh. *What would Chester like to do?* "Maybe we could...I don't know, go shopping together sometime?"

The guy's eyes lit up like Christmas morning.

"Of course!" he said.

"Really?" I said in surprise.

"Yes, oh my gosh," he said with a relieved laugh, waving a hand in front of his face. "I know it sounds super conceited. But at first, I thought you were trying to ask me out—like on a date!—and I was going to have to tell you I already have a boyfriend. Ugh, that would've been so awkward!"

I forced a laugh. "It totally would've been," I said faintly.

"Right?" he said then put his hands on my shoulders. "But I completely understand now."

"You do?"

Chester nodded. "You've come to me seeking fashion advice, and I won't let you down. Between you and me, makeovers are one of my favorite things. And I've wanted to get my hands on you forever!"

"That's so nice," I mumbled.

"Never fear," he said, taking a step back. "You're obviously in need of help."

I tried not to take offense at that.

"Here, take one of my business cards."

I gripped the card he held out to me with numb fingers.

Chester shot me a wink. "You're a friend, Lottie Lott, so I'll do your first consult for free. Just call whenever you're ready."

With one last squeeze of my hands, Chester left, and I glanced down at his card.

"Nice choice of font," I murmured.

Pulling out my list, I marked through another name.

Number three was Harrison Klein.

Harrison and I had been in the same homeroom every year of high school. I'd never actually spoken to him. However, he had a friendly smile. He carried a book around wherever he went. He never took cuts in the lunch line. And he had a car sticker that said *Good People Don't Bend Book Pages*.

"Third time's a charm," I said to myself then walked across the cafeteria to his lunch table.

Harrison was, as usual, reading.

A guy after my own heart.

He must've been very into his book too because he jumped when I put my tray down across from his.

"Hi Harrison," I said. "Mind if I sit with you?"

The guy blinked.

"Harrison?"

"Okay," he said. "Sure. It's not like I own this table or anything."

"Thank you," I said and took the seat across from him. Harrison's gaze had already gone back to his book. "What are you reading?"

Harrison said nothing but held up the book so I could see the cover.

"Ah, Stephen King. Nice."

He grunted in response.

I brought out my own book and placed it on the table, hoping it would further the conversation. But Harrison wasn't even looking.

"Must be good," I remarked.

Another grunt was my only reply.

"I brought this one from home. It's by one of my favorite authors," I said, tapping the book at my side.

Harrison glanced up briefly. "Yeah, I prefer

male authors."

"That's funny," I said. "I've always enjoyed books by women more."

After a few moments, I knew he wasn't going to say anything else, so I cleared my throat.

"Only a few pages in, and I'm hooked already," I said. "It's a romance novel."

Harrison chuckled at that.

"You...don't like romance?" I asked.

"Not really my thing," he said, and I noticed a red flush crawl up his cheeks.

"Maybe you should try it," I said. "I know some people think romance isn't as deep or thought-provoking as some of the other genres, but her characters are so real and relatable. They feel like friends, you know?"

No response.

"I can't wait to get back to it."

Harrison stood, tucked his book under his arm, and gave me that friendly smile. Then he said, "I'll let you get to it then."

I went to protest, but he held up a hand.

"No offense, Charlotte. But I only have so long to read before P.E. We're playing dodgeball today, and I really need this. It gives me an endorphin boost. Understand?"

I did.

Books gave me a natural high too.

I couldn't fault Harrison for wanting the same

thing—especially if it'd help him get through one of the worst, most sadistic games ever adopted by the educational system.

"I completely understand," I said seriously. "Sorry for taking up your time by flirting with you."

Harrison's face scrunched up. "Is that what this was?"

I nodded.

"Huh. Well, bye, Charlotte."

"Later, Harrison."

Pulling out my list again, I crossed his name off and realized I was now down to two.

Before I could get too down about it, though, Scarlett dropped into the seat Harrison had just vacated. Her smile was full of curiosity and mischief.

"Sooo?" she said. "How goes the man hunt?"

I laughed. "Not sure I'd call it that, Scar."

"Okay. How goes the suitor search?"

"Much better. Bonus points for alliteration," I said then sighed. "And as predicted, it went awful."

Scarlett smiled. "Come on, it couldn't have been that bad."

"And yet, it was."

"Tell me everything," she said, folding her hands. "Spill the tea. Spare no details, then I can assure you it wasn't nearly as bad as you thought."

I told her.

By the end, Scarlett's face was caught

somewhere between a grin and a grimace.

"I can't believe it," she said.

"Which part?" I asked. "The part where Trevor assumed I'm bad at science because I'm a girl."

"Physics isn't your strong suit," she commented.

"Thanks for the support, sis," I said.

Scarlett shrugged. "I love you too much to lie."

Rolling my eyes, I said, "Or was the unbelievable part where Chester ended up having a boyfriend and offered to give me a makeover?"

"Nah," she said. "I can totally believe Copperfield would have a boyfriend or girlfriend. He's a total catch."

"Yeah," I said. "Just not for me."

"Are you going to take him up on the makeover?"

"Still thinking about it."

"If you don't, can I?" she asked.

I shook my head. "Like you need it. You've always been fashionable without even trying. It's one of the many reasons I'd dislike you if you weren't my sister."

Scarlett huffed, pretending to be offended, but she ruined it by grinning.

"Or can you not believe that two bookworms—romance-hating Harrison and I—didn't hit it off?"

"None of those," she said.

I lifted a brow in question.

"I can't believe two of them already have

business cards," she said. "I've now made a mental note to get my own."

I elbowed her in the ribs.

"Hey! Like it didn't cross your mind?"

It totally had.

When Scarlett raised her brows, I said, "I may have considered the layout, colors, and font for my own cards. As a librarian's assistant, they could come in handy, obviously. But that's not the point."

"What is the point?" Scarlett asked.

"The point is I suck at this."

With a sigh, I bent at the waist, burying my head between my crossed arms.

"Did you expect everything to be perfect?"

I took a page from Harrison's book and merely grunted.

"Seriously, Lotte, don't be so hard on yourself." Scarlett lowered her voice then said, "I'm not trying to be mean, but you know next to nothing about flirtation or talking to guys. I don't either. There's always a leaning curve when you're trying something new, right?"

I mumbled something incoherent.

"What was that?" she asked.

"I said"—I lifted my face—"I studied before today."

Scarlett's eyes narrowed. "You studied? What does that even mean?"

With a huff of exasperation, I threw up my

hands. "What do you think, Scar? I did some research. I read every article I could find on 'how to talk to guys', 'how to flirt', 'flirting with your crush', 'how be less awkward', 'connecting with your crush', 'attracting a mate', 'the mating habits of teenage boys'—"

She smothered a laugh as I looked at her. "You actually searched the mating habits of teenage boys?" she asked.

"Yes, and?" I demanded.

"Nothing," she said. "Bet that search turned up some interesting results."

"It did actually"—I winced—"and I will forever be scarred by some of the disturbing images. Again though, not the point."

Scarlett took a moment then got her giggling under control.

"Scar, I really prepped for this," I said. "But when it came time, everything went right out of my brain. Even with all of my second-hand romantic training via books...nothing helped. I was still a disaster."

My sister shook her head. "You weren't, Lotte. You were brave, and that counts for something."

I forced a smile. "Tell that to Harrison. He looked pretty freaked out to discover that I'd been trying to flirt with him."

"Ah boo," she said, waving that away. "There are still more names. Who's next on the list?"

I didn't have to look. "Leif George."

"He's on the football team, right?"

"Yep."

"Don't you hate football players on principle?" she asked.

"I kind of do—but Leif is different," I said. "Once in the hall, I dropped my books, and he stopped to help pick them up. Granted he was the one who ran into me. But still."

"That was nice, I guess."

"It was." I smiled for real this time. "But he's absent today, so I can't talk to him."

"You look really happy about that," she remarked.

I hummed. "It's been a long day of flirting. I'm tired now and need a nap."

Scarlett laughed. "So, Leif is next."

"He is," I confirmed.

"And then my pick," she said, clapping her hands with a grin. "Bo is obviously the clear winner, but I hope all goes well with the other guy."

"It would take a miracle for it to go anything but horribly," I said then took a deep breath. "But happiness is a choice. I will not let this get me down."

"Yeah, don't," Scarlett said. "They're just guys."

I nodded.

"And if everything goes south, at least you tried. That's more than most people."

"Thanks for the positive," I said brightly.

"That's what I'm here for." Scarlett and I rose at the same time. "Besides, I hope all the others crash and burn. I'm pulling for Bo. You and he are meant to be."

I scoffed.

"You know I'm right 99 percent of the time."

She was, but... "You're wrong about this," I said.

"Am I?" she said innocently.

I was about to respond, but Scarlett hip-checked me, making me stumble and careen sideways into something.

Correction, someone.

A tall someone with broad shoulders, a firm chest, and large hands. Oh yes, and an undeniably attractive frown.

Karma must really hate me.

5

"Kent," Bo said, helping me right myself.

"Stryker," I said back. My cheeks were burning, and I was trying to forget the way his hard chest felt against my fingertips. As I looked back for my sister, she had disappeared. Coward. "It's such a nice day. Don't you think?"

"I guess."

"Did you know that a jacket like the one you're wearing is perfect for either a sunny afternoon or a slightly overcast one?" I rambled.

"No," he said.

I nodded. "Well, now you do. Ta-ta."

I turned away and closed my eyes. Had I actually just said 'ta-ta' to Bo Stryker? Wonderful, Lottie. Just wonderful.

"Hey wait," Bo said then stepped up to me,

holding something in his hand. "You dropped this."

My eyes widened as they landed on the little yellow note.

"What's it for anyway?"

I snatched my list from him and tucked it quickly into my pocket. "Nothing," I said.

Bo's eyes narrowed.

Before he could say anything else, I waved and got the heck out of there.

Unfortunately, after a few steps, I realized Bo was following.

"Something else on your mind?" I asked.

"Still curious about that list of names," he said.

I tried picking up the pace, but of course, Bo was in peak physical condition. The guy could probably run a 5K in his sleep. He lived and breathed soccer, looked like he could keep this up forever.

"What was all that about, Kent?"

"Like I said, it's nothing." I swallowed. "Don't you have a class to get to?"

"Yeah, psychology. The same one as you," he said.

Ugh.

"You're going the wrong direction by the way."

Double ugh.

Skidding to a stop, I turned to face him. "What?"

"The list," he repeated, giving me his trademark frown and crossing his arms. "I saw my name on there. I want to know what it is."

I shrugged. "Well, what do you think it is?"

"There was no title, so it could be anything."

I tried to mirror his passive expression.

"I saw all guy names, a few of them crossed out," Bo said.

I lifted a brow. "Maybe you're the one training to be a detective."

"Bodyguard actually," he said.

I smiled. "I could definitely see that."

"Was it a hit list?"

I choked on my tongue.

"I know girls sometimes do weird things," Bo said with a grimace. "Make voodoo dolls they stick with pins, crazy stuff."

"It was just a list of names," I said, "and this was your first thought?"

He shrugged. "Second. My first was actually much more grim."

Shaking my head with a laugh, I said, "It's a suitor list, Bo."

"A what?"

"A list I made of possible guys I might like to get to know better." Seeing his look of surprise, I added, "Not that I put your name on there. That was my sister."

Bo's jaw twitched. "The handwriting looked the same to me."

"Well, it wasn't," I said.

"Sure you're not in on that bet?" he asked.

"Absolutely not!"

"It looked like your handwriting."

"The ink isn't even the same color," I said, pulling out the list just to show him. "See?"

Bo squinted at the paper. "Maybe you switched pens."

"You wish," I said, belatedly realizing that he was teasing me. It was hard to tell with Bo. The frown masked a lot of his emotions. "Again, you're on there thanks to my sister, Scarlett. Not for any other reason."

"I see." His eyes lifted to meet mine, and he said, "You took my advice about the romance thing. Good for you."

"I'm trying," I said with a self-deprecating smile.

"So...Leif George?" he said. "Didn't think you'd be into jocks."

"Yeah well," I said, "that's not why I like him. He just seems kind."

Bo grunted at that.

"If my streak holds, I'll strike out with him too. Like I said, it hasn't been going well. Turns out I'm terrible at attracting men, hence the crossed out names."

"Maybe they're the ones striking out with you," he said.

I blinked.

Did he really just...give me a compliment?

Bo tilted his head. "Would've been cooler if it

was a voodoo list."

"Of all the men that wronged me? I'll keep that in mind for next time, Stryker."

I gestured to him.

"So, how's the bet going?" I said, making sure to keep my tone light so he'd know I was joking. "Anyone manage to melt that icy heart of yours?"

Bo's face tightened.

"That bad, huh?"

"Girls keep coming up to me. Trying to get me to talk. One even asked me to, and I quote, hook up." He faked a shiver. "It's a nightmare."

I bit back a laugh. "Sounds horrendous."

"Exactly," he said then ran a hand down his face. "It's like it's open season, and I'm the one being hunted."

"Good luck, Bo. You seem fit," I said, patting his shoulder. "I bet you can outrun them all."

Footsteps sounded, and before I knew it, two girls had joined us.

"Bo Stryker, you are a hard man to find," Elana Rigglesby said then nodded to me. Her eyes went back to him a moment later. "So, I think you're cute. Do you want to go on a date sometime?"

I blinked. Wow, she made that look so easy.

No stuttering or doubt.

Elana just did the thing.

I was impressed.

Bo on the other hand looked very

uncomfortable.

"Why don't you come out with both of us?" Portia Lowe said, grinning as Elana threw her a smirk. "We could all go to the movies or dancing. It'll be so much fun!"

As she reached for him, Bo stepped back, and her brows lifted in surprise.

"Uh...I...no, thank you," he finally said.

I watched it all in wonder. I'd never seen Bo act like that before. He was always so sure of himself.

"Gotta go," he muttered, walking away as the bell rang. "See you, Kent."

"Bye," I said to his back.

"Such a shame," Portia said. "I really wanted to win."

"I know, he's gorgeous but difficult. It wouldn't be a good bet if it was easy," Elana said. "Maybe we should try again? When he's not preoccupied?"

Portia nodded. The two linked arms, and off they went.

Amazing, I thought. They hadn't wallowed in misery after their failed encounter. They just bounced right back as if nothing had happened. Hopefully, I'd be able to do that too.

Two more names on the list.

Really one, but still.

Leif George wasn't here, and I would live to flirt another day.

Maybe I could do this.

Maybe I could talk to a possible suitor and jumpstart my HEA.

And if not, at least no one else would know about it.

#

Nothing fun ever happened on a Wednesday.

It was a slow day at the library and notoriously our least busy time of the week. But this one was doubly so because both my friends had called in sick. Apparently, Casey was taking a mental health day, and Natalia was down with the stomach bug. My boss had gone home early, leaving me to close up since I had a key. That meant I was all alone with the books.

Shelving took no time at all.

There were less returns than usual.

A quiet had descended, and the atmosphere almost reminded me of being inside a church.

A sanctuary.

I absolutely loved it.

I'd been reading for the last twenty minutes, was just getting to a really good part in my book, when the bell above the door tinkled.

Smiling, I used a bookmark to save my place, looked up—and froze.

There, holding out his phone to take what looked like a selfie, was Leif George.

AKA suitor number four.

After the picture, he looked around, seeming lost for a second, until he spotted me, and a slow grin appeared. Leif strode over and leaned one arm against the counter.

"Hey," he said, flashing me a set of pearly white, perfectly straight teeth.

"Hey," I replied.

"That was lame wasn't it?" Leif nodded to the door, raising his phone. "I mean, who takes a picture at the library?"

I'd taken tons of them. In fact, library pictures were one of my favorite things. Mine, other people's, didn't matter. Bookshelves were beautiful.

But I chose to focus on his first question and shook my head. "No, it wasn't."

"Come on, be honest."

"It wasn't lame," I said, trying not to stutter even though his light blue eyes were on me. "Actually, we encourage taking and sharing pics. It helps us get more people to read. Just make sure you tag the Chariot Public Library."

He nodded. "Will do."

I tried not to stare at his gorgeous face, but it was hard.

"I just have a lot of followers," he explained while turning his phone between his fingers. "They're insatiable, so I like to document everything. Which, naturally, includes my first trip to the library."

Leif winked, and I giggled.

Ugh. What the heck, Lottie?

"Can I help you with something?" I said. "Did you want to check out a book?"

"Yeah," he said, opening a note on his phone and showing me. "Do you have this one? I need it for a project that was due today. Forgot to do it, so I'm pulling an all-nighter. Hopefully, Mr. Warshaw won't bite my head off."

"Sure," I said and bent to look beneath the desk. "I actually think I have a copy right...here."

With a flourish, I placed the book on the counter as well as one of our standard forms.

"Just fill out this paperwork for a library card, and you'll be good to go."

Leif heaved a sigh of relief, running his hand through his hair in a way that was just so charming. "Thanks, you're a lifesaver."

"Sure."

As he began filling in the blanks, the bell above the door sounded again.

This time the person who filed inside was a familiar face.

Bo Stryker had a book under his arm, and when he saw who stood in front of me, his gaze grew flinty.

Leif threw a look over his shoulder, flashed a grin at Bo, then said, "Hey, Iceman. Didn't expect to see you here."

Bo just said, "Hey."

"Is the library one of your main hangouts? You go here to pick up girls or what?"

Stryker stayed silent, and Leif chuckled.

"Ah, that's right. They're the ones thirsty for a taste of you." To me, he mock-whispered, "Chariot High's a pretty big school, but everyone knows the Iceman. He must have some secret because all the girls are after him."

I laughed awkwardly.

"What school do you go to?" Leif asked.

My smiled wavered, but Bo just rolled his eyes.

"That's Charlotte Kent," Bo said, and when he got no reaction, his frown deepened. "She goes to school with us, idiot."

"Ah," Leif said, looking at me again, "sorry. I remember now. You're always carrying around all those books. Charlotte the Bookworm."

I shrugged. "Yep, that's me."

"Sorry again," he said with an apologetic smile.

I was willing to bet that look got him out of tons of trouble.

Leif passed back the paper with his information and twirled the book around in his hands. "Need anything else?"

I was debating in my head.

Should I or shouldn't I?

Leif hadn't remembered my name which stung.

But honestly, why would he?

Sure, we'd had a couple classes together over the years, but we'd never really spent any time together. Maybe he was really bad with faces. Or maybe I just hadn't done anything in high school to be memorable.

Blah.

Maybe it was time to change that now.

Even if Bo Stryker was standing there, hovering in the shadows like a dark storm cloud.

In the end, I decided to just go for it. If Elena, Portia, and a million other girls around the world could do this, so could I.

"Hey," I said after a moment.

Leif was taking another selfie with his book, but at that he looked up.

I couldn't bring myself to say it to his face, so I picked a point over his shoulder and plunged ahead.

"So, I think you're cute," I said in a rush. "And I was wondering if you'd want to go on a date? With me? This weekend?"

After a moment, I shifted my gaze to him—and Leif's mouth was gaping.

"Did you seriously just ask me out?" he said, shaking his head. "At the library? And after I didn't remember your name?"

I blinked as he grinned and raised his phone.

"Okay"—Leif laughed—"that was random and hilarious. I've gotta get this on video. Let's go from when I asked you which school you went to up until the date thing. Say it again just like that. Okay, Charlotte?"

My heart dropped. "You want to record this?" I whispered.

"Yeah, my followers will love it," he said.

Oh fudge.

He wanted to share this?

With his followers?

To forever memorialize my humiliation online?

This couldn't be happening.

"They eat this stuff up," he continued, fiddling with his phone. "Nerdy girl asks the clueless jock for a date. Priceless. I'm almost ready to record."

Honestly, I was a happy-go-lucky person.

I could see the bright side of just about any situation.

But this was too much.

I was about to tell Leif he could stick his phone and his followers where the sun don't shine...when suddenly an arm fell over my shoulder.

Looking up, I saw Bo staring down at me.

His eyes were dark, intense.

There was something in his face that looked determined.

And maybe even the slightest bit hungry.

In the back of my mind, it registered that, at some point, he must've come around the desk.

Technically, only employees were allowed to be

back here. I was just about to tell him that when Bo said...

"You really are an idiot, Leif."

His eyes stayed on mine.

"Why would she want you when she already has a boyfriend?"

Gentle fingers slid into my hair, his other hand tilted my chin up as he leaned down, and before I could do more than gasp, Bo Stryker was kissing me.

His lips met mine without hesitation.

Confident, slick, soft yet firm.

Bo kissed me like he knew my mouth and wanted to teach me a lesson or two.

And I was more than eager to learn.

When I kissed him back, Bo made a sound deep in his throat. He pulled me closer—or I moved closer because the next thing I knew I was pressed against his chest. Tugging on his neck, I dragged him down to my level, and he deepened the kiss.

My knees suddenly went weak.

I was scared I might fall...

...but Bo was there, lifting me up and up, until my feet left the floor.

Good Lord.

Was this really happening?

Bo nipped at the corner of my mouth, making me gasp, and I knew.

I was kissing my grumpy neighbor and loving every toe-curling second.

Why hadn't I done this sooner?

The sound of the bell over the door made us both freeze, our eyes snapping open.

Bo pulled back, his lips leaving mine as he lowered me back to my feet and straightened to his full height.

He cleared his throat.

I couldn't stop staring at him.

"I think Leif left," Bo said.

My brain was slow to start working again.

"He's a jerk. Don't worry about him."

I wasn't worried. The reality of what happened was just beginning to set in, and as it did, my brow furrowed. Stunned, I thought. That's what I was feeling. Dazed, confused, and just stunned.

Bo was frowning at me. "You okay?" he asked.

I swallowed.

"Kent?"

Finally, I regained the ability to form words, but they definitely weren't the ones I intended to say.

"You...I can't believe you stole my first kiss," I said softly.

Bo tensed.

"You're a thief, Bo Stryker."

As he nodded, turned on stiff legs and walked out of the library, Bo seemed like the one who was dazed. Couldn't blame him really.

That kiss...

It was...

My cheeks reddened, and as I closed up the library, turning off the lights and locking the door, I was still thinking about it. How I got to my car without incident was a mystery. But as I started the drive home, I racked my brain, running through everything that'd happened.

Leif had been about to reject me...but then Bo stepped in.

He'd kissed me, stolen my first kiss, and yeah, maybe I should've been mad about it.

Possibly I should've been furious.

But I wasn't either of those things. I'd always thought Bo didn't like me. I'd thought I felt the same way about him. It felt like up was down and down was up. I didn't know anything anymore, but I knew this.

Bo had given me the best first kiss ever.

And I would always remember that.

6

The after-kiss wasn't what I expected.

I awoke the next morning, surprised to find that my lips still tingled. They felt sensitive too, in the best way possible. It was like it hadn't been hours since *The Kiss*.

Oh, and I kept thinking of it that way.

Not really 'the kiss'.

But *The Kiss*.

Capitalized, bolded, and italicized.

As I went to the window, I told myself it was just to tidy my desk. I often enjoyed reorganizing my books, sometimes by size, color, or trope. But today, what I really wanted was another glimpse of Bo. He showed up like always, same time, same deep frown. He wore a black tee and jeans. I had to admit. The look was doing wonderful things for him.

Although I'd seen his morning workout a million times, I found myself mesmerized.

By the flex of his muscles...

Was that how his forearms looked when they'd been wrapped around me?

The slight sheen of sweat on his neck...

I'd touched him there.

The roll of his shoulders...

My hands had been there too.

I was on my third Twizzler, and Bo had just stood after completing his pushups. That was when he broke with tradition. Bo began walking toward his house—nothing unusual there—but after a few steps, he halted.

I sat up straighter.

In the next moment, Bo turned his head and looked over his shoulder.

Right at my window.

With a gasp, I shrank back—but I knew he couldn't see me.

My light was off, and the gauzy lavender curtains with yellow sunflowers I loved so much were only open the slightest bit. Just enough so that I could gaze at him. I did that now, watched as he kept staring, his face unreadable. After a moment (during which I may or may not have held my breath), Bo shook his head, turned, and went back inside.

I exhaled.

Maybe I wasn't the only one who kept reliving *The Kiss*. Had Bo stayed up all night, mentally rehashing every detail over and over?

The romantic in me insisted it must be true.

You couldn't just kiss someone and go back to normal.

Right?

Except...as I got to school that day, Bo treated me the same.

Or actually, that wasn't totally accurate.

Bo's behavior was strange. If I didn't know better, I'd even say he was actively ignoring me.

Bo being Bo—straightforward, no B.S., blunt usually to the point of rudeness—I'd expected at least a conversation. I'd thought he would, I don't know, meet me at my locker again or approach me in the halls.

But that didn't happen.

He'd had a ton of chances too.

Bo was near my locker when I went to exchange my books.

Not a word was spoken.

He was leaning against the wall outside my third period.

But he must've been waiting for someone else since he completely ignored me.

I'd also seen him standing close to where I usually sat in the lunchroom.

Again, nothing.

We had psychology together for goodness sake, but when he and I got to the door at the same time, we both stopped. I looked up at him, giving him a smile, waiting for him to say something, anything, to just look at me. But he never did. In fact, he was making a valiant effort to look anywhere else.

"Fancy meeting you here," I joked.

When it became clear he wasn't going to respond, I nodded.

"Message received," I muttered and walked past him.

So.

Bo didn't want to talk about *The Kiss*.

He wanted to pretend as if it never happened.

I could do that.

I could.

Even if he was my first.

Even if I could still feel the press of his mouth against mine.

This was Bo's way of brushing me off. In my beloved historical romance novels, they would've called his behavior "snubbing" or "giving the cut direct." Bo Stryker had snubbed me. He wanted nothing more to do with me or my lips. Well, fine. I may have had limited romantic experience, but I could take a hint.

Throughout the day, though, I kept getting the oddest feeling.

Like Bo's eyes were on me.

If it wasn't for Scarlett, I would've thought I was going crazy.

"Why does Bo Stryker keep looking at you?" she'd asked, meeting me at my locker after the last bell rang.

"What?" I said, heart fluttering at the sound of his name. "He's not looking at me."

"Well, he was," she said. "I caught him giving you this intense look at lunch."

She had?

"Did something happen between you two?"

"Nope, nada, nothing, nope."

Scarlett's eyes filled with suspicion. "You're smiling super hard right now."

"Of course, I am," I said, shutting my locker and turning to face her. "That's because I'm so excited about work today. We're getting ready for our Friends of the Library event. It's going to be book-tastic! Book-tacular! B-amazing?"

"You're acting strange," she said thoughtfully. "But that's normal for you. I liked book-tastic the best."

I nodded. "Great."

As we walked out to the car, Scarlett patted me on the shoulder. "I'm sure you'll tell me all about Bo when you're ready. Otherwise, I'll be left to imagine"—her lips tipped up in a grin—"and you know my mind isn't nearly as PG-13 as yours."

"Hey, I have R-rated thoughts!"

"Do you?"

"Sometimes," I said.

She released a laugh. "Let me guess. You dream of being ravished in the library?"

Cheeks pink, trying desperately not to think of how close she'd come to the truth without realizing it, I pulled my books tighter to my chest and sniffed. "I do not."

Scarlett bumped my shoulder with hers. "Try to sound a little more convincing next time. Maybe then I'll believe you. Also, you know I was kidding, right?"

"Yeah," I said then lifted a brow at her. "Besides, at least I don't have a list of all the romantic acts I'd like to complete before I graduate, including but not limited to: handholding, kissing, cuddling—"

Scarlett's eyes widened as she placed a hand over my mouth, glancing around. "Seriously, Lotte? What the heck? My secret list is not up for discussion—especially in public."

I held up my hands in surrender, and she dropped hers back to her side.

"Sorry," I said.

"No, you're not," she grumbled, "but I still love you."

"And I adore you from your awesome lists to your somewhat dirty mind."

She didn't bring up Bo again, thank goodness.

But that didn't stop me from remembering what she'd said about him staring at me.

I wanted her to be right. But I knew it was just wishful thinking. Whenever I'd looked, Bo was directing his frown at someone else. They were girls mostly. He hadn't lied the other day. Bo was getting a lot of attention. Each time I spotted him, a different girl was chatting him up. They were all gorgeous too. I was a firm believer that everyone was beautiful in their own way, and where I had struggled to find even one suitor, Bo could've had his pick. Blonde, brunette, redhead, thick, thin, curvaceous, freckled, tan, black, white, any color under the rainbow, the ladies and gentlemen of Chariot High were taking the challenge that was Bo very seriously.

Funny.

I'd never desired his attention before.

Never thought I'd miss his harsh looks.

But in my gut, I felt the absence of them now.

"Nope," I said to myself. "You are not allowed to miss Bo Stryker's frowns. The guy isn't some kind of fae prince who cast a spell on you. Be a boss about this, Charlotte, and shake him off."

I tried to listen to my own advice, but it was hard—especially when I had to return to the scene of the crime.

I'd been at the library a couple hours, daydreaming on and off about a certain someone, when Casey and Natalia called me out.

"Okay, what's up with you?" Casey asked, putting her hands on her hips.

I blinked. "Huh?"

She held out a hand to my face. "We're brainstorming for the Friends of the Library event—one of your favorite times of year by the way—and you keep getting distracted."

"I'm not," I said.

Natalia cocked her head to the side. "Casey just said we should have shirtless men at the event, painted to look like statues."

"And do you know what you said?" Casey asked.

"Um, it's a family-friendly event, and the library board would never let us do that?" I said.

"No, that's what you would've said had you been paying attention."

"What you said," Natalia added eyes alight, "was, 'Great idea. Very *Bridgerton*-esque.'"

I winced.

"You were also in favor of finally allowing beverages in cups this year rather than making everyone bring a reusable bottle."

"But liquid could get on the books!" I gasped.

Casey nodded. "Exactly! Which is what you say every year, but you didn't this time. Because, as previously stated, your mind was wandering."

"It's also better for the environment," I mumbled.

"You had the dreamiest look on your face," Natalia said.

"Almost like—" Casey's eyes widened. "Charlotte Kent, were you thinking about a guy?" she asked.

I scoffed. "As if."

Casey's smiled got bigger. "You were totally thinking about a guy."

"She was," Natalia agreed, and I shot her a look. "But now, I have so many questions. Who was it?"

"Have we met him?" Casey asked.

"Why are you thinking about him now?"

"Does he play sports?"

"Is he nice?"

Casey sniffed. "Come on, Nat. This is Lottie we're talking about. *Of course*, he's nice."

"You're right," Natalia chuckled. "He's probably all sunshine, sweetness, and sparkles just like her."

I gave a mental laugh at the description.

Bo was definitely more shade, broodiness, and raindrops.

"Wait, wait. Is he real or fictional?" Casey asked suddenly.

Natalia cocked her head. "Good question. Most days, I actually prefer fictional men."

"Same, but I really wanted him to be someone we can meet."

"Me too."

With their eyes on me, I felt the need to

respond but wasn't sure how. *I was thinking about Bo Stryker—you know, the guy who works at the flower shop across the street? The one who comes in, frowns at everybody, and checks out swoony romance books? The one who kissed me breathless the other day when you were both out sick?* Yeah, I definitely wasn't opening that Pandora's box. In the end, I ended up giving an awkward shrug.

"It's okay, Lottie," Casey said and handed me a stack of books. "Why don't you take some time for yourself, maybe read a little? Nat and I will keep coming up with plans for the event."

Natalia smiled. "And when you come back, you can tell us your ideas. You always have the best ones."

Nodding, I eagerly left to complete the task (and escape more questions about Bo). I knew the library like the back of my hand, so locating the right aisles was easy. After that, I went about reshelving each and every book. Making sure the books made it home, placing them back where they belonged, was one of my favorite things. It was my version of therapy. Climbing the library ladder was also something I loved. Even with my five-foot-five frame, it allowed me to reach the highest shelves. I pushed the ladder into position, stepped up to the third rung, and replaced the final book.

A few others had somehow gotten unalphabetized, so I made sure they were in the proper place as well.

Once it was done, I smiled.

There.

Now, everything was perfect.

Contentment settled over me, and I wasn't ready to return to the front desk just yet. So, I took Casey's advice. Still on the ladder, I spotted a romance novel right at eye level, pulled it off the shelf, and opened to chapter one. Reading never failed me. Unlike people, books were reliable; they always provided a welcome escape.

And I needed that now.

As my eyes drifted over the pages, I thumbed through the book and became engrossed in the story.

Lady Sophie and the Duke of Winchester were so deliciously wrong for each other. A once rich heiress turned servant girl out for revenge paired with the man who ruined her family and who might also just be her soulmate? The chemistry was scorching, and the banter fed my soul. Gah, it had everything.

And then I got to the kiss.

A stolen one.

In a library of all places.

Was it really any wonder I began picturing myself as Lady Sophie and Bo as the Duke?

He had always stared at her with contempt, disdain, or even worse, indifference.

But he was not looking at her that way now.

No.

The Duke's eyes were hooded as they took in her flushed cheeks, her red lips, and the flames dancing in her eyes. Sophie could not deny it. She felt that look everywhere.

"Did you like it, Sophie?" he asked in a gravelly voice.

"It was...adequate," she said finally.

"Only adequate?"

As his gaze caressed her lips, Sophie's body betrayed her with a shiver, and he chuckled softly.

"Well then, perhaps I should try again," he said, pulling her to his chest. "Does that sound like a good plan?"

As her hands began stripping him of his cravat, the Duke was the one who shivered.

"If you must," she said primly. "But do try and make more of an impression this time."

"Minx," he growled, lifting her so that her legs wrapped around his waist.

"Rake," she said back.

"You will be mine after this, Lady Sophie."

"Hmmm, or perhaps, you'll be mine. If you are so lucky."

As his lips descended on hers, the fire in the hearth seemed to burn hotter. Sophie could not seem to catch her breath. But strangely, she did not miss breathing. She only needed his lips on hers. His scent filling her lungs. The way his hands molded to her—

"Good book?" a voice said.

Startled and forgetting I was on a ladder, I screeched, wheeled around, and smacked the person standing behind me.

Or rather my book made contact.

The awful smack of book meeting face could probably be heard in the next town over.

"*Oof,*" Bo said as the hardback walloped him in the head, taking him by surprise and knocking him back a couple steps into a bookshelf.

The fact that I'd literally book slapped Bo did nothing to stop my momentum.

I squeaked again.

As my body swayed and my feet scrambled for purchase on the tiny rung to no avail, I accepted my fate.

I was going down.

I'd probably hit my head and fall to my death off this dumb ladder.

But at least, I thought, I'll have died reading a good book.

Those were my thoughts as I began to fall.

And then suddenly, Bo was there.

He moved so fast.

Bo's arms shot out, grabbing my waist and hip, as he pulled me to him. At the same time, he kicked the ladder away, and we kept falling together. It felt like it happened in slow motion. Bo turned us in midair, and as we fell on our sides, I felt Bo's hand get squished under my ...well my butt...and heard him grunt in pain. Once on the ground, Bo rolled us, so I was on top of him, our foreheads close. I was breathing hard from all the panic, but Bo looked cool as a cucumber.

A very grouchy cucumber.

"Oh my gosh," I breathed, bringing my hands up to cover my mouth. "Stryker, are you okay?"

Bo's eyes narrowed. "Am I okay? You just assaulted me with a book, Kent. My face is throbbing like a mother."

"I know, and I'm sorry," I repeated. "So, so sorry."

"Didn't know something so tiny could cause so much damage."

I nodded. "Actually, historically books have been used as weapons. Today, women even carry them around in their purses. It goes right in there with the pepper spray. I read something about that recently."

Bo grumbled, "I wasn't talking about the book."

Oh.

"Again, I truly apologize. I didn't mean to book slap you. It was just...I was reading, and it was so good...and I got startled."

There was an awkward moment of silence, then Bo sighed.

"I came to apologize to you actually," he said.

My brow furrowed. "For what?"

"For what happened yesterday. All that stuff with Leif." Bo cleared his throat. "The kiss."

I stared at him.

"I know you're mad, and you have every right to be," he said. "I should've never done that, stolen your first kiss. I'm sorry, Kent. Been trying to figure out how to say it all day."

"I'm not mad," I said quietly.

Bo's eyes snapped to mine. "You're not? But I thought—"

"That kiss made me feel a lot of things, Stryker. But mad was not one of them." I shook my head, the movement making me realize that yes, I was still on top of him. "It wasn't even in the top 10 emotions."

And oh goodness, now, his lips were turning up on one side. Was that...? Yep, that was definitely a grin. It was Bo Stryker's version of one, tiny, barely there, all lips and no teeth. But it was a grin alright.

"You don't have to look so pleased with yourself," I said.

Bo's frown fell right back into place. "This better?" he asked.

"Yes, it's very you."

As I reached out to touch his cheek, Bo's breath caught.

"Does it hurt?" I asked. "Where the book hit?"

"Not right now," he said in a low voice.

"Hurt anywhere else?"

"Honestly, Kent, all I can think about is the fact that you're on top of me."

I swallowed. Bo's eyes dropped to my neck, tracing the movement. Then our gazes locked. All at once, I realized how close our faces were, how if I leaned down just an inch, and if Bo were to lean up...

A new voice interrupted us before anything else could happen.

Another book slap.

The sky falling.

Me kissing Bo.

"You two okay down there?" Casey asked, and as I looked up, I saw she and Natalia standing there with surprised looks on their faces. "If you're busy, we can come back later."

Correction: surprised and smug.

Fantastic. Casey and Natalia would obviously want details. I barely understood what'd just happened. How the heck was I going to explain this to anyone else? At least, Bo was okay. I hoped.

The look he was giving me was a little less irritable than usual.

Oh bother.

Maybe I'd hit him harder than I thought.

7

Sometimes words weren't enough.

This was definitely one of those times. Accidentally hitting someone with a book (that turned out to be amazing by the way, a total knockout—no pun intended) and falling in a heap on top of them, required a bit more. Though I'd apologized to Bo, I woke up early the next morning to take him a gift, an olive branch if you will, in the form of muffins.

With a side of Twizzlers.

As well as a small bag of peanut M & Ms.

And ginger ale.

Oh, and I also included a hand-made card.

They were all things I loved. I even added a couple of my favorite romance books, knowing how much he seemed to enjoy them if the ones he checked out at the library were anything to go by.

Plus, though he'd said he was fine, I wanted to make sure everything was okay.

I got up early, so I wouldn't risk missing him. Walking over to his house, I rang the Strykers' doorbell at 6:30 AM.

Bo usually did his workout at 6:45, so I figured he'd be up.

Eyes down, I was checking the basket I'd made for him a final time when the door opened.

When I looked up, there was a woman silently staring back at me. Her hair was pulled back in a tight, no-nonsense bun, a few gray strands threaded throughout the black. Wrinkles lined her light tan skin, and her dark, serious eyes seemed to miss nothing. They took in my hair which was down, my smiling face, the clothes I was wearing—including my plaid blue-and-green cardigan, light blue tee, jeans, and chucks—before finally landing on the basket in my hand. The sides of her mouth dipped in a scowl.

The older woman was small, maybe five feet, but she was unnerving.

I'd opened my mouth, but before I could say anything, she shut the door.

Well then.

Gathering my courage, I leaned forward and knocked lightly.

When the door swung open again, her eyes met

mine.

"*Nuguseyo?*" she said.

My smile widened. I knew one day watching all those K-dramas would finally pay off.

"*Annyeong haseyo*," I said. "I don't really speak Korean, but I think you just asked who I am. My name's Charlotte, and I live next door. You can call me Charlotte or Lottie or Lotte—whichever you'd prefer."

"That's a lot of names for one person," the woman said still scowling.

Her English was near perfect. I'd definitely have to work on my Korean.

Shaking my head, I said, "It is! Though one of my uncles has four names, and I have a cousin with five. Guess it runs in the family."

She didn't laugh.

"I basically answer to anything," I added quickly. "It's nice to meet you."

"Why are you here?"

Okay, so she needed a bit more info. No big deal. I loved meeting new people.

"I came by to see Bo," I said.

Her eyes narrowed. "He got beat up."

My face paled, eyes going wide. "What?"

"He got beat up," she said slower this time as if I was hard of hearing and then gestured to her face. "Bo's face is all messed up. He's not taking visitors. You go home now."

"But I—"

"*Ga, ga*! Shoo!"

Okay, if I hadn't understood before, I got it that time. But I still hadn't given Bo his gift.

"I just wanted to—"

She shut the door.

Again.

"—give him this," I finished to no one.

As I turned, the door reopened, and I heard Bo say, "We've been over this, *Halmeoni*. You can't just slam the door on people. It might be important."

That was met by a "hmph."

At least now I knew who she was, I thought. *Halmeoni*, Bo's grandmother, had slammed the door in my face. Twice. Obviously, first impressions were my forte...not.

"Kent?" he said, his voice holding a hint of surprise. "What are you doing here?"

I turned, intending to just give him the basket and run—but then I got a good look at him.

Post-book slap Bo was a sight.

"Oh my gosh," I said, shaking my head in horror as my gaze moved over his face.

Bo frowned. "It's not that bad."

"Not that bad?" I gestured to his cheek. "Your face is all banged up and bruised—"

"Like I said, it's nothing."

"—and you're wearing one of those bandages wrapped around your head."

Bo quickly removed said bandage and cleared his throat. "Uh yeah, I forgot about that. Smacked the back pretty good on a shelf."

"And jeez, what happened to your hand?" I said, registering the black brace covering most of his right forearm. "Did I...*oh God*, did my butt break your hand?"

"No, Kent," he said. "Again, I'm fine. The doctor said I may or may not have a minor concussion"—I gasped—"and sprained wrist. It should be better in a few weeks. The head bandage was just a precaution."

Swallowing, I tried to hold back the tears that were suddenly welling-up in my eyes.

"I told you," the older woman repeated. "He got beat up."

"*Halmeoni*, please," he said.

My eyes moved to meet his, voice soft as a whisper as I said, "I am so sorry, Bo."

"Why're you sorry?" his grandmother said. "You're not responsible."

"Actually," I said miserably, "I am."

Bo's mom joined us then. She was kind and beautiful, and I'd immediately liked her because her name was Snow, but her personality was like a warm blanket; I'd always appreciated the dichotomy. She'd always been nice to me, but now, she looked at me in concern.

"Charlotte?" she said. "Is everything okay? It

feels like forever since we talked."

I shook my head. "No, it's not okay," I said.

"What's going on here?" a new voice asked, and Bo's dad joined the other three in the doorway. Ash Stryker was tall like his son with the same lean torso and broad shoulders. His hair was blond, the exact opposite of Snow's, which was dark brown, and he had an easy smile. Still, Bo looked like both his parents, and his frown was even similar to his tiny grandmother's. Mr. Stryker took in the scene then pointed to my basket. "Hey, Charlotte. What do you have there?"

Taking a deep breath, I said, "It's an apology basket for your son, Mr. Stryker."

"You didn't have to do that, Kent," Bo said.

While Mrs. Stryker said, "That's so sweet," and Mr. Stryker said, "Nice. Are those muffins?"

Bo's grandma just looked on in silence.

"Also, I feel the need to confess," I added.

Bo shook his head, but I plunged ahead.

"Bo didn't get beaten up," I said miserably. "I did that to him. With a book. It was all an accident, but it was my fault, and I feel absolutely terrible."

There was a moment of silence then...

"You did this?" Mrs. Stryker asked. "With a book, you said?"

"Yes, ma'am."

"Were you aiming at his face when it happened?"

"No ma'am," I said. "I was on a library ladder, reading, and when he spoke, it startled me. Then I spun, slapped him with the book, started to fall, and...it just happened so fast."

Bo's grandmother stepped up to him, gestured for him to lean down.

"Is that true?" she asked.

When he nodded, she drew back her hand and knocked him right in the back of the head. I winced along with Bo.

"Why didn't you duck?" she said. "You know how to block."

"It's true, Bo," his mom said. "You've been studying mixed martial arts practically your whole life. When you see something coming, you don't just stand there."

Mr. Stryker put his hands on his hips. "Hey, the kid was faced with a completely unprovoked sneak attack"—at this, he turned to me—"no offense, Charlotte."

"None taken," I said.

"Books can be heavy," he went on, "and I bet he even tried to catch her when she fell. Am I right?"

"I did catch her," Bo said, and Mr. Stryker gave his shoulder a pat.

"That's my boy," he said. "Now, about those muffins—"

"Sugar is bad for you," Bo's grandmother said.

"*Omma*, come on, it's a gift," Mrs. Stryker said

and threw me a smile. "There's nothing wrong with having something sweet now and then."

The older woman sniffed. "Bo's more disciplined than you, Snow. Always has been."

As Mrs. Stryker went to protest, her husband laughed. "You know it's true," he said.

"Ash, you're supposed to have my back," she grumbled.

"I do," he said, laying a kiss on her forehead which made her frown melt away. "I always have your back, ninja girl."

"Stop calling me that," she said, but it didn't sound like she meant it. "Let's go inside and give the kids a minute alone."

"I'll just take this," Mr. Stryker said and grabbed the basket. "You're a nice girl, Charlotte—even if you did hit my son with a book."

I gave him a weak smile.

As they left, Bo's grandmother stayed behind.

Pointing to his face, she said, "You duck next time."

Bo nodded. "I will, *Halmeoni*."

Her finger pointed at me next, and I nearly jumped. She stared at me for a long moment then said, "You're stronger than you look."

With that, she left, and Bo and I stood there in awkward silence.

"Thanks for the basket," he said.

"You're welcome," I mumbled.

"You really didn't have to do anything."

"Yes, I did." I lifted my eyes to his and shook my head. "I'm going to make this up to you, Stryker. I don't know how yet. But I will."

Before he could say more, I held up a hand.

"Enjoy the candy and muffins," I said then turned to walk away. "I'll leave you to your workout."

Bo paused. "How'd you know about my workout?"

Closing my eyes, I gave myself a mental slap.

Ugh.

With a forced smile, I looked back over my shoulder and said, "You had to get those muscles somehow, right?"

"Right," he said slowly. "What *Halmeoni* said was true, you know. I'm on a strict diet. No sweets."

I balked at that.

"But I might make an exception. Since you went to all that trouble."

"I really didn't," I said.

"Looked like you put a lot of effort into that basket, Kent," he said.

"Only a minimal amount"—I shrugged—"see you later, Stryker. Enjoy the extra calories."

I waved, leaving Bo on his doorstep, and went inside, my mind already churning.

Despite my flippant attitude, I was determined to make amends.

Bo may have a slight concussion. His wrist wouldn't get better for another few weeks, and I was responsible. There was nothing for it.

This apology would require more than sweets.

Now, I just had to brainstorm and figure out my next steps.

#

Scarlett wasn't any help.

When I told her about the incident, she started laughing then laugh-crying and didn't stop until we were at school.

"So you book slapped him?" she said finally. "Lotte, I just can't. It's too freaking funny for words. Too bad you didn't capture it on video."

"You're the worst sister ever," I said sweetly. "Now, what should I do?"

Scarlett shrugged. "You already took him the basket, right? He accepted and said it was fine."

"Yeah, but can't you see? It's not. The scales are still unbalanced."

She gave me a look.

"Scar," I said, "he gave me the most amazing first kiss."

"Which you neglected to tell me until now," she put in. "And I'm supposedly the bad sister?"

Ignoring her, I went on. "He gave me something priceless. And I gave him a bookcussion and sprained wrist."

"Did you just make up a new word?" she asked.

"Yes," I said and lifted my hands, "it's a mashup of the words book and concussion."

"Makes sense."

"I know, but Scarlett, please. Help me! I really want to help him."

She thought for a moment. "What about more kissing?"

I blinked. "More kissing...are you crazy? Stryker just did that to help me out of a crap situation. I'm sure he still dislikes me as much as he ever did."

She gave me a look, and I couldn't help but remember the way Bo stared at me as we lay on the ground together, our faces only inches apart. But...

"Maybe even more now," I said, "since the whole knocking him out with a book thing."

"Did he lose consciousness?" she asked.

"Well, no."

"Then technically you shouldn't say 'knocked out'. It's confusing and inaccurate. Plus, I think you're just saying it that way to make yourself feel worse. So..."

I rolled my eyes.

"Seriously though, here's my take," she said with a shrug. "If you want to help, the first thing you need to do is figure out what he needs help with."

"Okay," I said.

"And that means you need to do some

research—"

"Love doing research."

"—on Bo Stryker," she finished.

I lifted a brow.

"Which is also one of your favorite subjects." Scarlett winked. "Secretly."

The fact that my sister knew about my totally inconvenient, apparently not-so-secret fascination with Bo wasn't a surprise. Scarlett had always been way too observant. It was one of her more annoying traits.

Still, I couldn't just admit it.

"I don't know what you're talking about," I said.

"You try to resist, but you can't help your interest in him," she said while examining her nails. "And he's probably the same way with you. You're polar opposites. Of course, you'd be curious."

"Gah, you are such a know-it-all."

"Thank you," she said brightly, like it was a compliment.

"But I'll take your advice," I said.

Scarlett's smile widened.

"I'll do some recon on Bo today to see where I can be useful." I exhaled a long breath. "He's bound to need help in some areas."

"Like getting dressed and washing his back?" she said innocently.

"Like," I said unable to hold back a laugh, "I don't know yet. That's what the research is for."

My sister pouted which made me laugh again.

As we entered the school, though, my laughter died out.

Bo was walking down the hall, and I might not have even noticed him (okay, I would've totally noticed him; I always did for some reason), except he was wearing sunglasses indoors. He was also the only thing anyone was talking about. The rumor mill was in full swing.

"I heard he got jumped," someone said.

"Must've been a bunch of them," another voice replied.

"Yeah, Bo's a big guy."

"Could've been a car accident."

"Dude. Look at his face..."

"He used to be so pretty."

"Messed up his wrist too. Hope that doesn't jack up our soccer season."

"I heard a girl did it."

A laugh. "Yeah, right. Bet the other guy looks worse. Iceman is cold, on and off the field. He'd never go down without a fight."

Scarlett gave me a wide-eyed look, mouthed "Wow," then walked off to her first class.

I had to agree.

The rumors were wide-ranging, but none of their guesses were anywhere near the truth.

While I watched, the book on top of Bo's stack wobbled, and he had to scramble to right the pile before walking on. Naturally, I thought. His dominant hand was out of commission.

Taking out a notepad, I quickly wrote.

1) *Carry books.*

That was an easy one.

Now, I just had to follow Bo all day without him realizing and figure out more places and ways I could be of assistance.

Let the research begin.

8

It turned out I was an excellent sleuth.

Even though I kept tabs on Bo during school, he didn't seem to suspect a thing. There were a few times when he glanced over his shoulder—but I simply ducked around a corner or, when a hiding spot wasn't present, I laughed out loud and pretended to be talking to someone.

Not gonna lie.

I got a lot of strange looks.

But that was fine because my plan had produced results.

Bo's class schedule was different than mine. We only had the one class and lunch together. However, with the help of Ms. Deidre, the school's office assistant who loved me and my sister like we were her own, I was able to request Bo's schedule.

"Of course! Anything for you, Lottie," she'd said with a smile. "How's your dad doing?"

"He's good, Ms. Deidre. I'll tell him you said hi."

She nodded. "I still remember when Leo and his brothers went here. They basically ran the school. They were loveable but a bit rowdy. Not picture-perfect students like you and your sister, Scarlett."

I shot her a wink. "You should see us at the Kent family reunions. It can get a little crazy."

"I'll bet you all have a good time."

"We do—though I'm not a big fan of playing violin in public," I said. "But I also love it because the music gives me an excuse to catch up with my cousins."

"You're a sweetheart, Lottie," she said then tapped the paper that came out of the printer with Bo's schedule. "Now, what did you say you need this for again?"

"Bo's injured, so I'm going to help him until he's better," I explained.

"Uh-huh. And the school nurse told you to do this?"

I shrugged, giving her my best and brightest of-course-you-can-trust-me smile.

"You're not spying on another student are you?" she asked.

I swallowed, not wanting to lie to her but also knowing that schedule would help me a lot.

"Well...I...um..."

Deidre just laughed. "I'm kidding, dear. Here you go."

"Thank you so much," I said in relief and took the paper gratefully. "I owe you one."

"No, you don't," she said, a Cheshire cat grin appearing on her lips. "I was young once too, you know. I understand what it's like to have a crush."

"It's not like that," I stuttered.

She nodded in understanding but ruined it with a wink. "Sure, it's not."

I got out of that office as quickly as I could.

Having Bo's schedule made it that much easier to determine where he'd be and therefore see what he might need. He was pretty self-sufficient. But his wrist was obviously bothering him. As Bo walked between classes, there weren't many instances, but I did notice him fumble his books a time or two. I underlined my first list item for emphasis.

Bo also struggled to open his locker with his left hand.

It took him five tries.

He scowled menacingly at the lock—though that was basically his default expression.

At lunch, he didn't seem to have any problems. No bobbles, and he was able to easily eat everything in his sack-o-lunch. This included mostly vegetables and fruit: carrots, broccoli, celery, a block of cheese, an apple, and two sandwiches filled with some kind of meat. No dessert at all. Hmmm, maybe he'd been serious about the no sweets thing.

I couldn't imagine life without chocolate.

It just did not compute.

So, I chose to believe that maybe Bo had forgotten his dessert at home or was saving it for later.

I fully intended on offering him my notes for psychology. There was really nothing I could do about the classes we didn't have together. But I hoped he'd be able to get notes from someone else or record the lessons on his phone.

After school, Bo had soccer practice. I'd never actually gone to a game, never saw him play in person. And I didn't get to that day either. When I arrived at the field, I noticed him sitting on the bench, looking crankier than he had all day. A few other students sat in the bleachers watching practice, so I took a seat and made myself comfortable. My ball cap and large sunglasses were in place. I was the slightest bit nervous that Bo might look back and see me.

But his eyes were glued to the action on the field.

Just in case, I pulled out a book, pretending to be into it.

My gaze kept getting drawn back to Bo.

His face, though cranky, held something else I

hadn't noticed at first. A wistfulness, like he wanted to be out there more than anything.

"It's so sad," Heather Patel said. "The team is nothing without Bo."

Darren Minter nodded. "Yeah, Chariot's going to have a heck of time if he doesn't play."

"I heard he's only sitting out one practice," Antonio Mulroney put in. "Because of the concussion and all."

I winced.

"He should be good to go on game day."

Heather shook her head. "It's a good thing Bo's dad is head coach. He wouldn't make him sit out, knowing how much this means to him."

"I've heard Coach Stryker can be stubborn," Antonio said.

"He'll let Bo play," Darren replied. "He has to."

"I hope so." Heather sighed. "Bo looks pissed, more so than usual."

"Nah, he always looks like that."

The three of them chuckled, and I turned back to Bo.

He did look more sullen than usual. It would take a whole cheer squad to lift that guy's spirits, I thought. With a nod, I added another item to the list.

Cheer Bo up. Go to games.

I didn't stay for the whole practice. I had to get home and drop off my things before driving to the library early. There was something I needed to do before my shift started. Having watched Bo today, it struck me that possibly the best way I could help him was at the flower shop. I knew next to nothing about gardening. I wasn't a green thumb by any means. But I could learn.

And I would.

I just had to get hired first.

Instead of going straight to the library, after I parked, I got out of my car and walked across the street. *Mrs. Lee's Flower Shop* had a sign featuring pink cursive font set against a white background along with a pink and green awning. Beneath that, there was a shaded space with two chairs. The store window had original painted artwork every few weeks. Honestly, the whole setup was inviting, welcoming. As I stepped through the door, a chime sounded, and I was immediately surrounded by the smell of fresh flowers.

My eyes closed involuntarily to breathe it in.

The air was so fresh.

So pure.

As I exhaled, I felt my shoulders relax.

I opened my eyes and looked around, noting the colorful flower displays, walls painted a calming shade of light mint green, cream tiled floor, several mismatched yet somehow complementary chairs lining the small seating area. The curved archway behind the counter was lined with flowers as well. It was charming and gorgeous, and I regretted not having come here sooner.

"Be with you in a minute," a voice said from the back.

I was still taking it all in when a woman appeared.

Her lips had been tipped up at the corners, not quite a smile, but not a frown either.

Until she saw me.

"Oh," Bo's grandmother said, her lips turning down. "It's you."

I was thrown. I definitely hadn't expected to see her here, but there was nothing to do but smile and brazen it out.

"Hello again," I said.

"You want to buy some flowers?"

Walking up to the counter, I shook my head. "Not today but thank you. This is a beautiful shop."

She nodded.

"It's been here all this time," I said. "I see it when I go to work at the library but never come in. It's like a whole other world here, a magical one. I half expect to see fairies and sprites flying around."

Bo's grandmother simply stared me down.

Obviously not a fantasy lover then.

"Um...if it wouldn't be too much trouble, can I please talk to the owner?" I asked.

Her face didn't budge. "I am the owner."

Of course.

"That's awesome," I said with a nervous chuckle. "Women owned businesses rock."

"Yes," she said and crossed her arms. "Did you need something, Charlotte, Lottie, Lotte?"

I gave her a nod. "I was hoping you might hire me."

Her brow slowly arched, so I hurried on.

"Because of what happened to Bo"—I felt my cheeks heat—"I wanted to help out. Help him, I mean. Just until his wrist gets better."

I swallowed.

"And I wouldn't want or need to be paid. This would be purely on a volunteer basis."

"You would work for free?" she asked.

"Absolutely!" I said. "This is to repay a debt, make amends. It wouldn't be right if I was getting paid."

"But you said you already work at the library."

"Yes, but I can decrease my hours."

"Weekends? They're our busiest time."

I nodded. "I'll work those too."

The older woman gave me an intense, searching look. "Does Bo know you're here? Did you discuss this arrangement with him?"

Shaking my head, I said, "No, ma'am, and I don't think he'll want to accept my help. But too bad."

I lifted my chin higher.

"Your grandson isn't my biggest fan, but I'm determined to see this through. He'll just have to deal with my presence. Whether he likes it or not."

It could've been a trick of the light, but I thought I saw her mouth twitch, amusement shining from her eyes.

"So...what do you say?" I asked.

I waited for her to throw me out.

To tell me "shoo" again like she had this morning.

But she surprised me.

"Okay," she said.

I blinked. "Okay?"

"Yes, you're hired." Holding up a hand, she eyed me down. "But I expect hard work, one hundred percent effort."

I nodded.

"You'll take this job seriously. No being late, no fooling around. Do you understand?"

"Yes, ma'am," I said. "You have my word."

Her eyes stared into mine as she stated, "And you will call me Mrs. Lee. Not 'ma'am'."

I grinned. "What about Boss? Or Boss Lady?"

When she didn't smile back, I waved that away.

"Never mind, Mrs. Lee," I said, moving quickly to the door before she could change her mind. "I'll be the most dedicated worker you've ever had. You won't regret this. I promise."

"We'll see," she said. "You start tomorrow. 8:00

AM sharp."

"You got it. Thank you so much again. Have a good day, Mrs. Lee."

I waited to celebrate until I was safely back outside. I'd done it. I had gotten the job at the flower shop and followed Bo around all day and avoided detection. I'd also made the list currently in my pocket of all the ways I intended on helping him. Walking across the street, my fist-pump/happy dance was interrupted when a deep voice spoke out of the blue.

"Why have you been following me?"

I stumbled to a halt.

Bo Stryker leaned against the trunk of my car as if he owned it.

The frown on his face remained as I stared back at him like a kid caught with her hand in the cookie jar.

"Kent?" he prompted.

"I haven't been following—" At his look of disbelief, I said, "Fine. I did follow you today. Happy?"

"To hear you admit to something I already knew? I'm ecstatic."

Tilting my head, I asked, "When did you know?"

Bo pushed off of my car and came over to me. "The whole time. I can always sense when someone's tailing me."

"Yeah, right," I scoffed.

"It's true. Can't you feel it when someone's watching? When they've got eyes on you?"

Only when it's your eyes, I thought.

Ugh. I gave myself a mental slap. Sometimes being a hopeless romantic made you think/hear things differently. I had no idea where the thought came from, but I beat it back with relentless ferocity.

He tilted his head. "Does it have something to do with why you were at my grandmother's flower shop?"

"Yes actually," I said, "she just hired me."

Bo jerked back. "What?"

"I'm volunteering at the flower shop."

His brow furrowed.

"Don't look so upset, Stryker," I said.

"I'm not," he mumbled. "Just wondering what you said to get *Halmeoni* to hire you."

"I told her the truth." I gave him a shrug. "I'm going to help you while your hand gets better."

"No, you're not."

"Yes, I am," I countered. "I owe you, and a Kent always pays their debts."

"What are you a character from *Game of Thrones*?" he snarked.

"No," I said, "and if I was in a book, it would definitely be one of the following: a cheesy romcom where I'm the heroine—or more likely the heroine's loveable best friend—a cozy mystery where I'm the loveable detective, or an urban fantasy where I'm the kickass-yet-loveable MC. Could also be a paranormal romance."

Bo's scowl was so sharp it could cut glass. "Kent, I don't want your help."

"Stryker, I don't care. You've got it." I smiled as he stared me down, taking a step closer. "In fact, I'm going to be so helpful, that when I leave, you're going to wonder how you ever did life without me."

He grunted.

"No, you know what. You're going to miss me."

"Doubtful."

"See you soon, Iceman."

Before he could say another word, I skipped by him and into the library, proud of myself for not getting weak-kneed in the face of his bluster or that sexy frown. This was going to be so much fun.

9

I was wrong.

Fun didn't seem to factor into Mrs. Lee's vocabulary. I was pretty sure she didn't even know the meaning of the word. That was something I found out on day one.

Waking up early on Saturday, no big deal. I was determined to be on time for my first day of work at the flower shop. Driving there, no problem. I'd done it a million times—though I'd taken that route to go to the library. I did get behind a slow-moving bus, but it didn't affect my progress too much. Walking inside the shop, the bell above the door chimed, and I looked at my watch.

Ha. Right on time.

"You're late," Mrs. Lee said, and I snapped my head up. Even more than her words, the stern look on her face told me she was not pleased.

I gulped. "But...I thought you said 8:00 AM?"

"That's when work begins," she said. "You're not ready to work. You still need to put on your uniform."

With a smile, I said, "Oh! I can do that super-fast. No problem."

Mrs. Lee said nothing, just pointed to a small bathroom.

The uniform consisted of a mint green t-shirt sporting the flower shop's logo and a matching ball cap. There were also several aprons and sets of gloves. I changed in record time. When I walked back out, I was bright-eyed and raring to go.

"Where would you like me to start?" I asked.

Her gaze moved to the clock behind my head then came back to my face. "Your shift started five minutes ago."

Cheeks flushing, I gulped once more. "Sorry, Mrs. Lee. It won't happen again."

She said nothing.

Bo walked out of the back room, carrying a big bucket of flowers with one arm. "*Halmeoni*, where do you want these?"

Gesturing with her chin, she said, "Gerber daisies out front. The sunflowers go on that side table."

He nodded, placing the flowers where she indicated, completely ignoring me.

"Stryker," I said as he walked past. "Need any help with those?"

Bo grunted, and I took that as a 'no.'

When he came back out with more flowers, I tried again.

"Looking forward to working with you."

That got me something between a glare and an eyeroll.

Mrs. Lee cleared her throat. "Bo, you show Charlotte-Lottie-Lotte what to do."

"Why?" he said. "She'll only slow me down."

"I'm the boss. You do what I say."

"But *Halmeoni*, I told you I'm fine. We don't need her."

"And I told you, she'll work for free."

"Saturdays are our busiest time with deliveries," he said, keeping his voice calm and rational. "Kent doesn't know anything about flowers. She's a liability."

Mrs. Lee turned to me. "You know nothing about flowers?"

"No," I admitted while cutting my eyes at her grandson, "but I learn fast, and I'm great at customer service. The people who come into the library love me."

Bo scoffed.

"Well, most of them," I amended.

After a beat, Mrs. Lee said, "Bo, you show her."

His grandmother scowled when he went to

protest, and Bo's mouth snapped shut as he frowned back at her. Neither of them blinked. She was so tiny. Bo looked like a giant next to her. Despite myself, I was fascinated, wondering who would win this battle of wills. Just knowing him and his surly nature, I would've put good money on Bo. But after a few seconds, he caved.

"Yes, *Halmeoni*," he said with a sigh.

Mrs. Lee nodded. "She'll come with you on deliveries too."

Bo released another sigh then started walking past me.

"Let's go, Kent," he said.

I followed without a word.

The back of the flower shop was just as magical as the front. There were more flowers here in buckets like the ones Bo had been carrying as well as in little refrigerated glass cases. There were ribbons, baskets, and vases in various colors and shapes. Beautiful didn't cut it. This place was truly otherworldly. I couldn't resist reaching out to gently run my fingertips against some of the petals. They were soft and fragile. As Bo kept walking, and I saw his strong frame settle behind the long table that was obviously used to set up the arrangements, I was struck by how much he didn't fit in here. Like at all.

Bo caught me staring, and I shook myself out of it, quickly walking over to join him.

"What were you thinking just now?" he asked.

I shrugged. "Just that it's kind of odd. You, working at a place like this."

"Odd how?"

"This is such a beautiful, happy place."

"Ah," he said, "and I'm hideous and miserable."

"That's not—"

"It's fine, Kent. I got your meaning."

"Yeah, got it all wrong," I said with a huff. "Jeez, Stryker, all I meant is that this place is full of delicate, cheerful-looking flowers. You're so strong, rugged, and grim all the time. It's unexpected. That's all."

Bo tilted his head. "Rugged?"

"It means muscular or chiseled."

"Oh yeah?"

"Well-built," I added.

"Ah," he said. "So, you think I'm well-built, huh?"

I narrowed my eyes at him. "If I didn't know better, I'd say you were teasing me, Stryker."

"And why would I do that?"

"To throw me off my game," I said.

"You have game?" he asked, sarcasm coloring his tone. "I had no idea."

"Ha ha. Are you ever going to show me what we're doing?"

Instead of answering, Bo studied my face until I began to fidget.

"What?" I asked.

"Just filing it away," he said, and there was definitely a gleam in his eyes. "Charlotte Kent thinks I'm rugged and well-built. That'll feed my ego for a while."

"As if you need it," I mumbled. "And I also said grim. Let's not forget that part."

Bo shrugged his big shoulders like that description didn't bother him one bit.

"Okay," he said, "since you insist on being here even though your assistance is unnecessary *and* unwanted—"

I rolled my eyes.

"—here's what's going to happen. *I* will be cutting the stems off these flowers and then bring them out to the front of the shop. After that, *I* will load the van with the arrangements, most of which have already been put together, and at that point, you will accompany me in the van to make the deliveries. All of which *I* will carry to the door and deliver to the customers."

"Okay, so what do I do?" I asked.

Bo lifted a brow. "Watch."

"Watch?" I repeated.

"Yeah," he said.

"Come on, Stryker. I can do more than that."

"No."

"Why not?"

"Because," he said.

"What's with the one-word responses?" I asked.

Bo stared me down.

"I owe you."

"Wrong."

I shook my head. "Seriously, I'm here to make up for your wrist and the bookcussion."

His face grew curious for a moment, and he crossed his arms. "The what?"

Ha, I thought. At least that was more than one word.

"The book slap that left you possibly concussed. Book plus concussion," I said. "That equals a bookcussion. It's my fault that you're in your current state. You can't just expect me to watch."

Bo's frown only grew.

"Just so you know"—I gestured to his face—"that glare-frown combo doesn't scare me. I've come to think of it as your signature look."

"Kent," he growled.

"Okay," I said with a shrug, trying to exude careless nonchalance. "I'll just sit right here while you do your thing."

Bo looked suspicious at my easy acceptance, but he didn't question it. That was good. That meant my smile covered my true thoughts. I'd perfected the art years ago. It came in extra handy when things got tough. A happy disposition could mask just about anything. But oh, I was having feelings.

Annoyance was one of them, frustration another.

Why couldn't he just accept my help?

Whatever.

If Bo thought I was going to sit back, watch him work and do nothing, he had another thing coming.

I'd watch him alright.

Like a hawk, I'd track his movements, learning his ways, and if he faltered, I'd swoop in to save the freaking day.

"What's that look about?" Bo asked.

I wanted to laugh at his concerned expression. "What look?"

"Like you're planning something."

"Just doing what you said." I smiled. "Ready to watch."

Bo grunted but got down to business. He grabbed a handful of yellow flowers from one of the buckets, shook them out to release the excess water, then placed them on the table, spacing them out just so. Next, he lifted a set of scissors. I could tell it wasn't the easiest thing, using them with his left hand, but Bo took his time, carefully cutting the stems. Next, he removed extra leaves. When he was finished, he placed them back in the bucket. He repeated this process until all of the blooms were about the same height.

To my surprise, I actually enjoyed watching.

He handled the flowers with care, seeming to get lost in the repetition.

"What kind of flowers are those?" I asked.

"Daffodils," he murmured.

"Beautiful."

Bo nodded.

He lifted the container as if it weighed nothing then disappeared to the front of the shop. When he came back, his hands were empty. Bo marked something out on a clipboard hanging from the wall.

"What's that?" I asked.

"A list of tasks and today's deliveries," he said.

"Bet that comes in handy."

"Hmmm."

Bo then moved to one of the glass cases, opened it, and took out an arrangement filled with pink, orange, yellow, and light purple flowers.

"Ooh, those are pretty," I said. "What are they for?"

"I'd have to check the log, but probably a birthday or anniversary gift."

"That's awesome. What kind of flowers are in there?"

He cut his eyes at me.

"Okay, okay," I said, "no need for that look. If you don't know, you could just say so. Sheesh."

"I do know."

"Then what's the problem?"

"Too many questions, Kent," he muttered.

"Sorry," I said. "I was only curious."

Bo sighed. "It's a mix of day lilies, roses, and carnations with some zinnia."

I smiled, though he'd already turned away. They were gorgeous, and wow, Bo really knew his stuff. As he moved to a door that I assumed led to the side of the shop, that was where he encountered a problem.

The door was not one you could push or pull. It had a knob that had to be turned. Instead of asking me for help, Bo just stood there, looking at the door a moment as if it would magically open. He couldn't do it by himself. One of his hands was full, and the other was injured. As I waited, Bo tried to switch the arrangement to his injured arm while opening the door, but his wrist gave, and he nearly dropped the vase of flowers. Bo got his good hand back on it just in time. The boom of the door closing echoed in the space.

"What's that noise?" Mrs. Lee called back.

"Nothing," Bo replied.

"No slamming doors. It's bad for business."

"Yes, *Halmeoni*."

Jumping into action, I jogged over and propped the door open, keeping it from closing with my hip.

Bo lifted a brow. "I thought I told you to watch," he said.

I shrugged. "I did watch, and it was very illuminating. I've graduated to doorstop now."

His face contorted.

"Weren't you going out?" I asked.

Bo shook his head then walked past me. I let

the door close softly once he was back inside.

We continued like that for a while until all of the arrangements had been loaded into the van. There were a good bit of them. 13 by my count. Each one was more beautiful than the last.

"We're going now, *Halmeoni*," Bo said.

"See you later, Mrs. Lee," I called out.

The tiny woman dismissed us with a wave, keeping her head down as she filled out paperwork.

Once outside, Bo and I got into the van.

"Want me to drive?" I asked. "Your wrist—"

"I'm good," he said.

"But your bookcussion—"

"First, can you please stop calling it that? And second, it's been 24-48 hours, so like I said. I'm good."

Bo passed me a clipboard.

"Can you enter the first address into the GPS?" he said.

"Yeah, no problem," I said, trying not to grin too much. "Thank you for finally letting me do something."

Bo mumbled under his breath, but I thought I caught the words, "You wore me down. So many questions."

After entering in the address, I reached for the radio.

"Mind if I play some music?" I asked.

Bo shook his head.

"No, you don't mind? Or no, you don't want me to play anything?"

"You're doing this on purpose," he said.

"Doing what?" I asked innocently.

"Stop."

"But Stryker, I thought you liked my questions."

Bo's frown remained, but I swore I saw amusement flash in his eyes. I considered that a win. With a shrug, I hooked my Bluetooth up to the radio system and started one of my playlists. Bo, surprisingly, didn't complain. In fact, I caught him tapping the steering wheel after a minute. I couldn't hold back my smile.

We arrived at our destination about 20 minutes later. It was a two-story with a nice yard and garden gnomes. After Bo pulled over to the curb and turned off the engine, I turned to give him a look.

"You're not really going to make me wait out here, right?" I asked.

Bo shrugged. "Why not?"

"Because I'm good with people."

"And I'm not?"

"Well..."

"Kent, just sit here. I've got this."

"But I could get heat stroke."

"I'll crack a window."

My eyes narrowed. "You're not funny."

"Then why are you smiling?" he asked.

"It's my default," I said, though yes I did find his

dry, sarcastic sense of humor somewhat hilarious. But right now, I just wanted him to give in. "Stryker, we're a team here."

Bo looked like he was the one who wanted to laugh. Instead, he just scoffed.

"We are," I insisted. "We're partners in the flower trade, a new brand of superheroes bringing people happiness in the shape of bouquets. I've already started calling you Flower Boy in my head."

"Kent, you are so weird."

"All the best people are," I said. "Let's go do this delivery, our first mission together."

Bo was looking at me like he thought I was crazy, but after a second, he nodded.

"Alright, Kent," he said. "We go together."

I fist-pumped.

"But I carry the arrangements," he said, pointing to my face.

"Okay," I agreed.

"You just smile all sunshine-y and get them to sign for the flowers. We're in, and we're out. No muss, no fuss."

"Got it, Flower Boy."

Bo grabbed a ball cap. It was the same as mine except instead of mint green, his was black, and he'd obviously worn it before because it fit him perfectly. The hat shadowed his eyes, making the contours of his cheeks and angular jaw stand out even more. Not gonna lie. It was a very sexy look.

"You ready?" he asked.

I nodded, still entranced. "Yep."

"Is there something wrong?"

"No, why?"

"You're staring."

I forced a laugh. "Was I? It must've been because I'm so excited. To deliver the flowers. Obviously."

Bo's eyes narrowed, and that made him look even more hot.

Ugh, stop this madness.

"I'll meet you out there," I said, quickly getting out of the car.

Bo met me at the hood of the vehicle, and we walked up the driveway to the front door. I rang the doorbell, and we waited. A minute later, the door opened, and I saw a woman in her mid to late 40's. Her hair was in a messy updo, her clothes were rumpled, and her eyes looked a bit tired.

"Yes?" she said.

"Good morning," I said brightly, "I'm Charlotte, and this is Bo. We—"

"If you're here to sell me something, sorry. I don't need a new security system, and I'm not switching religions any time soon. I have three kids who are all home sick with a stomach bug, so I don't really have time to talk."

"Oh no, of course not. We have a delivery here for Jackie Adams. Is that you?"

The woman blinked. "Yeah, that's me."

"Oh yay!"

I held out the clipboard and pen for her signature. "If you'll just sign here...."

After she signed, Bo handed her the flowers. "Here you go," he said. "You'll find a card in the bouquet."

"Oh," Jackie murmured. Her face changed right before our eyes, going from wariness to surprised joy. "I didn't realize...thank you."

I smiled. "Someone obviously loves you very much."

Her happiness was a palpable thing. As she read the card, her eyes got teary. "Ah, my mom. She remembered my birthday—and I nearly forgot." Looking back to us, she said, "Thank you again. This really made my day."

"You're welcome," I said, "and thank you! Happy birthday, and I hope you enjoy your bouquet from *Mrs. Lee's Flower Shop*."

As Bo and I got back in the van, I grinned.

"That was amazing!"

Bo's jaw twitched. "Where's the next address?"

"Entering it now," I said, and then we were off.

On our way to deliver happiness to someone else.

10

"I can't believe that last guy tipped you."

I flashed my teeth at Bo. "Why not? I'm awesome."

He grumbled, "No one does that."

"Well, he did," I said, pulling out my ten-dollar bill and giving it a kiss.

We'd just completed our final delivery of the day and were in the van, driving back to the flower shop. Bo was in the driver's seat, and I was riding shotgun. Despite his surliness, it had been a surprisingly pleasant trip.

"Mr. Willard and I had a good talk," I added. "Did you know he walks to the park every day to feed the birds? He even invited me to go sometime. How sweet is that?"

Bo rolled his eyes.

"What?"

"He was hitting on you," he said.

"Stryker, please. He was like 80-years-old."

"And?"

I paused. "Though now that you mention it, he did say he used to be a ladies man..." Shaking my head, I sniffed as Bo kept his eyes on the road. "You're just mad because I got this little beauty, and you didn't."

I kissed the bill again then stuck it in my pocket.

"Do you know how many germs are on that?" he asked.

I scoffed. "There can't be that many."

"Yeah Kent, there can," he said. "Money is one of the dirtiest items we touch daily."

Crossing my arms, I hmphed.

"Look it up if you don't believe me."

I did believe him.

That was the problem.

I was actually regretting kissing the money as my mind pictured all the hands that'd touched it. Some of them likely unwashed. Ewww. I knew I'd end up brushing my teeth extra tonight even if it wouldn't do any good.

"I'm not looking it up," I muttered.

"Because you know I'm right," he said back.

Bo's voice was smug.

Jerk.

After surreptitiously wiping my mouth with the

back of my hand, I changed the subject.

"So," I said, "which was your favorite delivery?"

Bo was silent a moment then, "I liked the woman who yelled at us."

"Of course, you did." With a shrug, I added, "To be fair, though, Gertrude got nicer after we gave her the flowers. And her dog, that little Yorkie, Sir Lancelot? So stinkin' cute."

He made a noise.

Whether it was one of agreement or disagreement, I couldn't tell.

"It's crazy how you became friends with the customers so fast," Bo muttered.

I felt the corners of my lips tip higher. "Yeah, crazy amazing."

Bo shook his head.

"It's called socializing, Stryker. You should try it."

"I hate most people," he said seriously.

My first thought: Wow, that's bleak.

My second: I hope I'm not one of them.

It was a strange thing, but right when he said it, I realized how much I didn't want Bo to hate me. Because I didn't hate him. Not even a little bit.

"You're quiet," he said. "That's not like you, Kent."

"Just taking a breather," I said with a grin, telling my brain to shut up. "By the way, my favorite delivery was number seven. The Pietros baby shower. They gave us cake."

"They gave *you* cake," Bo corrected.

"Hey, I asked if you wanted any."

He sighed. "I told you. I'm in training. I don't eat that stuff."

I clucked my tongue. What was the big deal? It was just a tiny piece of cake, and Bo was built like a tank. One bite wouldn't have done any harm.

"Besides when I looked back, you'd already inhaled it."

My eyes widened. "I did not."

"Gone in 60 seconds."

"I'd appreciate it if you didn't time my eating habits. Thank you very much," I said, a blush rising to my cheeks. "And I'll have you know I ate that delicious slice of chocolatey goodness at a normal, polite speed."

Bo shrugged. "If you say so."

Ugh, he was so annoying.

"Surprised your favorite wasn't the last one."

"Nothing could beat that cake," I said with a smile. "Mr. Willard was sweet, though."

"You mean pervy," he said.

"You're just jealous, Stryker."

A scoff. "Nah, jealousy's not my thing. Plus, he wasn't my type."

I laughed in surprise. "Was that a joke?" I asked.

"No."

"It was," I retorted, studying his profile. "You're

kind of hilarious, you know that?"

"And we're back to the questions." Bo sighed, which only made me laugh again.

As we drove, the silence was cozy, settling over us like a warm blanket. I definitely hadn't seen this coming. Bo and I having a semi-friendly conversation. The two of us *not* tearing each other's hair out after being together in a confined space for so long? Now that was crazy. A few minutes later, during which I couldn't help but covertly watch him, he glanced over.

"We're back," he said.

Looking out the window, I saw that he was right. *Mrs. Lee's Flower Shop* looked just as inviting as it had when we left. The lights were on, and inside, I caught sight of Mrs. Lee talking on the phone.

"I can't believe you do this all the time," I said.

"Do what?" he asked.

"You make people's days brighter." I felt a smile appear on my face. "The customers we met today, every single one of them lit up when you gave them those flowers. It has to be the best job ever—well, besides working at the library."

"Never really thought of it like that."

When I turned to Bo, my smile fell. He was looking down at his injured hand, grimacing as he flexed his fingers.

"Does it hurt?" I asked.

His face went blank.

"Okay then"—I held out my palm—"can I see your arm?"

"Why?" he asked.

Rolling my eyes, I reached over, gently grasped his forearm and brought it closer.

"What are you doing?"

"Relax," I said, trying not to laugh at the alarm I heard in his voice. "If I wanted to hurt you, I would've done it by now."

"Says the girl who gave me a bookcussion" he grumbled.

Biting back a smile, I concentrated on his forearm, running my fingers over his skin to find the correct spot. This took a few moments. When I found it, I leaned closer, using my thumbs to press down, gently at first, then adding a little more pressure. Bo didn't tense. He didn't move a muscle. I might've thought he'd stopped breathing he was so still. But then I felt his breath against my neck.

The sensation sent shivers down my spine.

I counted the seconds under my breath and then released him.

"What was that, Kent?" he asked softly.

"I looked up how to treat a sprained wrist," I said with a shrug. "It was nothing, just one of the techniques they recommended."

"You looked that up?"

Meeting his eyes, I nodded. "Does it feel any better?"

Bo glanced down at his wrist before looking back up, locking me in his intense stare. "Yeah, it does. Thanks, Kent."

For some reason, I blushed. "No problem."

I didn't know what made me say it.

But I added, "Maybe now, you won't be so opposed to working with me."

Bo shook his head. "It's not that."

"It's not?"

"No," he said. "I just don't like the idea of you taking care of me out of some misplaced sense of guilt."

Oh.

I hadn't even considered that possibility.

"I thought you hated having me around," I admitted.

"I don't."

"You even told me how much you hate people."

"Not you," he said.

My heart skipped a beat.

"I could never hate you, Kent."

"That's..." I swallowed then tried again. "Well, that's a relief. I don't hate you either, Stryker."

Bo lifted a brow. "But I thought I was a thief."

I couldn't believe he brought it up, our kiss. **The Kiss.**

Keep it together, Lottie.

"You are a thief," I said. "But I've heard that first kisses are sometimes terrible. So, all things considered, I'm glad it was you."

"Yeah?"

I nodded. "It definitely could've been worse."

"Good to know," he said with a gleam in his eyes.

"Yeah well," I murmured. "I guess I'll see you around, Flower Boy."

"Bye, Kent. Drive safely."

As I got out of the van and walked to my car, I was dazed, confused, and fluttery.

Was this what it felt like to *not* hate someone?

If so, I couldn't recommend it highly enough.

#

The rest of the weekend went by in a flash. It was relaxing, uneventful, and overall boring—which didn't bother me at all. People often underestimated boring. It could be a good thing. Personally, I loved having time to myself. Hours to read or reminisce.

Or try to untangle my feelings for a certain someone.

I'd had a wonderful time delivering flowers. I'd enjoyed our conversation in the van. I could totally see why people would make a bet about being the one to break down Bo's walls. He'd only given me a glimpse, and if I was being honest, I liked what I saw. Going against the norm, I was even looking forward to school on Monday.

And I was currently trying to convince myself it had nothing to do with Bo.

There was no connection. Why would there be? Just because I'd felt *something* didn't mean I knew what that something was. And Bo...

Well, he obviously wasn't into me like that.

This was fine because I didn't have feelings for him either.

Just because we didn't hate each other didn't mean it was more.

Why did my overly-romantic brain insist on making it more?

It was *The Kiss*, I decided. Had to be.

I was looking at Bo differently because we'd kissed. My emotions were all over the place because of that one incident, and I just needed to keep reminding myself of that.

"Lotte," my sister said for what clearly wasn't the first time. Scarlett's tone and body language gave off a frustrated vibe. "We've been idling here in the parking lot forever. Are you ever going to turn off the engine?"

Snapping out of it, I said, "Yeah, of course. Sorry."

Scarlett furrowed her brow. "Seriously, are you okay?"

"Hmmm, why do you ask?"

"You want me to go down the list?" she said then proceeded to count off on her fingers. "One, you got home Saturday with this dopey grin on your face—"

"Yeah, right," I mumbled.

"—two, you didn't get mad Sunday when I interrupted your reading to suggest we practice violin—and I know you dislike both of those things."

"No one likes being interrupted when they're reading," I said. "Book time is sacred."

"Which makes it extra suspicious that you didn't argue."

"And I like practicing my violin."

"Yeah, by yourself, alone in your room where no one else can see."

I opened my mouth, but she talked right over me.

"Three," she said, "you haven't said anything about the flower shop. Four, you haven't said anything about Bo—who, as you know, I added to your suitor list. And five, as your sister, I know you have a secret you're not telling me."

I blinked. "How could you possibly know that?"

"Because I know you," she said with a sniff.

"Scar, you're a nut."

"No, I'm perceptive"—she held up a hand—"and before you try to dismiss everything I just said, let me remind you. I love you, but you're the worst liar ever."

My brow scrunched. "I could lie if I wanted to."

"Yeah, and your face would give you away every

time."

I wanted to deny it but couldn't.

"So...?"

With a shrug, I said, "There's no secret. Bo and I had a good time. Flower delivery is now on my list of top jobs ever. He told me he doesn't hate me, and for some reason, my mind turned that into something romantic."

"Hold up," she said, her eyes bright, "he said that?"

"Yeah."

"I need more context."

I sighed. "Bo said he hates most people. But not me. He said he could never hate me."

Scarlett let out a squeak. "Oh my God, that is so romantic."

I squinted my eyes, thinking she was kidding.

"Seriously," she said. "In broody Bo speak, I feel like that's a declaration of love or something."

I had to disagree. Though she hid it better, obviously my sister and I suffered from the same affliction. Hopeless romantic syndrome. Shaking my head, I focused back in on what Scarlett was saying.

"So, you've been caught up in your feelings all weekend." Scarlett nodded. "Makes sense. You should've discussed this with me sooner."

"Maybe," I allowed, "but no worries. I figured it out."

She lifted a brow.

"Kissing Bo messed with my mind."

Scarlett scoffed, but I went on.

"It's a real thing," I said. "To prove my theory, I searched online—"

"Of course, you did," she mumbled.

"—and the internet did not let me down. I found out that kissing can affect your brain chemistry. It promotes feelings of safety and intimacy through the release of neurotransmitters."

"Are you serious?" she asked.

"Yes"—my eyes widened—"it's science, Scar. Oxytocin, dopamine, and serotonin, all linked to kissing, all chemicals that make you feel good. My research has led me to one indisputable conclusion."

"Oh, I can't wait to hear this," Scarlett said.

Sarcasm practically dripped from her tone, but I didn't let it distract me.

She was my little sister. She hadn't kissed anyone either—that I knew of. Maybe this info would help her down the road.

"Kissing is like a drug," I said. "One touch of Bo's lips made me high. I had a hit, and I'm still experiencing the aftereffects."

Scarlett stared at me.

"Ready to go inside?"

"Sure," she said, but while we were walking toward the school, she shook her head. "You've never done drugs have you?"

"No way," I said. "Have you?"

"No," she said. "But...you know, you're only fooling yourself, right?"

"Meaning," I said.

"Lotte, you can't blame your feelings on science. It's okay to admit it. You like the guy. I like him too."

My eyes shot to hers.

"For you," Scarlett added, her eyes twinkling.

"Whatever," I mumbled, dismissing the whole idea. Because Bo and I? We were still as different as night and day. One good conversation and one earth-shattering kiss did not a relationship make. Bo didn't seem to be suffering from the same kiss-induced feels that I was.

Nope.

No matter what Scarlett said, I needed to snap out of it.

I had nearly no romantic experience. I was prone to romanticizing things. Maybe I'd done that with regard to Bo as well.

Maybe the kiss hadn't been as good as I remembered.

I smiled because I was finally thinking about it like a normal person. Lowercase, no bolded font. It was the first step to recovery.

As Scarlett and I walked through the doors of Chariot High, however, there was something strange. I couldn't put my finger on it. It was just a weird feeling, an almost imperceptible shift in the air.

"Why is everyone looking at you?" Scarlett muttered.

"They're not," I said.

"Uh, yeah, they are."

The farther we moved down the hall the more I realized she was right. I wasn't imagining things. People really were watching us, whispering behind their hands, glancing at their phones, smiling like they knew something we didn't.

"What is going on?" I said to myself.

I found out a moment later.

Scarlett pulled out her phone then nudged my side.

"Lotte, you might want to see this," she said.

"Wha—" My words cut off as I caught sight of her screen and the video playing on it.

Bo and I in the library. Bo's hand touching my cheek. Bo's lips moving, his voice clear as he said...

Why would she want you when she already has a boyfriend?

Bo leaning down, his mouth touching mine, and...

"You weren't kidding," Scarlett said, and I looked over to find her eyes glued to the screen. "That kiss would've addled my brain too."

I elbowed her, but my eyes were drawn back to the kiss. My arms were twined around Bo's neck, and he'd lifted me off the ground. Oh.

"Did your research say anything about getting a second-hand high from kissing?"

"Not funny, Scar," I said.

"Wasn't joking."

My gaze snagged on the amount of views, and I nearly choked.

"At least we know why everyone's staring at you," she said. "Bet they've all watched it at least ten times."

My cheeks reddened. How did this even happen?

And why, oh why, couldn't I stop rewatching my first kiss?

The answer came easily.

I'd been wrong. I didn't romanticize. The kiss had been just as amazing as I remembered.

And now, everyone knew it.

11

I stood frozen as the video played for a third time.

As I watched, Scarlett's finger pressed the heart icon.

"Did you just love that video?" I accused.

"Yep," she said.

Then her finger hit the save button. And was she...no, she wouldn't.

"Saved and shared it too." Scarlett smiled up at my shocked expression. "Oops."

I pinched her arm, making her yelp. "I can't even...you're terrible. You know that, right?"

"Hey, it's a kissing video," she said, laughing while she rubbed her arm. "You know I love those. Plus, I'm supporting my sister."

"Thanks," I grumbled under my breath.

"Besides, be real, Lotte. If you had social media,

you would've loved it too."

I swallowed my retort because it was true.

As I watched Bo lean down to onscreen me again, I admitted it if only to myself. I would've watched the heck out of that video. I probably would've broken the replay button. In fact, I might need to reconsider my stance on social media and create an account to do just that.

My sister and I sighed in unison.

"You're thinking about making an account aren't you?" Scarlett said.

"Yeah, right," I replied.

"You totally were."

"This is actually one of the reasons I hate social media," I mumbled. "No one needs permission. They just post stuff about people."

"Including awesome first kisses," my sister added. "At least, they couldn't tag you. But..."

I saw it the same time as she did.

"Ugh, they tagged the library?" I said and then groaned. "Seriously? Mrs. Welks is so going to fire me."

"Hmmm, doubtful," Scarlett said. "You're her favorite."

"Yeah, because I'm good at my job. Really good," I said. "I match people up with their favorite books, and nine times out of ten they come back to the library. Not because I'm caught kissing during work hours."

I closed my eyes, took a deep fortifying breath, and shook it off, the fear of being sacked, the stares of my classmates, my sister's look of concern. It was all placed on the back burner.

There was only one person who could've taken that video.

And I was going to find him.

Right after, I went to Bo's locker to see if he needed help.

"I'll un-share it if you really want me to," Scarlett said.

"Nah, it's alright," I said, waving her words away. "I'm sure it's been shared a few times already."

"Oh yeah, with that many views it had to have been...sorry," she said.

I shook my head. "I'm off to assist Bo," I said. "Bye, Scar."

"Bye," she said then added, "and hey, if the 'assist' involves your lips touching his, I wanna be the first to know."

Flipping off your sister was wrong, right?

I held up a peace sign instead.

"That video deserves a part two," she called which made some of the people within hearing distance giggle.

Despite my chagrin, I ducked my head and gave a small smile. I knew if Scarlett thought I was truly upset she would've never shared it. Still. I looked forward to the day when I could tease her about something.

Bo's locker was only a few feet away.

Eyes followed me every step in that direction.

When I got there, however, I pulled up short.

The sight that greeted me was a surprise.

Bo was standing with his arms crossed, glowering at Leif, whose back was pressed up against the lockers. Though Leif was trying to play it cool, his pretty-boy smile wobbled at the edges. And Bo...well, his glare held the fire of a thousand suns.

Time to lower the temperature.

"Hey guys," I said as I walked over to them. "This looks like a fun discussion. Mind if I join?"

"Charlotte," Leif said with a sigh of relief, "I'm so glad it's you. I was just telling your boyfriend it's no big deal. I wasn't trying to upset anyone by posting that video."

I was about to correct his use of the word 'boyfriend' but didn't get a chance.

Bo's glare remained on Leif as he said, "You embarrassed her."

"Really?" Leif said, turning to me then back to Bo. "She doesn't look embarrassed."

"You need to take the video down," Bo said. "Now."

"I told you I can't."

As Bo seemed to expand before my eyes, Leif held up a hand.

"Well, I could," Leif amended, his voice rising a

few octaves. "I absolutely could, but it wouldn't do any good at this point."

His eyes shifted to me then as if I would be the voice of reason.

"Charlotte, listen. Everyone's already seen it," he said. "The video's a big hit. Deleting it won't do anything."

I cocked my head. "I don't even get how you captured it. If I remember right, you said you were *almost* ready to record."

Leif grinned. "Ah, well, you get better performances out of people when they don't know they're on camera. It's a little trick of the trade."

Bo looked like he was ready to breathe fire, but I wasn't quite done questioning Leif.

"Why'd you do it?" I asked. "Seriously Leif, I thought you just wanted to commemorate your first visit to the library."

"I did," he said with a nod. "I posted the selfie, but it didn't get much love. Apparently, people aren't interested in stupid things like books."

Okay, now, even I wanted to smack him.

"But they go crazy over a little mouth-on-mouth action," he added with a wink. "You and Bo know what I'm talking about. It was getting hot up in that library. You feel me?"

I struggled for words. "You...you're such a...I can't believe you just said that about books."

Bo's eyes shifted to me then. "Really, Kent?

That's what you're mad about?"

"He's a total idiot—"

"Hey!" Leif said.

"—and yet, he has the audacity to call books stupid?" I said with a huff. "How dare you, Leif George. Saying such horrible things, recording us like a sleaze and releasing it without our consent? You are not the guy I thought you were."

"I'm sorry?" Leif scratched the back of his head. "I figured you guys wouldn't mind. Again, I'll take it down, but other accounts have reposted it already. Without giving the original aka me any credit," he sniffed. "Thieves."

My cheeks grew pink as Bo looked to me.

That word had taken on a whole new meaning, and I knew we were both thinking the same thing.

"Kent," he said, "it's your call."

I shrugged. "I guess he has a point. The video's already out. Not much we can do about it now. Though I always thought if I ever went viral it would be for something like having the world's largest collection of romance novels."

Both guys blinked then looked back to each other.

"Don't do it again," Bo warned.

Leif's easy smile came back as he inched away from the locker. "You got it, Iceman. I'll never mess with you and your girlfriend again. Sorry for hitting on her the first time. Though I thought she was hitting on me because...well, I'm me."

Bo didn't laugh. He let his glare speak for him.

Leif got the message and got the heck out of there.

Using Bo's distraction, I asked, "Hey, completely off topic, but what's your locker combination?"

"17, 29, 5," he said, rattling off the numbers as his eyes tracked Leif until he was out of sight. "Why?"

"No reason," I said, but before he could stop me, I had his locker open and was pulling out his books.

"Want to tell me what you think you're doing?" Bo asked, stepping up to me.

I swallowed then lifted my chin. "I'm carrying your books."

His brow furrowed. "Like hell you are."

"I've developed excellent upper body strength from my work at the library," I said. "The hardbacks are basically like lifting weights. Oh, don't give me that look."

Bo's face cleared. "What look?"

"The one that says 'You're crazy, Kent. I do all these pushups in the morning. I'm a guy. I can carry my own books.' Newsflash," I said, "I can too. These arms may struggle to do anything resembling a pushup, but I'm tough."

I flexed my biceps.

"See? Totally ripped. Just accept the help and let's go."

Bo seemed to be choking on something.

"Are you okay?" I asked in concern.

He was doubled over, good arm wrapped around his abdomen, and I was getting worried at the choked gasps he was making. But then, suddenly, the noises resolved themselves into something sounding like...no. It couldn't be. Could it?

"Are you...*laughing*?" I asked.

As he stood to his full height, the sounds of his laughter, deep and smooth, poured from his mouth which was stretched in a grin.

"You—" Bo gasped, seeming surprised by his own laughter, before he managed to get himself under control. "Yeah, Kent. I am."

"I didn't know you could do that," I said.

He tried pulling on his typical frown, but his eyes danced with delight. "Guess you don't know everything."

"Apparently not," I mumbled, still staring at his face.

Bo's smile was like some kind of hidden treasure.

Rare, dazzling, and hard to find. But once discovered, you wanted to bask in it, thankful for even a glimpse of something so beautiful.

I wondered if I'd ever get to see it again.

Bo was saying something. I was pretty sure it was my name, and I blinked, coming out of my daze.

"Come on," I said, turning before Bo could argue or make a grab for the books. "Don't want to be late to first period."

Bo kept pace with me easily. "Just so you know, I wasn't calling you weak back there," he said.

I shrugged.

"Wouldn't want anyone carrying my books, girl or guy." Bo's brow scrunched. "Hey, how did you know which ones I'd need? We're not even in the same classes."

Because I have an inside woman in the front office, I thought. But I kept my mouth shut, not wanting to give Ms. Deidre up. I also didn't want him knowing I'd gone through the trouble of getting his schedule.

"Kent?"

"You could just say thank you," I said.

He let out a long exhale.

"Think of me as your private nurse, or wait." I smiled. "Your fairy godmother."

As he placed a hand on my arm, I stopped and looked up. We were already at his classroom. Other students were still walking the halls. The first bell hadn't rung yet, so I'd have plenty of time to get to my class which was only a few doors down.

"If I need your help, I'll ask for it," Bo said.

I tilted my head.

"Would you?" I asked.

He didn't respond, but I saw his answer as

clearly as if he'd spoken.

'No' was practically stamped across his forehead.

"That's what I thought," I said with a sigh, handing over the books. Bo cradled them in his good arm. "Have an awesome day, Stryker."

He looked from the books to my face. "Thanks, Kent," he said then cleared his throat. "Also, sorry about Leif."

I flushed. "Why are you sorry? You didn't release the video."

"Yeah, but still. I know it hurt your feelings."

"Why would you say that?" I asked.

"Because you're into Leif," he said and cocked his chin. "I saw him on your list, remember?"

I gave a mental groan. "Seriously, it's not what you think. I—"

"Hey, Charlotte!" Shonda Lawrence came up and stopped in front of me. She was the girls' soccer team captain, and I didn't think we'd spoken since fifth grade. "I just wanted to say congrats."

"Thanks, Shonda," I said baffled. "But what's the congratulations for?"

"You won the bet," she said, throwing a grin over her shoulder at Bo. "No one even knew you were playing. But there's no denying the proof."

"I don't—"

"The bet about Bo." Shonda rolled her eyes with a laugh. "The video clearly shows you two together. I didn't even know he was your boyfriend!"

I was stunned speechless.

"And *you*," she said, turning to point a finger at Bo. "You should've just told us you were already taken. It would've made things a lot easier."

Her eyes landed back on me.

"So, we'll get you your prize soon," she said. "But yeah, I just wanted to congratulate you."

Finally finding my voice, I said, "I think there's been a mistake. I didn't win anything."

Shonda frowned. "What do you mean?"

"I'm not...well, we're not together," I said, gesturing between myself and Bo.

"You're not?" she repeated then crossed her arms.

I shook my head.

"That would mean the HUBS is still on."

I could've sworn I saw Bo's eye twitch at that.

"The what?" I asked.

"HUBS," she said, "you know, Hook Up with Bo Stryker. It's what we decided to call the bet."

"Wasn't aware it had a name," I murmured.

"Me neither," Bo growled.

Shonda's gaze moved from me to Bo and back again. "Well, if that's true, then the bet's still going. You guys seriously aren't a thing? I would've sworn you were. I mean, that kiss..."

I knew exactly what she meant. The kiss had been fire, but it was only Bo trying to help me save face in front of Leif. I was about to tell her that, getting ready to explain the whole misunderstanding, when Bo stepped up next to me.

"We are a thing," Bo said.

My eyes snapped up to meet his.

"My girl's just shy. Doesn't like all the attention."

My heart stuttered over the words *my girl*. Plus, the way he was looking at me was... different. Softer somehow, more tender. He leaned down and pressed a kiss to my temple, stealing my breath.

Bo's mouth moved lower, and he whispered in my ear, "I need your help, Kent."

I swallowed.

"Please, Charlotte," he added.

As if I could say no.

I was pretty sure Bo had never used my first name. And he'd even said please.

When he leaned back, my smile had returned full force.

"He's right," I said to Shonda. "Sorry, it just happened so fast. I'm still getting used to the idea."

She nodded like she completely understood. "I knew it," she said with a grin. "You two are the cutest."

"Aren't we just?" I said as the first bell rang.

I glanced up and gave Bo a meaningful look.

"Bye, Flower Boy. We'll talk soon."

"Oh, that's such a sweet name," Shonda said then walked into class.

"Kent, I—" Bo said.

I pretended like I didn't hear and kept walking. Once I was safely in my classroom, however, I dropped into my chair. Chester Copperfield leaned over to say, "Well alright, Lottie Lotte. Word on the street is you caught yourself one Bo Stryker. I'm almost jealous."

I gave a weak laugh.

"Anyway, you go, girl. I'm an 8.5, but your guy? He's a 10."

Yeah, I thought, except he wasn't.

Bo wasn't my guy.

He wasn't *my* anything.

None of what Chester said was true, but I couldn't say that.

Instead, I smiled and murmured, "Thanks, Chester."

"No offense, but Bo's kind of uptight. I was shook when I heard the news," he said.

"Trust me, I was too."

As my literature teacher started her lecture, I laid my head down on my desk. It wasn't until about 10 minutes later that I came to a startling realization. Bo Stryker had stolen more than my first kiss. He'd become my first boyfriend.

Fake, yes.

But a boyfriend nonetheless.

Bo and I trying to fake a relationship?

Yeah, this couldn't end well.

12

Bo let me carry his books from first to second period.

He didn't even put up a fight—which let me know guilt was eating him up. As we walked, from the corner of my eye, I saw him glance my way several times as if he wanted to say something. But he never spoke. Bo had always been a man of few words, yet he always spoke his mind, was never hesitant. Until now. Our classmates watched us, of course. They tracked our progress through the halls, likely wondering how broody-yet-popular Bo 'Iceman' Stryker and sweet-yet-awkward Charlotte 'Bookworm' Kent had become an 'us'. I was wondering the same thing, but whatever.

This was what Bo needed from me.

I'd certainly read enough fake romances.

I could do this.

I would do it.

My mantra stayed true in my head until we stopped outside his second class. Instead of taking his books and disappearing, Bo placed a hand on my arm and addressed one of his teammates.

"Hey Riconne," he said.

The other guy paused and lifted a brow. "Yeah?"

"Can you put my books on my desk?" Bo asked.

"Something wrong with your leg too?" he said. "We got a game coming up."

"My legs are fine."

"Glad to hear it. Heard about the arm, and you can't miss that shiner."

I winced. I hadn't forgotten how bad it was—I'd just been trying not to look. As my eyes took in the bruise on Bo's cheek, the one I'd accidentally created, his skin was a mix between blue and green. Riccone was right. It looked terrible.

"Don't know who got the drop on you, Stryker." The other guy grimaced. "But I hope you didn't take it lying down.

A cough. "Uh yeah, actually, I did."

The memory of my body lying on top of Bo's, his breath mingling with my own, being discovered by my friends at the library, flashed through my mind. It was a good thing no one got *that* on video. Just the thought had me shifting anxiously from foot to foot.

"So, the books?" Bo asked, gesturing my way with a tilt of his head. "I just need a second."

Riccone's eyes moved to me, and he grinned. "Ah, I got you, Captain. Have fun with your girl."

My jaw dropped as he took Bo's books and walked into the room, leaving Bo and me alone.

"I can't believe he just called me your girl," I said.

Bo raised a brow. "I called you that too."

"Oh, I remember."

He stood there for a moment, seeming at a loss for words. During that time, sparks continued to race up and down my arm, and I looked down at his hand. He was still touching me. It was light, barely there. Most of his hand was covered by the brace, but his fingers rested against my skin. Warm tingles radiated from every point of contact.

"Sorry," Bo muttered as he jerked back, looking at his own hand as if he didn't know how it got there. "Kent, I just wanted to say..."

"Yes?" I asked, trying to make my breath sound less shaky than I felt.

He stared at me, opened his mouth, and—

"Mr. Stryker."

We looked to the open door, and there was Mrs. Taggart. She eyed the two of us with a bored expression then tapped her watch.

"Were you planning to join us?" she asked.

"Ah yeah," Bo said, "sorry, Mrs. T."

He looked to me and ran a hand along the back of his neck.

"Guess I'll see you at lunch."

I hummed in agreement. "Sure thing. Bye, Stryker, Mrs. T."

Mrs. Taggart's mouth lifted to one side. "See you in fifth period, Ms. Kent. If you're late, at least I'll know the reason"—when she shot Bo a significant look, I nearly died—"and I'll be sure to check the library first."

I laughed nervously then practically ran in the opposite direction.

My haste was partly due to humiliation. There was no doubt in my mind that Mrs. T had seen the video. Her knowing look and reference to the library said as much. Ugh. Weren't teachers supposed to discourage rumors?

The other part was I hated being late. I'd had enough eyes on me today. I didn't want any more. Walking into class right as the bell rang, I slipped into my seat, which thankfully was in the back row. Our teacher gave us time to read—usually one of my favorite things—but instead, I did something I knew I'd regret later. It only took a minute to create an account and even less time to find the video of Bo and I kissing. I refused, absolutely refused, to believe that many people had actually viewed the video. There was probably something wrong with the counter, I decided. After watching a couple times, I couldn't stop my gaze from wondering down to my arm. Why had I reacted to Bo's touch like that? During those moments, I'd been so aware, my skin completely alive with the feeling. Bo, on the other hand, forgot he was even touching me.

Rubbing my arm, I tried to quell the worry rising in my chest.

But it was no good.

I needed time to think, to be alone with my thoughts.

Unfortunately, that meant I'd have to break the promise I made to Bo.

When lunch rolled around, I didn't go to my usual table. I didn't enter the cafeteria at all. Instead, I made a beeline to the girl's restroom, locked myself in an empty stall, and tried to breathe.

What would Scarlett do in this situation?

My sister always knew the right course of action for any problem.

I could've walked into the lunchroom and asked her in person, but honestly? I didn't want to deal with the onslaught of questions or the stares I knew would come my way, not just from Scarlett but from other students too. So, here I was, trying my best to solve my own issues.

Just think rationally, Lotte.

Scarlett told me this on countless occasions.

Take the emotions out of it.

I gave a mental nod.

And when in doubt, write it out.

"Okay," I murmured, grabbing my notepad and pen. "Here goes nothing."

When I flipped open the cover, a little yellow note slid down to rest on my thigh. I picked it up, skimming the names of my so-called suitors, and shook my head. Five guys, each of them crossed out—except one.

The irony of the suitor being Bo and the situation we currently found ourselves in wasn't lost on me.

Folding the note, I read the writing on page one. This was where I'd compiled my list of all the ways I could help Bo. Funnily enough, pretending to be his girlfriend was nowhere to be found.

I shut the notebook, shaking my head. Writing lists was really my sister's thing. I decided to talk myself off the ledge instead.

"This really isn't that complicated," I whispered, doing my best to believe the words. "So, you're fake dating Bo Stryker. Big deal. People do it all the time, right?"

Or at least they did in books.

"And yeah, your feelings went a little crazy when he called you his girl and touched you. It's only natural. You've never been with anyone, and he's the first person you've ever kissed. There's no way you'll catch real feelings."

I lifted my chin.

"Don't make it into a thing."

I was helping Bo because of the book slap. He asked me to fake date him to get out of that stupid bet. Now, I was in a pretend relationship with my next-door-neighbor. Simple. Nothing to worry about.

"But it might be best to end it quickly," I muttered.

With that thought in mind, my breath started coming easier, the weight on my shoulders lifting and replaced by calm. Might've sounded strange, but I didn't want to experience love. Not the real, heart-in-your-throat, miss-you-when-you're-gone kind of love. I wanted to experience some things (hence the suitor list). But I didn't want to fall. It was one of my number one fears actually. Romance was something I enjoyed reading about, but I had no desire to get my heart broken. This thing with Bo, the pretending would end eventually. I knew it, and there was some comfort in that. If you knew something was coming, you could prepare for it. I took another deep breath and smiled.

My serenity was interrupted when someone entered the bathroom.

Or actually several people.

"It's just really hard to believe," a familiar voice said. "That's all I'm saying."

"Why?" a second voice asked.

"Because Bo Stryker is so gorgeous, and she's...so

weird."

There was some shuffling, and then, "Lottie's okay. We had a few classes together last year. She's a cool chick."

A snort. "Yeah, if you think reading is cool."

I scrunched my nose at that.

Who didn't think reading was cool?

A third voice spoke then, "Come on, Aspen. She reads books, so what?"

Ah, Aspen Vanderbilt.

That meant the other two were likely her best friends, Sierra Flemming and Mya Williams.

Naturally. Now, it all made sense. Aspen had hated me since elementary school when I got the lead as Mary in the school's nativity play, and she was cast as the male innkeeper. You know, the one that turns Mary and Joseph away? No room at the inn? Yeah, that was Aspen. Far as I knew, she'd never gotten over it. Must've been the moustache and beard—or possibly the shabby costume. Since we hit middle school, Aspen had starred in every school play, and she wouldn't be caught dead in anything that wasn't designer.

"Charlotte Kent acts like she's better than everyone," Aspen said with a sniff. "And the way she smiles all the time? So fake. Everyone knows the world is crap—at least for poor, middle-class weirdos like her and her sister."

Again, was weirdo supposed to be an insult?

I'd always liked that word.

"Remember what we used to call her?" Aspen sounded like she was smiling when she said, "Loser Lottie."

I rolled my eyes.

"Her hair and clothes sucked. I mean, didn't her mother ever teach her how to use a brush?"

Now, that struck home. My hand went to my chest, rubbing the sudden tightness I felt there.

"She never had any friends, so she had to carry around all those books. Poor, Loser Lottie," Aspen repeated. "Maybe we should bring that back."

"Um correction," the second voice said, which I now knew was Sierra, "only you used to call her that. Mya and I took no part in your mean-girl ways."

"Why are we friends again?"

"I wonder the same thing sometimes," Sierra replied.

"Sounds like you really wanted Bo for yourself," Mya (voice 3) said.

"No," Aspen said, "I just wanted someone else to win the bet."

"Yeah, you."

"Whatever."

Sierra said, "Well, I like them together. Maybe she'll soften Bo up a bit."

"Good luck with that one," Mya said. "My brother's on the team with him, says Bo never lets his guard down."

"I heard he never smiles," Aspen put in.

"Yeah," Mya said, "he's so intimidating. That's what makes Iceman a killer on the soccer pitch."

"That and those abs," Sierra said, and the three of them laughed.

Aspen sighed. "He's too good for Loser Lottie."

There was a pause.

"Do you think that kiss was staged?"

"If it was," Sierra said, "that was some good acting."

"Definitely made me blush," Mya put in.

"Me too," Aspen admitted then added, "but there are ways to make it look like you're kissing someone when you're really not. We learn them in drama. Maybe Bo was just faking it."

Making sure my smile was at 100, I stood and stepped out of the stall.

The three girls watched me, open-mouthed, as I went to one of the sinks and washed my hands. I took my time, making sure to scrub really well and dry each finger off before balling up and throwing away the paper towels. Then I turned to face them.

"Hey Lottie," Aspen said with feigned pleasure, as if we were old friends. "We didn't know you were in there."

"I gathered that," I said.

Her smile faltered then got even wider. "Ah, you know how we girls like to talk. It's all in good fun."

"Hmmm."

Sierra hesitated then said, "Congrats on winning the bet."

"And on that kiss," Mya said while fanning her face. "I liked the part where he picked you up."

I lifted a brow. "Thanks, I liked that part too."

Sierra and Mya laughed, but Aspen wasn't smiling anymore.

"It must be nice, always getting things you don't deserve," she said.

"I don't know about that," I said. "I think everyone decides what or who they deserve, in life and in love."

I shrugged.

"Also, I wasn't trying to win any bet. The kiss was real. I don't mind you calling me Loser Lottie—I'm a fan of alliteration. My family is middle-class, but we aren't poor. Half the people in this town will probably end up working for my sister. Scarlett is a freaking superstar. Oh, and weirdo isn't a good insult. Calling someone weird just means they're passionate about something you don't understand. Weirdos are the ones who make life interesting."

"Wow. That was deep," Mya said, and Aspen poked her in the ribs.

"Sorry for all that, Lottie," Sierra said.

"No problem," I said.

The bell rang, and I moved to the exit. Pushing on the handle, I stood in the open doorway a moment and then turned back to face them.

"My smiles aren't fake, you know. I just choose to be happy."

I shook my head.

"Oh, and the rumors aren't true. I've seen Bo's smile. It's gorgeous."

I thought back to that brief moment of him laughing.

"Like when the sun comes out after a storm."

With that, I walked away.

I was practically skipping I felt so buoyant. Aspen hadn't gotten to me (much), and her friends were nice. Chalk one up for weirdos everywhere, I thought. If I had a soundtrack, I would've thrust my fist into the air.

"Gorgeous, huh?" a voice said so close to my ear that I almost tripped.

"Stryker," I gasped, turning to face him, a hand on my heart. "What the heck? Where did you come from?"

"I was waiting for you," he said.

"Well, don't do that."

"Do what?"

"Sneak up on people, all quiet and stealthy like a ninja," I said.

"Guess it's a good thing you weren't on a ladder this time," he said.

"Funny."

"So"—Bo lifted a brow, and I saw that his eyes

were alight with something—"you think my smile's gorgeous."

"I mean, you're no Ian Mackenzie. But it's okay," I hedged, continuing to walk with him.

"Who's Ian Mackenzie?" he asked, and his smile was nowhere in sight.

I scrunched my brows. "He's the main character of that book you checked out a couple weeks ago. *The Madness of Lord Ian Mackenzie*. Didn't you read it?"

"Ah," Bo said. "Nah, ran out of time."

"Well, you could see if it's available," I said. "Though it's one of my favorites, so I recommend it a lot."

"I'll keep that in mind. Now back to my gorgeous smile."

"Eh, it's alright."

"That's not what you said."

I huffed. "Yes, but that's because I'm playing the part."

Bo cut his eyes at me.

"Oh my gosh, fine! You have a nice smile."

"I know," he said, and I couldn't help but laugh.

"Was there some reason you were waiting?" I asked.

Bo cocked his head. "Thought we were meeting."

"Oh, that."

"When I didn't see you in the lunchroom or the

library," he said, "I figured you must be in there. Hiding out."

"I wasn't hiding," I said quickly.

Though yes, if you wanted to get technical, I kind of had been.

Bo looked like he didn't believe me, but he let it drop.

"Listen, Kent," he said and gently pulled me to the side of the hall, so we were out of the flow of people. Lowering his voice so only I could hear, he went on, "I appreciate you doing this. I know I sprung the whole girlfriend thing on you."

"Shonda kind of sprung it on both of us," I replied. "But it's okay."

"It is?" he asked, searching my face.

"Yeah, but I think we should lay out some ground rules."

Bo looked curious. "What kind of rules?"

"Ones that'll keep us on track, make sure no one gets hurt," I said, looking around. "But we can talk about it later at the flower shop."

He waited until I met his gaze.

"You gonna run again?" he asked.

"If I did, you'd probably just track me down," I mumbled.

"Yeah," he agreed.

My eyes widened. "Is that one of your bodyguard skills?"

Bo didn't answer.

So, I took that as a yes.

"You're not scared, right?" he said.

"No," I said, crossing my arms. "Are you?"

"You're funny, Kent."

"Hey, if you're Iceman, does that make me Icewoman?"

Bo's jaw twitched, but he didn't smile. Dangit.

"I'll see you later," he said.

"Can't wait, Flower Boy," I said back.

Bo shook his head. "Rule one, don't call me that."

"Ah, you love it."

He didn't respond, but I thought I saw his lips tick up on one side.

13

"Can we please move on?" Casey asked.

"But I haven't even gotten to the theme, colors, and fundraising initiatives," I said, holding up the packet I'd printed out. "We almost didn't reach our goal last year. Libraries everywhere are struggling. We've got a lot of work to do."

She and Natalia groaned.

"What's that for?"

"Lottie, come on," Natalia said. "There's another very important matter we need to discuss."

I shot her a look. "More important than our Friends of the Library charity event, the one we hold every year to raise funds so underprivileged schools and children in shelters can have books to read? What could possibly be more important than that?"

Casey blinked. "Are you seriously trying to guilt us? We've been working on this for months. We love the event as much as you do. But you and Bo—"

"I told you we can talk about it after," I cut in.

"Why?" Natalia asked. "You know we want to hear all your event ideas and hash out the details."

"Doesn't seem like it," I muttered.

"We just really, *really* want to talk about that kiss," Natalia said.

Casey nodded, but I shook my head.

"Friends of the Library first, then the kiss," I said.

"But—"

"That's the deal. Take it or leave it."

They looked to each other, communicated some silent message, and then Casey spoke.

"Fine," she said with a glint in her eye, "but you will answer every question honestly, at length and in detail."

I opened my mouth to respond, but she wasn't done.

"Particularly the ones about Bo."

"And what a good kisser he is," Natalia added.

My brows lowered. "What makes you think he's good?"

Casey grinned. "Well, we did watch the video before you got here."

"Only like 20 times," Natalia said, and my jaw

dropped as she shrugged. "It would've been more, but my phone died."

I looked at the two of them; neither showed even a hint of remorse.

"Please place your hand on this copy of *Pride and Prejudice*," Casey said, setting the hardback on the counter.

I rolled my eyes but did as she asked.

"Do you swear to tell the truth, the whole truth, and nothing but the truth?"

"I do," I said, "but just so you know, I think you went too far by dragging *P & P* into this."

"And I think it was just far enough," Casey said with a clap of her hands. "Back to the charity event. Hit us with your thoughts, Lottie."

"Okay," I said.

"Then we can get to the kiss-and-tell."

With a sigh, I proceeded to tell them my plans. This year's theme was *A Night Out with Austen*. My idea was for us to hold a regency book ball, right here in the library, where the guests could dress up as their favorite characters. We'd already asked and secured local businesses who'd be willing to provide food and decorations. To raise funds, we'd have to reach out to more sponsors. We still had a ways to go. I'd never been good at asking people for money, but I knew this was for an amazing cause. The right book could change a person's life forever. Kids needed books to remind them, even in the toughest of times, that life could still be good. Our problem, being a small public library, had always been visibility.

"If more people knew about our cause, I just know they would give," I said.

"I agree," Natalia said.

"The question is: how do we make sure our message gets heard?" Casey asked.

I closed my packet and lifted a shoulder. "That's what we have to figure out."

"We can send out fancy ball invitations," Natalia suggested.

"Awesome," I said and wrote down the idea.

"In addition to social media, we could also try to get local press coverage," Casey said and then muttered, "though they've never responded to our requests before."

"Still," I said, adding that as well, "it's worth a shot."

After going back and forth, we made some adjustments to my initial plan, added several new ideas, and came up with a rough estimate of the timeline to reach our fundraising goal. Now, we'd just have to execute. I sat back, placing my pen down, with a grin.

"Well, that was productive," I said.

When there was no response, I looked up. Casey and Natalia were staring at me with expectant looks.

"What do you want to know?" I said with a sigh.

The questions came at a rapid pace.

Casey: "Well first off, on a scale of one to mind-blowing, how good was that kiss really?"

Me: "Mind-blowing times infinity. Next."

Natalia: "Why did he kiss you?"

Me: "To help me out after I got rejected by someone else."

Casey: "Who was recording?"

Me: "The guy who rejected me."

Natalia: "Jerk."

Casey: "Douchebag."

I didn't deny either.

Natalia: "Were you mad about the video?"

Me: "A little."

Casey: "Was that your first kiss?"

Me: "Yep."

Natalia: "Do you think it was *his* first kiss?"

Me: "No way, it was too amazing."

Casey: "Would you do it again?"

Me: "In a heartbeat."

Casey: "Would you do it again *with Bo*?"

Me (mumbling): "Same answer."

Natalia: "Bo said something about being your boyfriend. What's up with that?"

I gulped.

Casey: "Is he your boyfriend?"

A pause.

Casey: "You promised you'd answer, Lottie."

Me: "Then yeah, he kind of is."

I didn't add that it was temporary or that it was all fake. It wouldn't have mattered anyway. Before the end of my answer, Casey and Natalia were jumping up and down with giddiness. I crossed my arms.

"Is that really necessary?" I asked.

"Yes," they said in unison. When they broke apart, Casey grabbed one of my hands, and Natalia took the other.

"You guys were totally making out when we found you in the stacks," Casey said.

"We were not," I said back, blushing wildly.

Natalia gave me a dimply smile. "I believe you, Lottie."

"No, you don't," Casey said. "You were the one who suggested the idea in the first place."

The other girl elbowed her in the ribs, but I shook my head.

"You know, we're only teasing you because we love you," Casey added.

"Yeah, we do," Natalia said. "Your happiness is all we want."

"That and for you to spill the tea whenever anything juicy happens."

A laugh escaped my lips.

"I love you guys too," I said. "And I promise to spill the tea if there is any to be spilt."

My friends gave me a group hug, and not for

the first time, I wished we went to the same school.

#

Mrs. Lee was behind the cash register when I walked into the flower shop.

"Hi, Mrs. Lee," I said.

She looked up, first to the clock on the wall then to me, and nodded. "You're on time today, Charlotte-Lottie-Lotte."

"Yes," I said with a smile. Technically, it was 10 minutes earlier than the time we'd agreed upon, but after the other day, I wanted to make a better impression. Gesturing to my ensemble, I added, "And I remembered my uniform too."

"Good," she said.

"I guess I'll go find Bo, see if he needs anything."

She nodded again then looked away.

I took that as my dismissal.

Walking to the back room, I spotted Bo. He was wearing a black apron over his uniform, standing at the table, frowning in concentration as he attempted to tie a pink ribbon around a batch of carnations. His sprained wrist wasn't helping.

"Hey boyfriend," I said brightly.

Satisfaction rolled over me as I watched his head snap up in surprise. The scowl as he lost hold of the ribbon was an added bonus.

"Need help with that?"

"No," he muttered.

Rolling my eyes, I waved him aside. "Make room, Stryker."

Bo scooted over but only slightly as I sidled up next to him.

"Does this have to be done in a certain way?" I asked, and he shook his head. "Well then, when we were younger, my sister desperately wanted to be a cheerleader. She was always practicing the routines around the house. Scarlett is a lot louder than you'd think."

"She doesn't cheer now though. Right?" Bo said.

"Oh no, she literally calls those 'the dark days'." I chuckled. "It ended up not being for her, but she didn't know that until she tried it."

Bo didn't interrupt, just watched my fingers as I worked the ribbon.

"Anyway, my dad—who is awesome—always tried his best to give us what we needed. And for the most part, he did," I said. "But Dad didn't have any clue how to do hair, makeup, fashion, or things like cheer—specifically the importance of hair bows."

I looked over to him.

"Do you know about cheer bows, Stryker?"

"Do I look like I'd know something like that?" he deadpanned.

"No, no you don't," I said. "Finger please."

Bo held out his hand, and I placed his index finger in the center of the bow to hold it together.

"Have any zip ties or wire?"

"There's garden wire in the drawer next to you," he said.

"Thanks." After locating the wire, I continued. "I ended up checking out craft books from the library and, of course, watching online tutorials. The first three bows I made were terrible. By the tenth, I had the technique down, and Scarlett's friends wanted to know where she got her awesome bows. Anyway, this led me to figure out how to do other bows too, for birthdays, presents, etc."

I finished the ribbon off with a flourish.

"Ta-dah."

Bo glanced my way. "Thanks," he said. "Looks great, Kent."

I shrugged.

"I spent way too much time on that, and you finished it in like two minutes."

Before I could tease him, another guy walked into the room. He just appeared out of nowhere. At first, it seemed like magic, but then I realized there must be a back entrance for employees. Dark brown hair was spiked all over his head; his eyes were dark too yet held a lightness to them; and he had a tall, lean build. The thing that stood out most, though, was his playful smile.

"After a brief but brutal brush with death," he said to which Bo rolled his eyes, "I'm back and better than ever. Ready to fluff, cut, and arrange some floral. Bo man, I thought you would throw me a welcome back party or something."

"You were gone three days," Bo said.

"Yeah, but they were the longest of my life."

The guy flopped onto a stool in the corner.

"For a second, I thought I was a goner. But I knew I had to hang on for your sake, Bo. Your life would be so sad without me."

He shook his head.

"I couldn't leave my cranky, socially challenged BFF behind."

Bo lifted a brow. "Who said we were best friends, Shin?"

The guy, Shin, smirked and pointed a finger at Bo. "Don't play, man. I know you still have that friendship bracelet I gave you back in the day."

I swallowed a laugh, picturing Bo and Shin wearing matching friendship bracelets. That was so cute and unexpected. But Bo's face looked pained. Shin's eyes landed on me a moment later.

"Hey," he said, "you look familiar, but I don't think we've met. I'm Shin."

"Charlotte, but most people call me Lottie," I said back. "It's nice to meet you. I didn't realize Bo had a BFF."

"Because I don't," Bo said.

"He says these things just to hurt me," Shin said cheerfully. "But I know he loves me in his own way."

"I'm sure he does," I said.

Bo grunted his displeasure.

"Did you two grow up together?"

"Oh yeah," Shin said with a smile. "We've known each other since we were in diapers. Bo used to beat my butt—and everyone else's—in youth soccer. Karate too. Oh yeah, and Taekwondo, Krav Maga... He basically whooped us in everything. But I could tell you some very embarrassing stories, Lottie."

"Really?" I asked with interest.

Before he could say more or Bo could protest, Mrs. Lee stepped into the room. Her eyes zeroed in on Shin. "You're late," she said.

"I know, *Halmeoni*," he coaxed, "but I've been deathly ill. The flu, remember?"

"You look fine to me."

"Yes, now. But—"

Her eyes narrowed. "You talking back?"

"I would never—"

"You sweep floors for being late, Shin," she said. Then her gaze moved to Bo and me. "You two, work together and cut the flowers. We need to be ready for tomorrow."

"Yes, Mrs. Lee," I said, and Bo nodded.

Once she was gone, Shin turned back to us.

"She missed me," he said.

"Obviously," Bo said sarcastically.

Shin waved him off, his eyes settling back on my face. "I recognize you," he said, looking deep in thought. "But I just don't know from where."

I swallowed, having a hunch but hoping he wouldn't get there.

But a second later, Shin snapped his fingers.

"Oh shoot," he said, his smile growing, "it's you! You're that girl from the video."

"No, I—"

"It is. You're Bo's girlfriend."

Shin came over and shook my hand.

"I have to say Lottie, I never thought I'd live to see the day," he said. "And not just because I almost died. But because, well, Bo is...kinda harsh, if you know what I mean. Underneath the scowl beats a heart of gold, and I'm so glad he finally found someone who can see that."

Bo sighed. "Shin, stop."

"I'm serious," he said back. "Lottie is now my friend by proxy. We're going to be besties too."

I gave him a faint smile. "You seem like a good friend, Shin."

"Thank you so much, Lottie," he said. "Can I officially dub you BOLO? Or would you rather your couple name be LOBO?"

I blinked, hearing a groan somewhere next to me. Pretty sure it came from Bo.

"Too soon?" Shin asked.

Thankfully, we were saved by Mrs. Lee.

"Shin," she called. "Stop slacking off. You come work up here, under my supervision."

Shin winked. "Told you she missed me."

With one last squeeze of my hand and a wave, Shin left, and an awkward silence descended. It lasted all of five seconds. That was when Bo turned to face me.

"So, *girlfriend*," he said.

Heart fluttering, I looked up at him.

"I've been waiting to hear these rules of yours."

"Really?" I asked.

He cocked his head to the side. "What do you say we talk while we water, feed, and arrange these flowers?"

"Sounds good, Stryker."

"Watch and learn," he said.

"I'll try and do what you do."

He shook his head. "There is no try, Kent."

Rolling my eyes, I scoffed. "Yeah okay, Yoda."

"*Halmeoni* swears she came up with that line first."

"Then I bet she did," I said. "Your grandmother's awesome."

Bo ignored me, but I noticed his eyes brighten. It was clear he loved her and his parents very much. Even with Shin, I'd noticed a clear affection beneath his pretense of indifference. I copied Bo's movements, trying my best to do exactly as he was. Soon, I was cutting the stems at what Bo called a careful 45-degree angle, changing out old water for new, and adding packets of flower food where necessary. Bo also did all the heavy lifting while I worked on more decorative bows. Taking a deep breath, I decided to jump right in.

"So Stryker, I've thought a lot about our situation," I said.

Bo nodded.

"And like I said, I came up with a few rules I think are a must."

"How'd you come up with them?" he asked.

I shrugged. "Tons of research via reading has taught me a thing or two."

He paused with his brow furrowed. "You've read about this?"

"Oh yeah," I said. "Fake dating is a whole thing. But you already knew that."

"What do you mean?"

Surprised, I shot him a look. "Well, you've checked out multiple books on the subject. I think half the romances on your lists involve some form of fake relationship."

He didn't say anything, so I elbowed him gently.

"It's okay," I said. "Not a lot of men are brave enough to read romance. I think it's cool that you do."

Bo lifted his chin. "Back to the rules."

"Yeah, so I came up with three." I set aside the ribbon I was working on and listed them off on my fingers. "Rule one, no physical intimacy. The kiss was a one off, no more of that."

Bo placed his batch of flowers in a bucket, turned to me, and crossed his arms.

"I don't like it."

"Why not?" I asked.

"Because everyone's already seen us kiss thanks to Leif," he said. "If we're a couple, who's going to buy that we don't even touch anymore?"

My brow furrowed. "I hadn't thought of that."

"We should negotiate rule one."

"What did you have in mind?" I asked.

Bo shrugged. "We do the normal things. Hold hands, hug, kiss—"

I shook my head. "I'm a hard no on the kissing."

"Why?"

How was I supposed to answer?

"Didn't you enjoy it?" Bo asked.

Yes, I enjoyed it. So much, too much. Kissing you felt like fireworks and symphonies and put every romance novel I've ever read to shame. I'm not sure I could do it again and not want more.

My cheeks filled with heat, and his eyes seemed to see everything.

"What kind of question is that?" I said. "Did you enjoy it?"

"Honestly, yeah. I liked kissing you," he said then added, "Kissing's a fun pastime."

Ugh. Seriously?

"*That* is why," I said, holding out a hand. "I don't see it as a pastime, Stryker. A kiss means more to me than that. Okay?"

"Okay," he said.

"But I see your point," I admitted begrudgingly. "Maybe we can just play that part by ear?"

He nodded. "What are the other rules?"

"Rule two, no faking it beyond one week, two tops," I said. "That should be long enough for people to believe us and forget the bet."

"I don't think we need an end date."

"We definitely need an end date," I replied.

He frowned. "Why?"

I didn't get why he was being so difficult. "That way no one will get hurt—which is also the reason for rule number three."

He gestured for me to go on.

"And finally, rule three, no falling in love. Obviously."

"If it's obvious, I don't think we need rules," he said.

I blinked. "But...we've got to have rules, Stryker."

"You afraid of falling in love with me, Kent?"

How he said it made me nervous.

So did the way his lips tilted up ever so slightly.

My shock only lasted a moment, then I said, "No, of course not. I may have had a few confusing feelings after kissing you, but that was all because of science."

Bo stared into my eyes. "You had feelings, huh?"

"Yeah, but like I said, I looked it up. There are neurotransmitters and hormones involved; plus it was my first kiss. Plus, I'm a hopeless romantic. My feelings were totally out of my control."

He lifted a brow.

"Rule three is for you just as much as it is for me," I added.

"Oh," Bo said. "So, you think I'll fall in love with you? In one to two weeks? That's pretty cocky, Kent."

"Ugh, I'm not saying that either."

"Then what are you saying?"

I took a deep breath for calm. "I'm just saying I don't want anything beyond a fake relationship, not just with you but with anyone."

His silence was clearly one of disbelief, but I shook my head.

"I don't."

"Thought you were a romantic," he said.

"That's right," I said, giving him a bright smile, "but love and relationships—real ones—never end well. They're too risky. Happily-ever-after doesn't exist in real life. That's why I love books."

Bo studied me a second.

"You're serious," he said.

"Well, yeah."

After a beat, I shrugged.

"So, do you agree or what?"

Bo stared at me a moment then held out his

hand. "I agree—but I still think your rules are stupid."

As I put my hand in his, warm tingles raced up my arm.

I liked the feeling entirely too much.

And that, I thought, is exactly why we need those stupid rules.

14

My sister looked at me like I was crazy.

"So, you're in a fake relationship? With Bo Stryker? And you told him you don't want to kiss him again?" she asked after I'd explained everything.

I nodded. "Pretty much."

She shook her head with a scoff. "Lotte, I don't understand you."

"That's okay," I said, "I don't understand myself half the time either."

"If you like the guy—which you obviously do," she said before I could cut in, "why are you pulling away?"

"I told you, Scar. We're just faking."

"Uh huh."

"It'll all be fine."

"Will it, though?" she asked.

"It will," I said with more assurance than I felt.

"For the record, it's clear Bo likes you too, if that's what you're worried about."

It wasn't clear at all, and I was worried. I couldn't decide whether I wanted Bo to be interested or not. But I didn't argue. My sister would debate just about anything if given the chance, and I was already tired from a sleepless night, dreams of Bo running wild in my mind.

Scarlett sighed. "I'm here if you need me."

"Thanks," I murmured.

As we parted ways, I headed for Bo's locker. My intent was to carry his books again. But before I could get there, two guys who looked like they'd just been in a fight were sprinting up the hall, coming directly at me. I flattened myself against the wall just in time. Shaking my head, I turned back—and saw Bo reach down to help someone to their feet. The kid looked like a freshman from his slightly nervous expression to his gangly body which hadn't quite grown into itself yet. He blinked up at Bo then took his hand, standing back up on wobbly legs. Bo bent down again, scooped a pair of glasses off the floor, and handed them to the kid who now stared at him with something akin to hero worship. Before he left, Bo reached into his locker and passed the kid a bright blue piece of paper.

The freshman nodded, started walking, and another guy joined him then said, "Do you know who that was? Bo 'Iceman' Stryker literally just saved your ass!"

"I know," the kid said. "Those other guys didn't stand a chance."

"What'd he give you?"

"A flyer, said I could take a class at The Academy for free."

"Martial arts is so cool," his friend said.

"Right? I heard Bo's a triple black belt or something."

They kept going until I couldn't hear, but it was clear Bo had fought back on the freshie's behalf. Gah. How was I supposed to keep my feelings in check when he did kind things like that?

Bo caught sight of me, standing frozen a few feet away, and lifted his chin.

"Hey," he said.

"Hey," I said back, closing the distance and stopping in front of him. "That was nice what you did back there. Do you know that kid?"

He shrugged. "No. The guys who were picking on him were twice his size. Thought maybe they'd want to try me instead."

"And how'd that turn out?"

"You saw them running."

"I did."

Bo's lips pressed into a thin line. "They won't mess with him again," he said.

I swallowed the huge lump that rose in my

throat.

Goodness.

Who knew confidence could be so freaking attractive?

"Practicing for your future as the world's #1 bodyguard?" I asked.

"Nah," he said, "just a normal day."

"You got your black belt when you were 10, right?"

Bo's eyes shot to mine. "How'd you know that?"

I shrugged. "Because I pay attention—and I still remember the day your family threw that party. Your dad put that bumper sticker on his car. *My son's an honor student and a black belt.* Though I like the one on your mom's better, *My son kicks ass—literally* with the cute little ninja."

Bo groaned, but my smile widened.

"They love you. It's sweet."

"Yeah, if sweet is code for embarrassing," Bo mumbled.

"It *is* sweet, like what you did for that kid just now," I repeated.

He shook his head.

"Good job, Flower Boy," I said, giving his shoulder a friendly pat.

He stared at my hand, and I dropped it, forcing a laugh.

"Sorry."

"For what?" he asked.

"Touching you," I said.

"No apology necessary." Bo coughed then lifted a brow. "I'm your boyfriend now. Remember?"

"How could I forget?" I muttered.

The dreams that'd kept me up last night were about us, our fake relationship, and every single one of them ended badly. There were some swoony bits in between sure. But the ending... I brought a hand to my temple and closed my eyes.

"You okay?" Bo asked.

"Yeah," I said, eyes still squeezed shut, "I'm just not feeling well all of a sudden."

In the next instant, there was a warm touch to my forehead.

Opening my eyes, I saw that it was Bo's hand. He'd reached out and...put the back of his hand against my skin.

"Stryker," I said, "what are you...?"

"Checking your temperature," he murmured, frowning with a look of concentration.

"Why?"

Instead of answering, he took me completely by surprise. Bo wrapped his hand around the back of my neck and gently pulled me closer, until my forehead rested against his cheek. We stood like that for several moments. He was so close I felt every rise and fall of his breath. My breathing grew shallow, my heart beating nearly out of my chest, as my eyes closed once more. His warmth surrounded me, and in that moment, I felt protected somehow.

After a beat, Bo hummed then stepped back.

"I don't think you have a fever," he said with relief.

It took me what felt like a lifetime to respond.

"Well...that's good," I said.

"Shin had a hard time with the flu, so..."

"Yeah." Of course, that made sense. Shaking myself out of it, I said, "Hand me your books?"

"I've got it," he said. When I gave him a dubious look, he added, "No really, I'm a quick healer."

My frown couldn't be contained.

"Plus, I brought this." Bo tugged on the strap of a messenger bag he had looped over his shoulder. By the outlines of square objects, his books were obviously inside. "Want me to take yours too?"

"Thanks anyway," I said.

I didn't know why I was being weird. I was glad Bo's hand was feeling better. Really, I was, but I'd wanted to help—and okay, maybe I'd been looking forward to spending time with him. Now, however, without the excuse of carrying his books...

"Guess I'll just go to class then."

"Not so fast, Kent," he said.

When I looked over, Bo was standing next to me.

"The bag also makes it so I can do this."

I jumped a bit as his fingers wrapped around mine, as our palms touched.

"This okay?" he asked.

It was better than okay.

Bo's hand in mine was wonderful, thrilling, the stuff that inspires the best love songs to be written. That was how it felt.

"It's fine," I managed. "What now?"

"Now, I'm going to walk my girlfriend to class," he said.

And right there, my heart melted.

#

Bo wasn't playing. He met me at the end of each of my classes, and we walked the halls, hand-in-hand. He also looked at me a lot more. Or at least, I caught him giving me these little glances, as if to make sure I was alright, adjusting his longer stride to match mine, making sure we didn't lose each other in the crowd. It was surreal. Our peers were watching—apparently, the novelty of our couple status hadn't worn off yet—and I knew the goal was to convince them. I just hadn't thought he'd find it so easy to pretend.

Especially with me.

Bo didn't bat an eyelash at the whispers, the attention. When I asked him about that, he shrugged.

"You get used to it," he said.

"Ah, I see," I said. "Everyone loves a superstar

athlete."

"That include you?"

I sputtered, but Bo just lifted a brow.

"It was a joke, Kent."

"Oh."

"Relax," he said quietly as we stopped.

I nodded but then froze as he pulled our joined hands up to his lips.

Bo laid a soft kiss on my knuckles.

The result: my knees went weak; my breath caught; and I was pretty sure hearts were coming out of my eyes.

The group of girls standing near us released a collective sigh, and Bo grinned.

"I think they liked that," he whispered.

They weren't the only ones, I thought.

"See you at lunch."

"Okay, Flower Boy," I said softly.

Bo gave me a stern look then. "No hiding in the bathroom."

With a laugh, I said, "That was a one time thing. I'm starving, and there's a new book I want to start. Plus"—I lowered my voice—"I have a fake boyfriend now, so I'll see you there."

Bo's frown didn't change, but somehow I knew he was pleased.

Lunch was...interesting.

Scarlett was already at our usual table when I arrived. She had her earbuds in, listening to music, and we nodded a greeting.

"Hey sis," she said, "how goes the dating game?"

"Shhh," I said, looking around.

"What? As if anyone could possibly guess what I'm talking about."

"They might."

Scarlett rolled her eyes as she took out her buds and then smiled at something over my shoulder.

"Hey there, neighbor," she said.

I felt Bo's approach before I saw him.

"I was wondering when we'd get a chance to chat."

Bo lowered his tray to the table and took the seat next to mine. He nodded to me then to my sister.

"Hey," he said to her. "I'm Bo."

"Yes, I've heard that name a lot over the years," she said with a grin, and I kicked her under the table. "I'm Scarlett, your future sister-in-law."

Sighing, I shook my head. "Sorry about her. She has no filter. We try our best to keep her away from actual people."

"Not true," Scarlett said, "I keep myself away from people because most of them are terrible."

"She has a point," Bo said.

"Thank you, Bo."

He shrugged then began taking out his lunch. This took a long time, and my eyes widened with each new item he placed on the table.

"Is it magic?" my sister asked.

Bo scoffed. "What?"

"I was thinking the same thing," I said, watching as he pulled out yet another container. "That bag seems bottomless, like the ones owned by Hermione or Mary Poppins."

"Or like a niffler's pouch," Scarlett put in.

"But Stryker doesn't have a pouch. It's clearly a bag."

"Yeah, but he fit a lot of stuff in there."

"True."

"And nifflers hoard shiny things like your boy Bo seems to hoard food. Hence the reference."

Bo blinked at the two of us. "Was I supposed to follow any of that?"

"No," we said in unison.

"Okay." Shaking his head, he opened all the containers—seven in total—then sat back, starting with some sushi. My book forgotten, I watched as he made quick work of that then moved on to the next bowl. Broccoli and carrots. Raw.

"Don't you want some dressing with that?" I asked.

He shook his head. "Empty calories."

"That make veggies semi-tasty," my sister put in.

I nodded.

Ignoring us, Bo kept going, past the veggies onto grilled chicken, two breasts with lemon juice squeezed over the top. There was something green in there too. Looked like asparagus.

"No mac n' cheese?" Scarlett asked.

"Or mashed potatoes?" I added.

"Nope—but I do bring a plain sweet potato sometimes."

Bo looked totally happy with his lunch, and it wasn't like my sister and I hated vegetables. But come on. All that, and not one tasty item in the bunch? Spying another container with something that looked a little odd, I pointed to it.

"What's that?" I asked.

"Kimchi," he said, pointing to the right side. "On the left, there's pickled cabbage, carrots, and cucumber."

My sister and I leaned over to get a closer look.

"You want to try some?" Bo asked.

My sister shook her head. "No, thanks. I already ate."

"Sure," I said, using the plastic fork I'd brought from home.

Bo lifted a brow. "Full warning, it's an acquired taste."

I shot him a smile. "Ah, kind of like you and your grumpiness."

He scowled in reply.

"And there's the frown I love so much," I said.

"Glad to hear it," he replied, "though I know you like my smile better. What was it you said before? Oh yeah, it's like the sun coming out after a storm?"

"Good memory," I said, coughing to hide my blush.

Scarlett's eyes were shining with interest, but before she could ask any questions, I shoved a bite of kimchi into my mouth. Salty, sour, flavorful with a hint of heat.

"I like it," I said.

"You sound surprised," Bo said back.

Disregarding that, I took a bite of the pickled cabbage next, and my eyes widened.

"Ooh, I love that!" Pointing at it, I told Scarlett. "This one's my favorite, but you'd like the kimchi. Here."

Scarlett chewed then smiled. "That's delicious."

Bo hummed in agreement as he polished off another container.

"We'll have to look up the recipes so Dad can try," I said.

"I'll bring you some," Bo said. "My grandma makes enough to feed an army—which is basically enough for my parents because they love the stuff, especially my dad. But I know she wouldn't mind making more. Especially since you're her favorite new employee."

I shot him a look then turned to my sister. "Mrs. Lee barely talks to me when I'm at work."

"She says more to you than most," Bo said.

"And she always frowns whenever I'm around."

"Again, that's just *Halmeoni*."

Scarlett grinned. "So, she's tight-lipped and stern?"

I nodded. "She is, but I like her. A lot."

"Sounds like someone else we both know," she said, shooting Bo a pointed look.

Rolling my eyes, I turned to Bo. "We would love some kimchi and pickled cabbage. Thank you, Stryker."

He nodded at me and packed up his now-empty dishes in record time. "No problem. Aren't you going to eat?"

"Well, I was going to read first, but you distracted me with your magic sack-o-lunch."

Bo cocked his head. "If your sister wasn't here, I can think of a ton of other ways to distract you."

My jaw dropped.

"Fun ways," he added, throwing me a small grin.

Dang.

The playful words, the tilt of his lips. Note to self: In addition to pushups and frowning sexily, Bo was also an expert at flirting. Who knew?

Scarlett shook her head. "Oh please, don't stop on my account."

"Maybe later," I said with a flick of my wrist. "I can't be distracted right now. Lunch is almost over."

Reaching into my bag, I pulled out my lunch. The cinnamon roll was calling my name. But before I had lifted the first forkful to my mouth, I felt Bo's stare. He watched as I slowly brought the bite to my lips.

"What...what's that?" he asked.

"Only the best thing ever, a soft, sweet, perfectly cooked cinnamon roll," I said.

Bo was practically drooling as I placed the food into my mouth and chewed, closing my eyes.

"Umm."

When I reopened them, he was still staring.

"Would you like a bite?" I asked.

"No, no. I shouldn't," he said, but Bo was learning forward. I didn't think he knew he was doing it—but he was. "Too much sugar. Not enough nutritional value."

"Are you sure?" I put a good-sized bite on my fork and brought it closer to him. "Even though I made them this morning, it's still kinda warm."

"Is it?"

"Yeah."

"Smells good."

"One bite, Stryker."

"But I don't..."

"On second thought, maybe you're right," I said, drawing the fork back, nearly laughing at Bo's scowl. "You'll have to run off all those calories later or your abs might disappear."

Frowning, Bo wrapped his hand around my wrist and brought the fork back to his lips.

"My abs are solid," he said. "I'll prove it to you later if you want."

Ooh yes, please.

He took the bite into his mouth, groaning as the sugar hit his tongue, chewing so slowly, savoring the sweet like it was a little piece of heaven. After he swallowed, his eyelids flipped open, and his gaze landed on mine.

"You made that?" he asked.

"Yeah."

"It's worth the calories."

"Thank you." On reflex, I reached forward to wipe the side of his lip then stopped with my hand hanging awkwardly between us. "You've got sugar right there."

Bo turned his head, letting me brush the side of his face, but when he turned back, his eyes were burning with something.

"I gotta go," he said almost to himself.

"O-okay," I replied.

Taking my hand, he placed a kiss on my thumb, removing the leftover sugar with a brief but devastating brush of his tongue. I couldn't have spoken then even if I'd wanted to.

Before he could leave, Scarlett said, "Hey Bo, you should come over for dinner sometime."

His eyes moved from my sister to me. "If Kent wants me there, I'll be there," he said.

"She does."

I did, but I wasn't sure how I felt about Scarlett actually saying that.

Bo lifted a brow, and I smiled, giving him a nod.

"Cool." To Scarlett, he said, "You two should come to the soccer game tomorrow."

"Oh, fun," Scarlett said, and I shot her a look of disbelief.

She either didn't see or chose to ignore it.

"We'll be there," I said. "Thanks for the invite."

Bo tilted his head. "You're my girl, Kent. I'd love to see you at all my games."

"You would?"

"Of course."

With a clearing of his throat, he stood, grabbed his bag, nodded to us, and then he was gone. Scarlett and I watched him go. When I turned to her, Scarlett's face was alive with all the things she hadn't said.

"What?" I asked.

"I like him," Scarlett said.

"I know," I said back. "You invited him to dinner—and called soccer 'fun'."

"You're welcome for that."

"You have literally zero interest in sports, Scar."

She flipped her hair over her shoulder. "Yes, but Bo will be playing. And as previously stated, I really like him."

"Hmmm. Too bad he's already taken."

She crossed her arms with a smug grin. "Jealousy is a good look on you, Lotte."

"That wasn't jealousy," I retorted.

"Whatever you say. You two are so smitten. It's disgusting."

The bell rang, and we stood.

"Will you at least admit that you like him too?" she asked.

I sighed.

"I do like him, Scar," I confessed then shook my head. "So much more than I should."

"I got that when you gave him some of your roll," she muttered, twining her arm through mine as we walked. "You practically growl when I skim your fries."

"Conditioned response," I said. "You steal my food all the time, and Bo looked like he hadn't seen dessert in a million years. Those eyes of his were begging for a taste."

Scarlett's smile was wicked. "Yeah, he wanted a taste of something."

I elbowed her side.

"You like him," she said.

I scoffed, but it was true.

No use denying the facts. I was crushing on Bo Stryker—even though I knew we were just pretending. Maybe there was a book on how not to fall for your fake boyfriend?

15

I couldn't find a book to help me with my current problem. Apparently authors, and people in general, didn't write or think about "how not to fall in love." And there definitely weren't any how-to books on fake boyfriends.

It was only the second time the library let me down.

The first was years ago when I looked up "how to make your mom love you."

Turned out people didn't write books on that subject either.

A strange melancholy tried to swamp me, but I forcefully pushed it to the back of my mind. Huh. That was weird. I hardly ever thought about my mother anymore.

Pulling my shoulders back, I inhaled deeply,

taking in the smell of old books, and then smiled.

The library was truly my favorite place in the world.

Nothing would bring me down today.

People always assumed libraries were quiet. And yeah, they were sometimes. But if you ever had a chance to work in one, you got to meet the most interesting people. Today, there was more traffic than usual. I wasn't sure what was going on, but there was clearly something in the air.

"It's been like this all day," Casey said.

"Looks like a lot of new faces," I commented.

"Yeah," Natalia said, "we could've definitely used your help earlier, Lottie."

"I know." I gave her an apologetic glance. "I told Mrs. Lee I'd alternate days, sometimes going first to the flower shop then library and vice versa. But I'm here now."

She grinned as someone took one of our A Night Out with Austen flyers. "At least, we're getting the word out."

"I've had to refill my tray twice," Casey confirmed.

"That's awesome," I said. "Hopefully, we can keep the momentum going."

A woman wearing big round sunglasses, a brown trench coat, and a silk scarf approached the library counter as I settled in. She had a determined stride.

"I'm looking for the latest release by Liv

Lamoreaux," she said so low I almost couldn't hear.

"*Foolish Love*?" I said.

She shushed me then whispered, "Yes, that one."

"We have it. It's wonderful, but so are all of Lamoreaux's books."

She looked around like someone might hear us.

"I think it's her best—and spiciest—yet," I added.

"Well good," she murmured, "I could use a little spice in my life. Can you tell me where to find it?"

"Aisle 18," I said.

"Thank you." With a nod, she marched away.

"I think that was my Sunday school teacher," Casey said.

Natalia whooped. "Coolest Sunday school teacher ever."

"Definitely the one with the best book taste," I added.

"I guess," Casey said.

"Even Sunday school teachers need romance, Case."

"I know, I'm not judging," she said. "But why not just own it? She's a grown woman. She doesn't have to be all shifty."

I nodded. "I did get kind of a secret agent, keep-it-on-the-DL vibe."

"No need to hide. She can read what she wants."

"Yep," I said, "but if she really was hiding, I don't think she would've even come to the library. Maybe this is her little rebellion."

The girls murmured in agreement, and when the teacher came back, she had the book in hand. I scanned it, put one of our event flyers on top, then said, "Thank you so much for coming in today! Please consider supporting our Friends of the Library charity event where we raise funds to give books to underprivileged children. There's a QR code if you'd like to donate. Happy reading."

"You too," she said, giving me a small smile before she readjusted her shades and left.

The family I helped after her was totally different.

"So, you're looking for an adventure in book form," I said to the man standing on the other side of the library counter, "preferably PG, middle grade with humor, featuring mythology because that's what your kids are into right now?"

The 40-something-year-old nodded. "Yes, and because I need to distract them, so I can finally get some work done."

I bit back a grin as the little girl and boy he'd brought with him chased each other, running circles around his legs.

"Guys," he said calmly, "if you don't stop that right now, I'm calling your mother."

The two looked up in alarm.

"I mean it." He leaned closer to me and dropped his voice. "I don't really mean it. My wife needs rest. That's why I told her I'd take them for a few hours. It's only been one, and it feels like a year. But I love the little heathens."

Either they heard what he said, or the warning had worn off because his children were now engaged in a pretend sword fight, involving two rulers they got from who knew where.

The man sighed then lifted a brow. "So miss, can you help?"

I nodded. "Absolutely! Try the *Percy Jackson* series by Rick Riordan. Also, the *Warriors* series by Erin Hunter; it's not gods and goddesses, but I hear the warrior cats are pretty awesome. The children's section is just that way on aisle five."

"Warrior cats," he repeated, sounding dubious, but the young girl paused.

Her t-shirt, featuring Hello Kitty, glinted under the lights, and her eyes held interest as she asked, "Did you say cats? I love them!"

I shrugged. "Then I guess you better go snag the books before someone else does. But no running," I added. "This is a library after all."

Her brother said, "Slo-mo zombie race?" and off they went, walking with their arms stretched out like extras from *The Walking Dead*. Dad followed after them, throwing a hasty "Thanks" over his shoulder.

The next person I helped was one of my favorites. A true romantic at heart, Mrs. Jenkins could read a book a day. She was in her late 70s, her salt-and-pepper hair always pulled back from her face with the prettiest pins, her eyes a deep chocolatey brown. But what I loved best about her was that Mrs. Jenkins was a book dragon just like I hoped to be when I grew up.

"Hi Mrs. Jenkins," I said as she came forward. "How are you today?"

"I'm floating on a cloud, Lottie," she said, holding up the last book she'd checked out. "This beauty kept me up well past midnight. I was stumbling into the ladies' bridge game, but I don't regret a thing."

"So you enjoyed Count Montague and his wicked ways?"

"Oh yes," she said then winked. "He's the main reason I had to stay up."

"Who needs sleep when you have amazing books to read?" I said with a grin.

"Hear, hear." Mrs. Jenkins patted her hair. "I always say there'll be plenty of time to sleep when I'm dead."

I tilted my head in thought. "True...but I think there'll also be time to read. If there is a Heaven, it must be filled with books. Don't you think?"

Her eyes sparkled at the thought. "See, this is why you and I get along—despite the huge age difference."

"Age is just a number," I said then held up a finger, "and besides you just turned what, 40?"

"Pssh." Mrs. Jenkins waved me off, but she was

grinning like a lark. "For that girl, I think you just earned the right to a complimentary one of my pecan pies."

Ooh, yum.

"But only"—she lifted a brow—"after you give me another good rec?"

I gave her an affronted look. "Just one? Mrs. Jenkins, what do you take me for? I've got three for you right here. They're all series starters too."

Mrs. Jenkins smiled then passed the book she was returning across the counter along with her library card. I scanned it and the three novels I just knew she was going to love. When I handed them to her—along with our event flyer—she nodded.

"You're the best, Lottie," she said.

"No, you are," I said. "And you should definitely come to our charity event."

"A Night Out with Austen?" she said. "Sounds right up my alley."

"Me, too. Hopefully, we'll have at least one soul brave enough to come as Mr. Darcy."

"Or Count Montague!"

"Seriously, Mrs. Jenkins, you should come," I said. "It's going to be so much fun for an amazing cause."

"I'll mark the date on my calendar, so I remember," she said.

"Oh yay! That's wonderful."

"I also wanted to say, I greatly enjoyed your

video. Library kisses are so incredibly swoony."

She walked away with a spring in her step—but I was left gaping. Had she just said what I thought she said?

Shaking my head, I refused to believe it. There was no way Mrs. Jenkins had seen the kiss, no reason to think she'd referenced the video of me and Bo. Nope. She must've been talking about something else.

"Well, that was odd," Casey said.

"Right?" I replied, forcing a laugh. "Mrs. Jenkins and I are usually on the same page. But I don't know what she meant by that last part."

"Um, I think you do."

"What?"

Casey put a hand on her hip. "Come on, Lottie. We all know what she meant."

Our eyes shifted to Natalia as she gasped.

"Oh my gosh," she said. "I think someone else mentioned it!"

"No," I said.

"Yes, this girl who looked about 14 asked if this was the library with the kiss, and I said sure." She shrugged. "At the time, I thought she was asking about romance, kissing books—which we definitely have. But now...oh, this makes so much more sense."

"I disagree one hundred percent," I said. "This doesn't make any sense."

"It's the library kiss challenge," Natalia said, eyes

twinkling.

I shook my head in confusion. "Am I supposed to know what that is?"

"She's talking about the challenge you and Bo inspired," Casey explained. "The one where people go to a library and film themselves kissing someone they're into."

My jaw dropped. "That's an actual thing?"

"It is." Casey nodded with a thoughtful expression. "And it would explain a lot. Just look around."

I did, and immediately saw what she was getting at.

The Chariot Public Library was never this full. On top of that, the people who came, though diverse, usually fell into one of two age demographics, children with their parents or older adults. But on this day...teenagers. Here, there and everywhere, as far as the eye could see, girls and guys in their teens seemed to be leaning against shelves, skimming over books, or sitting around reading them. And there were definitely more couples than usual.

"No wonder I saw more people hooking up in the stacks," Casey said.

"I did too," I said, thinking back to when I went for a bathroom break and passed two kids kissing, "but I just let it go. I didn't think..."

"That you were the cause?" Natalia said.

"Good grief. Don't say that," I said.

Casey grinned. "You and your boyfriend started a kissing cult."

"Ugh."

Natalia shook her head. "They inspired people to come to the library—and yeah, to kiss. That's pretty cool, Lottie."

"Mrs. Welks won't see it that way," I mumbled. "I'll be lucky if she doesn't throw me out and ban me from ever coming back."

"She's a tough nut," Casey agreed.

"She's our boss," Natalia put in then added, "but yeah, she is strict."

"Strict? The woman's got a stick up her—"

"Girls," a new voice said, and a shadow fell over the three of us, "how's it going out here?"

We each responded with some version of good as our boss, Mrs. Welks, surveyed the scene, staring unsmiling at the three of us, her stark gaze coming to rest at last on me.

"Ms. Kent," she said, voice soft yet clanging like a gong in my mind, "I'd like to see you in my office."

"Yes, ma'am," I said softly, tidying my space to play for time.

"Don't worry about that. This will only take a second."

I gulped as she walked away, the sound of her high heels like a countdown to my demise.

"Show no fear," Casey said as I moved to follow.

"Remember, you did nothing wrong."

"Well, she did let Bo behind the counter..." Natalia trailed off, and her eyes shot wide. "I mean, of course, you did nothing wrong, Lottie. Everything will be fine."

"Thanks guys." I sighed. "Besides the books, you were both my favorite parts of this job."

"She's not going to fire you," Casey said.

"She's not," Natalia agreed.

"And even if she does, it's not like she can ban you from the library forever. We'll still get to see each other."

"And I bet that kiss was worth it."

As I forced my feet to walk, their words ran through my head. Could Mrs. Welks ban me from the library? Did she have that kind of power? What was I going to do if I didn't have my safe haven? And...was the kiss actually worth it?

It was, I decided.

But I wasn't giving up my dream job without a fight.

"Mrs. Welks," I said, stepping into my boss's office with my hands out, "I know this looks bad. But I want to let you know that I've never done anything like that before, and I never will again. I take my job as a librarian's assistant very seriously."

"Shut the door please, Ms. Kent," she said.

"Yes, ma'am." I did as she asked but kept talking. "I really love working here. The Chariot Public

Library has been like a second home since I was a child. I would never do anything to jeopardize—"

"Charlotte."

"—my place here. And I even like working for you, though you once called my smile annoying and say I talk too much."

"Ms. Kent."

"And...it was only a kiss," I finished lamely. "You wouldn't fire your best employee over a kiss, right?"

Sitting back in her chair, Mrs. Welks surveyed me with her usual pinched expression. Her dress was a black and grey plaid, her sweater dark burgundy which matched her shoes, and she was also rocking black cat glasses. The overall look was kind of like a librarian angel of death. Mrs. Welks struck fear into the hearts of anyone who was caught talking too loud or disrespecting the books. Oh yes, and into employees who'd stepped out of line.

"What exactly do you think is happening here?" she asked after staring me down.

I deflated like a punctured balloon. "Well, I assume you saw the video?"

"I have," she confirmed.

"So, aren't you going to fire me?"

Mrs. Welks tilted her head then slowly began to smile. "Not today, Ms. Kent."

"Huh?"

"Why would I fire my best employee, who I might add has breathed new life into the library?"

I couldn't take my eyes off her as Mrs. Welks leaned forward, a full, bright smile like I'd never seen on her lips.

"Just look out there," she said, gazing through her open doorway. "Those are teenagers, Ms. Kent. *Teenagers!*" The way she said it made teens sound like a completely different species. "Your age group is overly sarcastic, woefully underread, and basically hates everything. Besides you, Casey, and Natalia, I can count on one hand how many high schoolers we typically see in a week. Your kiss wasn't just a kiss."

Her eyes were bright.

"The stunt you pulled with that boy started a literary movement."

"I don't know about that," I said.

"Well, I do," she said, leaving no room for argument. "And I know you'll continue to be dedicated to your job and this library."

I nodded. "Absolutely."

"And that you'll take advantage of this opportunity to introduce the aimless young people of your generation to the joy of books."

"I'd love to, Mrs. Welks."

"And," she said, holding up a finger, "that you personally will ensure this year's Friends of the Library is the best one yet."

"You have my word," I promised. "I'll do all I can to make it a success."

She gave a nod. "Then you can go."

It took a moment to set in, but once it did, elation poured through my veins. I wasn't getting fired. The fates had smiled upon me. It was a freaking miracle, and I wouldn't take it for granted.

"Ms. Kent."

Looking over my shoulder, I said, "Yes?"

"Remember, no visitors allowed behind the counter," she said. "Not even your cute boyfriend."

With a nod, I hurried out before she could change her mind.

As if she'd conjured him, Bo was standing with his elbows on the counter when I came back. He looked at me and lifted a brow.

"Everything okay?" he asked.

"Yeah," I said, "of course. Did you need something?"

"Do I need a reason to come visit my girl?"

Heat rising in my cheeks, I ignored the twin sighs I heard from my friends.

But I couldn't deny the effect his words had on me. Every time he said the words "my girl" or called me his "girlfriend," my heart took flight. It happened without fail. This was fake, I reminded myself. But the very real flutters remained in my chest.

"Missed me already, huh?" I joked, thinking he would scoff, roll his eyes, or, dare I hope, laugh again.

But Bo did none of those things.

He just said, "Yeah, maybe I did."

"I wasn't expecting"—*you to say that*—"to see you so soon."

"Good or bad surprise?" he asked.

"Good," I said softly.

His eyes grew bright. "Glad to hear it. I'm also returning these"—Bo passed some books across the counter—"and picking up a few more."

The books on today's list were familiar.

"Some of my favorites are on here," I said.

"Oh yeah?"

I nodded.

"Then I'll be sure to read them," he said.

For some reason, that made my eyes soften. I knew Bo probably noticed, but it couldn't be helped.

"Hey," another voice said, and I turned to see a girl about my age. "Weren't you two in that video?"

I looked to Bo, and he nodded.

"That's us," he said.

"You know that has over a million views, right?"

I nearly choked. "Really?"

She nodded, gesturing to the girl beside her. "The library kiss challenge is why we even came. It's cool to meet you."

"Good to meet you too," I said somewhat in a daze.

"Can we get a picture?" she asked. "Honestly, I didn't expect you guys to be real."

I nodded then walked around the counter,

holding in a gasp as Bo wrapped a hand around my waist.

"Well, we are," he said, giving me a small smile. "Right, Kent?"

"Right," I said.

He was so close. His eyes were so familiar and warm.

Leaning up, I gave him a kiss on the cheek, and Bo froze in surprise. That was right when the other couple snapped a pic. I asked if they would send it to me, and they said yes. Again, I knew I probably shouldn't have done it, just kissed Bo out of the blue like that. But I couldn't resist.

He was quickly becoming something that I didn't want to resist.

Which was a problem for several reasons.

The biggest one being: If I gave in, I knew, somehow, I just knew I wouldn't want to give him up.

16

Fact: Holding hands was seriously underrated.

I didn't know if it was because I'd read so many romance books or because I could basically live off K-dramas, rom-coms, and swoony movies for the rest of my life and be content. But holding Bo's hand was quickly becoming one of my favorite things.

Whenever we walked through the halls, he reached for me.

His hand was larger, his fingers longer, the skin a bit rougher than mine.

But my hand fit perfectly in his.

I loved it when he entwined our fingers together.

Now and again, he also ran his thumb up and down the center of my palm, ending in a soft circle against my wrist.

The gentle movement made my pulse jump, eyelids flutter, and sent a shiver of pleasure down my spine.

It was crazy.

That small touch affected me way more than it should have. I had a feeling Bo knew this which was why he kept doing it. But I couldn't be sure because whenever I glanced his way, Bo's face was completely blank.

Just to see what would happen, I tried the move on him once.

Bo hadn't moved an inch.

His jaw tightened the slightest bit, but other than that?

Nothing.

Oh well, I hadn't expected him to react the same way. Bo wasn't the one currently fighting back feelings. My fake boyfriend was a master of detachment. When we were switching classes for the last time, I decided to try mirroring his unreadable expression, hoping maybe his serious vibe would rub off on me.

But when Bo looked at me, he blinked.

"What's that face?" he asked.

I shrugged. "Just trying something new."

"No."

"No?" I repeated.

He shook his head. "That's not you, Kent. Stop

it."

"Why?"

"You're scaring the freshman."

"Ha ha," I said.

"Seriously, stop," he said.

"Mad that I stole your look, Stryker?"

When we got to my final class of the day, he'd turned to me and waited until I met his gaze.

"I'm not mad," he said.

I tilted my head.

"It's just...why would you want to be anyone else? You're you, and that's good."

Placing my hands on my hips, I said, "Seriously? No cracks about me being fake or smiling too big, too often?"

Bo just shook his head. "I never said that."

"Oh yeah, that's just other people."

"Who cares what they think?"

Bo pushed a strand of hair behind my ear, and I felt my detached expression melt away. It was impossible to remain blank. He'd literally just made my day. I'd always wondered what that would feel like—someone besides me brushing the hair behind my ear—and it was just as magical as I'd imagined.

"There," he said, watching as my lips curved into a surprised smile. Bo's own lips kicked up a bit at the corner. "There you are. Screw the haters. You do you, Kent."

"Wow, Stryker," I said, feeling myself staring

and trying to shake it off. Voice quiet, I added, "You're really selling the whole fake boyfriend thing."

Lips falling into a straight line, Bo took a step back. "Yeah," he said, "yeah. You coming to the game later?"

"I wouldn't miss it."

Bo nodded.

"Good luck," I said, but he was already walking away.

After working at the library and flower shop, I had just enough time to go home, get ready, pick up Scarlett, and drive to the game. We made it on time. But Scarlett—who'd always hated being late to anything—was still grumbling as we made our way to the stands.

"What if there are no seats left?" she said.

"We'll find seats," I replied.

"Not sure if you remember, but soccer's a popular sport in Chariot."

A total understatement, and Scarlett's tone was laced with sarcasm.

I did know. Of course, I did. You couldn't grow up in Chariot, North Carolina, let alone the Kent household, without getting swept up in soccer mania. My uncle had gone to CHS at the same time as Bo's dad, and the stories of the two of them, Becks Kent and Ash Stryker, their unstoppable talent, the championships they'd brought home to CHS, were the stuff of legend. It didn't hurt that both of them went on to have super successful careers in college and then professional soccer. Anyway, Scarlett had a point. No doubt there would be a lot of people. But...

"The games always sell out," I said, "but luckily, we already got tickets. Relax, sis. It's all good."

"Kickoff, jump ball, or whatever-the-heck-they-call-it is in five minutes," she said. "We're like the last ones here."

I peered around then said, "I don't think so. People were parking at the same time as us."

"Yeah, but I bet they weren't personally invited by the star of the team."

"Stryker just did that to keep up appearances," I said.

"Hmmm."

I shot her a look. "I know that sound."

She shrugged. "Then you should know I call B.S. He wants you here, Lotte. That's why he asked you to come. Period."

"If you say so."

"I do," she said, holding up her hands. "You're his girlfriend."

"Fake girlfriend," I muttered.

"What's Bo going to think if he looks to the stands, and you're not there?"

Before I could answer, Scarlett literally clucked her tongue at me.

"And I still don't get the outfit."

"What's wrong with how I look?" I asked offended.

Scarlett eyed me up and down, pursed her lips then shook her head. "I don't even know where to start."

With a huff, I picked up the pace. We'd both been right. The Chariot High Trojans drew a big crowd, but I was able to find us an empty stretch of bleachers, half-way to the top, that afforded an awesome view of the field. Tugging her down next to me, I turned to her.

"Happy now?" I asked.

"Very," she said with a grin. "We're not late."

"I told you we'd be fine." I lowered my voice. "And why are you giving me a hard time? I specifically chose this look for tonight."

I pointed to my hair.

"The Princess Leia buns are for empowerment and good luck."

Scarlett sighed.

"I made this t-shirt to show my school spirit."

"The tee is okay," she said.

"And I wore the hoodie and sweatpants—"

"The frumpy, shapeless hoodie and sweatpants," she cut in.

"—because, unlike you, I looked up tonight's forecast. It's supposed to be cold and windy," I finished.

My sister crossed her bare arms which I could already tell had goosebumps. "Your fitted jeans are warm too. Plus, they make your butt look amazing."

I smiled. "Not sure if I should be weirded out or flattered that my sister just said that."

"Whatever," she said. "You didn't wear them—or leave your hair down, like I suggested."

"I made an executive decision."

"But you look so hot with your hair down."

"Again, not sure how to feel about that, Scar."

She huffed out a breath. "I know Bo would've liked it."

I shook my head, making sure to keep my voice quiet so only she could hear. "Scar, we're not actually together."

"Then why are we here?"

"Even before Bo and I were..."

"Dating?" she supplied when I struggled to find the right word.

"*Fake* dating," I whispered. "Even before that, I'd already decided to go to his games and cheer him on, at least until his wrist and face heal."

Scarlett bit back a smile. "Ah yes, the infamous book slap. I'd almost forgotten."

"Well, I haven't. I'm doing what I can to make up for it."

"Okay—but be honest about the outfit. You're hiding, at least a little."

I sniffed because there was a small thread of

truth in what she was saying. Instead of fessing up, I said, "This is my fan gear. People dress like this at sporting events."

"Have you ever been to a soccer game?"

I shrugged. "I've attended virtually."

Scarlett gave me a nod. "Ever watch Bo play?"

Only almost every game he was in in high school. My blush must've given me away because suddenly my sister was all smiles.

"I do love the little soccer ball on your cheek," she said.

I rolled my eyes. "Yeah, because you painted it."

"Did I?"

Shoving her with an elbow, I laughed.

"I guess you're right," she said. "It doesn't really matter what you wear. Bo likes you, quirks and all."

"Scarlett," I groaned.

My sister shot me a sweet smile. "What?"

Before we could bicker more, I spotted Bo warming up on the sidelines. He and the rest of the team were stretching. Thanks to his morning ritual I'd seen him like this tons of times. But there was something about that uniform. The shirt accentuated his broad shoulders and trim waist, and those shorts were doing amazing things for his muscular legs. Goodness, even his forearms were attractive. Was that a thing? Yep, I thought, as he clenched and unclenched his hands.

My eyes moved back up to his face, catching

that familiar frown, though this time it was directed out to the field, more focused, his mind completely on the game.

As the refs and players got set up for kickoff, my gaze was on Bo.

The whistle sounded.

Though I'd watched several games via livestream, this felt different.

Everything was more alive. The air was charged; the crowd was pumped; and as the Trojans ran up the pitch, Bo had possession of the ball. He controlled it like he owned it. Shaking off players left and right, he was unstoppable. Bo passed to his teammates, working their way to the goal, but he was obviously their captain. His confidence, agility, and sheer athleticism was unmatched. When he got the ball back, he turned up the speed, and there was no one but him and the goalie. The side of his foot connected with the ball with a whack, and the next sound everyone heard was the swish of the net.

"Woo! Let's go, Stryker," I shouted.

I didn't know if he'd hear me. The rest of the Chariot fans were going crazy too. But for some reason, I could've sworn I saw Bo look right at me as he ran to the other side of the field, his lips quirking before they went back to a forbidding scowl.

"Jeez," Scarlett said, "I thought soccer was supposed to be a slow game."

"Not when Stryker's playing," I said.

"No kidding. He scored in what? The first three minutes?"

Two-and-a-half, I thought.

But that wasn't the only time he gave us a reason to cheer.

Bo kept scoring, and every time he did, I hooted and hollered my ass off. At one point, Scarlett looked the tiniest bit embarrassed. But I didn't care. The other Chariot fans were just as hype.

"Can I borrow your jacket?" she asked about 20 minutes into the game.

"I thought you hated my hoodie," I said.

Scarlett shot me a frown. "It's so I can hide and pretend we don't know each other when your voice gets too loud."

"Then no, you may not."

"Come on, Lotte. I'm freezing," she said.

"Fine," I said, removing my outer layer, glad I'd worn a turtleneck underneath the t-shirt, "but no more cracks about my clothes—which are practical and comfy."

"Sure, sure," she said, tugging on the hoodie.

There wasn't really a nice way to say it. The Trojans annihilated the other team. Our offense and defense were just better. At half-time, we were up by four goals (three of which had been scored by Bo). He scored two more in the second, and the game was over after that. CHS took the win 7-2. I watched as the players of both teams shook hands, and Coach Stryker pulled his son in for a hug.

"Ah, that's so sweet," I said as we descended the bleachers.

"It is," Scarlett agreed, "oh, and look. There's his mom and Mrs. Lee."

As they met up with Bo on the sidelines, both his mom and grandma took turns hugging and patting him on the back.

"I didn't notice them during the game," I commented.

"That's because you were too busy geeking out every time your man did something noteworthy," Scarlett said, examining her nails. "Which was a lot."

"Did you see them walk in?"

"Yeah, a little after us."

I nodded. That made sense. Mrs. Lee must've had to close the flower shop, and then they came straight here. Someone tapped me on the shoulder, and I turned, only to see the smiling face of my cousin.

"Vi!" I said, throwing my arms around her in a hug. "How are you here right now?"

"Well," she laughed, hugging me back and then moving to give Scarlett a squeeze, "I had a free night, so we came to check out the competition."

"We?"

"Me and Dare," she said, nodding to the guy standing with an arm around her waist.

Wavy dark brown hair, blue eyes, and a

charming smile, I'd met Viola's boyfriend at the annual Kent family reunion. But it didn't matter. Dare Frost was one of those people who just made you want to stare. He was pretty, and he knew it. His attractiveness wasn't quiet or undercover. The cool thing about him, though, was that he wasn't a jerk, which made me like him for my cousin.

"Hey," he said with an easy smile, "it's my two favorite Kent sisters. How's it going?"

"Going good," Scarlett said, "considering I just had to sit through a sporting event."

Viola laughed. "I so hear that."

"Hey now"—Dare pulled her in closer—"I thought you liked watching me play?"

"I do," she said, staring up at him with a soft smile, "you know, I do. But you weren't out there today, so it wasn't as fun for me."

He placed a kiss on her nose. "I love hearing that, flower."

"You would."

I sighed, couldn't help it. "You two are so cute together."

Viola blushed, and Dare looked like he was enjoying every second.

Scarlett leaned over to me and said, "They are, but I swear, on the adorable scale, you and Bo give them a run for their money."

Viola's eyes lit up. "What's this about you and Bo?"

"So you actually do that?" I asked, pretending as if I hadn't heard her and speaking to Dare. "Come and watch other teams play. Is that normal?"

"Yeah," Dare said, "it's pretty common, especially when you're going to be coming up against someone like Stryker."

I tilted my head with a smile. "He's amazing. Isn't he?"

"They call him Iceman for a reason. He's brutal on the field."

"Glad to hear you think so," Bo said, appearing behind me. When he lazily draped his arm around my waist, I felt my breath catch, tried not to let it show. "You here to spy on us, Frost?"

Dare laughed. "Like you don't do the same when you gotta go against Durham?"

Bo was silent a beat then, "We do sometimes. But I usually just watch game film, like all civilized people."

"You calling me *un*-civilized, Stryker?"

"Maybe."

"I'll remember that come game time."

"Wouldn't want you to forget."

"It's going to be an all-out battle."

"I know," Bo said. "I'm not the only one who's brutal, *Killer* Frost."

After a pause, the two guys walked forward, clasped hands, and patted each other on the back like guys do. What the heck? For a second, I'd honestly thought they might fight.

"You two know each other," I said, coming to the realization belatedly.

"Yeah," Bo said, looking down at me, "mainly through my dad and Coach Kent."

"Ah, the rivalry that turned into a lifelong friendship." My smile widened. "I can totally see that for you guys."

Bo and Dare glanced at each other—then both shook their heads.

"Nah, Kent, I'm not seeing it," Bo said.

"Me neither," Dare retorted.

I crossed my arms, and Viola rolled her eyes.

Scarlett, though, laughed. "Ooh, your boyfriends aren't getting along. We'll have to do something about that before the next reunion."

Maintaining my smile was an effort, but I kept it together as Viola squealed at the news.

"What?!?" she said, looking from me to Bo and back again. "You two are together now?"

"We are," I said, nearly jumping as his fingers flexed against my waist. "It's kind of a new thing."

"I had no idea."

Dare lifted his chin at Bo. "That's awesome, man. Congrats."

"Thanks," Bo said.

Viola's eyes were full of wonder when she asked, "How did this happen?"

I tried to form words, but nothing came out.

Scarlett just grinned, enjoying this far too much, and Bo was the one who came to the rescue.

"It started at the library," he said, and when I looked up, he was gazing down at me with an unreadable expression. "Then it grew from there. Right, Kent?"

"Y-yeah," I stuttered, still lost in that intense gaze and the sheer closeness of him.

"My girl loves books."

"I do."

Someone sighed.

It must've been Viola because then she said, "You're right, Scar. They are adorable."

"Told you so," my sister said.

Clearing my throat, knowing there was a blush on my cheeks, I looked away.

"Well," I said, "it was great seeing you, Vi. Are we still on for story time this weekend?"

"Of course," Viola said. "The dogs and cats at the shelter love it."

I grinned. "Well, the readers do too."

Scarlett gave a nod. "Some of the kids from my mentoring program signed up. They're really excited."

"Everyone gets something out of the deal," I said, "which is what makes it the best."

Bo was looking at me curiously, but before he could say anything, Viola stepped forward.

"Well, we better head out," she said, sweeping

Scarlett into a hug. "I'll see you guys soon."

"Can't wait," Scarlett said then leaned back and pointed a finger her way. "Don't forget we're also playing at the library charity event. So practice."

"Duh."

Viola loved playing the cello almost as much as she loved working at the shelter. Plus, she was a heck of a lot better at it than I was at violin. I had no worries at all that she'd be ready for our performance.

When she pulled me into a hug, she lowered her voice then said, "Lotte, seriously. Bo Stryker?"

"Yeah," I said.

"I didn't even know he could smile."

"He can, and it's beautiful."

"I'll take your word on that," she laughed then pulled back. "You two seem really good together. I'm happy for you."

"Thanks," I said with a smile. "I'm happy for you too."

Dare and Bo tapped fists.

"See you soon," Dare said.

"Yeah," Bo said. "Hoping we beat you again like last year."

"I was sick last year," Dare called back, even as Viola pulled him away.

"Sure, you were."

"Come on, Dare," Viola said with a sigh.

"Flower, I was just talking to the man," he said

back.

"Well, I want you to talk to me."

"Can't argue with that."

Once they were gone, Scarlett tapped me on the shoulder. "I'm going to go say hi to some friends. You two have fun." And before I could protest, she'd disappeared as well. Bo gazed down at me.

"You came," he said.

I turned to face him and tilted my head. "I said I would."

"You cheered for me," he said next.

"And?" I replied. "So did everyone else."

Bo studied my face. "But you were louder."

That startled a laugh out of me, the sound ringing in the space between us. Bo was still frowning, but it seemed softer somehow. Or...maybe the way he was looking at me was softer.

"I can tone it down next time," I promised, but he shook his head.

"I liked it," he said.

Oh.

Trying to lighten the mood, I said, "I wouldn't have expected it. You and Dare, being friends."

"Not exactly friends," he said.

"He's like the you of Durham High."

"There's only one of me."

I smiled at his cocky tone. "I know that, Stryker."

Bo touched the soccer ball on my cheek, and I

felt my pulse leap. "So, you liked the game?"

"I liked seeing you play," I said. "It was truly incredible. You're...incredible."

"What were you talking about before?" he asked. "Something about story time and a deal?"

I exhaled and shrugged, glad to be back on sure footing.

"Oh that," I said. "It's just something we do sometimes."

"Can I come?"

I blinked. "You want to come to story time?"

"Yeah," he said with a shrug. "If you'll let me."

"Okay, but why?" I asked.

Bo cocked his head. "Well, it seems like I'm getting a lot out of this deal. You coming to my game, working at the shop, doing nice things."

"But—"

He placed a finger against my lips, effectively stopping my next words.

"I just wanted to do something for you too," he finished. "Make sure we're both getting something out of it."

When he took his hand away, I rubbed my lips together, still feeling the warmth from his skin.

"But I owe you," I whispered.

Bo was looking at my lips. I both saw and felt his stare.

"You don't," he said after a moment. "You never did. Plus, I stole your first kiss, remember?"

Did I remember?

Was that a serious question?

I was remembering it now, as the desperate urge to feel his lips against mine suddenly hit me, watching as Bo slowly leaned forward. Or was that me who was leaning?

"Awesome game, Iceman," a voice called, and that broke whatever trance we'd been in.

"Thanks for coming," Bo said, voice rough.

"Yeah, congrats on the win," I murmured.

As I started to walk away in search of Scarlett, I heard Bo chuckle. I whipped back around just in time to see him, covering his mouth. Those lips of his were now pressed into a line again, but I knew what I'd heard.

"What?" I asked.

"Nothing," he said, but his eyes were dancing. "Nice shirt."

My smile was full of joy. "I thought it was a nice touch."

"No doubt who you're rooting for."

I sniffed. "Why should anyone doubt it? Good job, boyfriend. Now, I'm off to find my sister."

"Bye, Kent. Drive safe."

As I walked away, I made sure that my back was facing him, so he could really take in the awesomeness. My t-shirt was green and white—Chariot High's school colors—and on the back, I'd added the iron-on letters to form a word.

Icewoman.

It had gotten a laugh out of Bo, so I considered that a win.

And I hadn't kissed him.

Even though I'd really, *really* wanted to.

Which was another win—right?

17

If not kissing Bo was a win, I deserved a freaking medal.

We fell into a rhythm at school, and though the "relationship" was new and totally fake, no one, as far as I could tell, was questioning it. No doubt that had something to do with how fantastic Bo was at pretending.

I was good.

It didn't take much for me to act like I was affected by Bo's presence. I was—even if I wished it wasn't the case. My faking it wasn't so much faking as, well, an unintentional, real reflex.

But Bo?

He was a master.

The handholding, the little touches, the way words like "girlfriend" rolled off his tongue with seemingly no effort at all. Sometimes, I'd catch him looking at me. His expression blanked the second he realized I was looking. But during those times, even I wondered if maybe...

This was a side of Bo I'd never seen before. All of it, basically everything Bo did, made me want to do crazy things, like kiss him. All the time. But I held back because:

1) I really wasn't interested in putting my heart out there.

And 2) Bo couldn't, in a million years, have feelings for me.

If I needed proof of that, I got it when we were talking about the bet.

Shonda Lawrence had come up to me while Bo and I were walking in the hall.

"Glad I found you, Lottie," she said with a huge grin. "Here."

As she passed me an envelope, I looked to her with a clear question on my face.

"It's your prize for winning the HUBS bet."

"Oh," I'd said in surprise, "well, thanks."

"Courtesy of all the people who wanted a shot with your boyfriend." Shonda threw me a wink. "Have fun with that."

I shrugged at Bo as she left then opened what she'd given me. It was filled with money. My eyes widened as I counted then looked up to Bo.

"There's $300 in here," I said.

"Really? Didn't know I was so popular."

I shot him a look of disbelief. "Having all those girls after you? Admit it, you enjoyed the craziness."

Bo's frown deepened, but I wasn't sold.

"It has to be nice knowing someone wants you," I said.

"Not unless you want them back," he grumbled.

I tilted my head in thought. "But who'd actually make up a bet like that let alone participate?"

"Exactly, Kent." Bo shook his head. "Whoever it was, I hope they had a good laugh."

"Maybe they just wanted an excuse to get close to you," I suggested.

He shot me a look then shrugged. "Like I said, people are crazy."

"Come on, you loved being the center of attention."

Bo let out a long, deep sigh. "I didn't, Kent."

"Why not?"

"Because there's only one girl whose attention I've ever wanted," he said.

My jaw dropped in surprise. Not noticing this, Bo continued, but I was still stuck on what he'd inadvertently implied.

"Stryker," I said, pulling him to a stop. "I can't believe what I just heard."

"What?" he said.

"You, my grump-tastic boyfriend, are a romantic at heart."

He was shaking his head, but I wasn't having it.

"Oh my gosh, you have a crush!" I said.

"Shut up."

"But it's true. You're in looove."

Bo narrowed his eyes as I smiled. "You're having way too much fun with this."

"Yes, but can you blame me?" I said in delight. "You didn't like the bet because your heart already belongs to another. Iceman, ha! You are so much more the Flower Boy I've come to know and I—like."

Bo coughed, but it sounded like he was trying to cover up a chuckle.

"Thought you were going to say loathe," he said.

I forced a laugh. "Yeah, had to change it up because I know you better."

"And?" he prompted.

And I hadn't been about to say loathe. I'd almost said love. Because I love what I know, the Bo I'd learned more about, the guy who had already fascinated me and was now becoming so much more than that.

I wanted to ask.

Oh, I was dying to know who she was.

Who was this girl who'd won Bo's heart?

But something, maybe some sense of self-preservation, stopped me from uttering the words.

Instead, I just said, "And now, we have to decide how to spend this money."

Bo grunted.

"You want your half now or later?" I asked.

"Keep it," he said. "You won the bet by landing the Bo Stryker."

"I should since you just added 'the' before your name."

I shook my head, unable to hold back my smile.

"But there's no way you're not getting some of this. We'll spend it together. We only have a few more days before the week ends on our arrangement"—I gave him a significant look—"Maybe we can do dinner and a movie, go out as friends, once this is all over?"

Bo's face went stony once more.

I got the feeling I'd said something wrong but had no idea what.

After a beat, he reached out and tucked a strand of my hair behind my ear, making shivers race down my spine.

"I'll think about it," he said.

I'd wanted to kiss him then, feeling the time on our deal ticking away, afraid I'd never get the chance if I didn't act—but I'd held back. I'd wanted to tell him that the reason I actually sought to set something up was so that we'd have time together after this, an excuse to see him again. But I remained silent.

See? Totally worthy of a gold medal.

I'd also said *friends* like that was all I wanted from him.

I only wished that were the truth.

With Bo all but confessing he was in love with someone else hence his aversion to the HUBS bet, I needed to get over whatever these feelings were and fast.

It still didn't stop me from wondering who she was.

Or getting jealous when I saw another woman flirting with him on our flower deliveries over the weekend.

When I stepped into *Mrs. Lee's Flower Shop*, I paused just inside the door. Mrs. Lee was nowhere to be found. Instead, there was a girl I'd never seen, sitting on a medium-sized ladder beside the storefront window, bobbing her head to the music blasting through her sky blue headphones as she wrote something. It took her a second to catch sight of me, but when she did, the girl's eyes widened, and she lowered the headphones to hang around her neck.

"Hi," she said in what had to be the softest voice I'd ever heard.

"Hi," I replied, taking in her pink retro 90s t-shirt with Sailor Moon on the front, the baggy jeans, and her sylish-yet-well-worn sneakers. There was a smudge of something purple, looked like paint, on her face. I smiled, liking her already. "I'm Charlotte. Most people call me Lottie, but my cousins typically go with Lotte. Mrs. Lee calls me all three. So basically, I'll answer to anything." Pointing to my uniform, I added, "I'm her newest volunteer/employee."

Her return smile was genuine. "Nice. I'm Mi-Cha, but my friends call me Meech."

"I love that," I said.

"Fits me better than Mi-Cha. In Korean, that means gorgeous, and"—she ran a hand down her front—"as you can see, my parents greatly exaggerated."

I shook my head. "Not sure what you mean. I think you're lovely—also, Sailor Moon is the best."

"Right?" she said her eyes animated. "She and the sailor scouts don't get nearly enough credit."

"So much girl power," I agreed.

"Truth."

"Which character would you be?"

She thought about it a second then said, "Any of them, but probably Sailor Mars. You?"

"Good one. I'd probably pick Mercury—Ami is a powerhouse. Though I do love Serena."

"And she gets to be with Tuxedo Mask."

We both sighed on that one, and I knew I'd found a kindred spirit.

"Sorry if I was staring before," I said with a laugh. "Usually, Mrs. Lee is right there when I walk in."

Mi-Cha gave a solemn nod. "Clocking your time?"

"Yep."

"Yeah, that's just Mrs. Lee," she said. "She had a meeting today but told me she'd be back before close."

I nodded, walking over to the window, gazing at it with awe.

"Did you do all this?" I asked.

"Yeah," she said with a smile. "I love art, so Mrs. Lee lets me come in every few weeks to do my thing. She even pays me."

"Yeah, I can see why." Her work was bright and beautiful, colorful swirls in all different shades of lavender and plum with white highlights. It looked like real flowers hanging from the top of the window, cascading down, soft petals clinging to small vines. "Wisteria, right?"

She nodded. "I also do roses, tulips, orchids, anything really."

"This is amazing, Meech," I said, turning my gaze back in time to see her blush. "You're a wonderful artist."

"Thanks," she mumbled, "but I'm really not."

"How long did this take you?"

"Twenty minutes, give or take."

"Seriously? It takes me that long to dry my hair in the morning—and most days it still turns out terrible."

A door slammed, and Bo came in from the back then, startling us both, with Shin following right on his heels. They were carrying bags of what looked like soil. Bo had two and didn't seem to be struggling. In fact, I noticed he wasn't even wearing his brace. But Shin, who was shouldering one, panted a bit as he dropped it to the floor.

"I still don't get why *Halmeoni* won't spring for more workers," he said.

"Because we can handle it," Bo said.

"Speak for yourself," Shin mumbled.

"And hiring people to do the manual labor would cost too much."

Bo had a point.

Labor (aka movers) didn't come cheap. I'd researched that very subject for weeks, hoping to find an option for A Night Out with Austen. But everything was so expensive. We'd planned to bring in tables, chairs, and various regency props to set the mood. The budget was at maximum capacity. Looked like my girls and I were in for some heavy lifting.

If only I had my fake boyfriend's physique, I thought, I'd be set.

My eyes betrayed me, latching onto him, watching the ripple of his biceps as he grabbed a towel to wipe dirt off his hands.

Hands that had held mine in a firm grip.

Solid.

Just like the rest of him.

A sigh escaped my lips.

Hearing this, Shin turned his eyes to me and Mi-Cha. "Oh hey, ladies. What have you two been doing while we were lugging in dirt, nearly breaking our backs for minimum wage?"

Stryker rolled his eyes, but I just grinned.

"We've been getting to know each other," I said then pointed to his arms. "Is that how you got all those muscles?"

Shin's smile returned brighter than ever. "Actually, I've been working out since the age of three, Lottie. Mostly in the dojo. Thanks for noticing."

"Apparently lifting dirt is good exercise," I stage whispered to Meech, who laughed, but when I looked to her, she seemed flustered, not really looking at the guys, avoiding eye contact. It made me wonder if maybe she liked one of them.

Shin's chest puffed out at the compliment, but then Bo walked by and poked him in the stomach, causing his best friend to grunt.

"Still need to work on that core," Bo grumbled.

"And his high round kick," Meech added.

Shin scoffed at that. "I've got the best kicks at The Academy. It's a well-known fact."

"If you say so," she said.

"I do. My legs are lethal."

Shin looked so serious I had to bite back a laugh.

"Meech," Bo said, nodding to the window. "That's looking good."

Good? Such an understatement.

But Bo didn't give out compliments easily.

Brow scrunched I looked from him to Meech and wondered... Was Mi-Cha the girl? Could she be the one whose attention he wanted so badly?

"Don't you think so, Shin?" he said.

The other guy looked up and tilted his head. "It's nice, but Meech always does awesome work."

"True," Bo said.

"Thanks guys," she said in her quiet voice.

As she blushed, again, I got the feeling that maybe there was a crush.

Confirmation came when Meech missed a rung on the ladder, but before she could fall more than an inch, Bo was there, wrapping an arm around her waist and steadying her. It was all so graceful, so unlike what'd gone down in the library between him and me.

"You okay?" he asked as Meech turned fire engine red.

"Yeah," she said, taking the final steps down to the ground, "I'm fine."

"Clumsy as always, Mi-Cha," Shin teased, and she threw him a tiny glare. "Gotta be more careful. Bo might not always be there to catch you."

"You'd probably just watch me fall," she snapped.

Shin shrugged. "I probably would. Might laugh a little too."

"Maybe," she murmured, "you should work on your reflexes."

As I watched, she chucked her paintbrush at him. Shin, not expecting this, didn't duck. The projectile bounced harmlessly off his skin, leaving a purple line against his cheek. The shocked expression on his face was priceless. I gave Meech a high-five as she left the room, and Bo nodded at her.

Shin threw up his hands. "What did I say?"

Nobody answered, and after a moment, Bo walked over to me.

"Hey boyfriend," I said.

He didn't smile.

"You know you're right about the cost of manual labor." I shook my head. "I've been searching here, there, and everywhere for someone to help us with the charity event. But we can't find anyone affordable."

He grunted, still staring at me in this unnerving way.

"What's on tap for today? More flowers, smiles, giving people cheer?"

When he lifted his hand to my hair and ran his fingers gently through the strands, I nearly choked.

"Wh-what are you doing?" I asked.

Bo took his time answering. "Curious about something."

All the while his hand went through my locks, and my heart pattered like a drum against my chest.

When he finally dropped his hand, he looked me in the eye then said...

"Your hair doesn't look terrible."

My mouth opened but then closed again, having no idea how to respond.

It took me a moment, but then I remembered what Meech and I were talking about before the guys walked in.

"I didn't realize you'd heard that," I said breathlessly.

"Well, I did," he said and took a step back, plunging his hands into his pockets. "And like I said, your hair...it's not bad."

"Oh."

Holy cheese on a cracker. There was something seriously wrong with me. There had to be because those words were barely even a compliment. Yet, his voice and the way he said them, the way he was looking at me, made flutters erupt inside my chest.

I didn't know what made me do it.

Probably a temporary insanity brought on by Bo's anti-compliment.

My arm moved on its own, and we both watched as my fingers ran through his hair. Soft, I thought. So soft and a bit spiky and did he just make a noise? Seeing if he'd do it again, I gently brushed my fingers through his hair and...yep. There it was; a deep hum emanated from the back of his throat.

"Your hair's not bad either," I breathed.

"Hmmm," Bo said, his eyes looking a bit hazy.

When Shin stepped around the corner, I quickly moved backward, putting some distance between myself and Bo. I wasn't even sure what'd just happened. But I knew my skin felt alive in a new way, from the tips of my hair to my fingers.

Shin was grinning like a kid in a candy store while he looked down at the clipboard with today's deliveries.

"Hey Bo, you checked out the list?" he asked.

Bo shrugged. "Not yet. Why?"

"Got another order for Bianca Briggs."

I stared dumbstruck as red seemed to climb up Bo's cheeks. I'd never seen him look so abashed, almost shy.

"Stryker, are you blushing?" I asked, unable to resist.

He scoffed. "No."

"Looks like it to me," Shin put in and then patted Bo's shoulder. "Don't be embarrassed, man."

"I'm not," he said, shrugging out of reach.

"Wish I had an admirer—especially a hot one like Miss Briggs."

Meech, who'd made her way back to the window, rolled her eyes. "Stop giving him a hard time."

I looked from one to the other. "Who's Bianca Briggs?" I asked.

"Just a client," Bo said, moving to take the clipboard from Shin. "I'm going to go bring a few more arrangements out to the car then we'll be ready to go, Kent."

"Okay," I said.

When Bo was gone, Shin leaned in closer to me. "Bianca's got a thing for Bo," he said. "Don't tell him I told you. He'll go apeshit, but it's true."

"Really?" I asked, looking from him and then to Meech. "What's the story there?"

She gave a small shrug. "I'm not sure if she's into him—"

"She is," Shin put in.

"—but she orders something from the shop at least once a month."

"And specifically requests Bo be the delivery man."

I nodded, feeling a bit off kilter all of a sudden. "That must be good for business. I'm glad Mrs. Lee gets repeat customers."

"But there's nothing going on between them," Meech hastened to add.

"Right," Shin said. "But that doesn't mean Bianca wouldn't like there to be."

I looked to him when he placed a hand on my shoulder.

"I just didn't want you to be surprised. Don't be worried or anything. Far as I know, Bo's never made a move. Okay, Lottie?"

Swallowing, I shook my head. "I'm not."

He grinned. "Besides, it doesn't really matter what she wants. Bo's with you now."

"Yeah," Meech said. "Don't worry. It's all good."

"Team BOLO for the win."

Shin and Meech gave me encouraging smiles, but I was still struggling to process the new information. The feeling only increased when we pulled up to a two-story house, our first stop of the day, and Bo said, "I got this one." He left me in the car—which actually had never happened—and rang the doorbell. A woman came out with a bright smile, flowing red hair that hung to her waist, dressed in a pretty white fitted halter-top dress and nude heels. I wished I could pull off that look. Bianca accepted the arrangement from Bo, placed it inside her house, and then they stood there talking. It was funny because Bo hardly ever spoke to anyone, not at length anyway. Five minutes went by. Then seven. At eight-and-a-half, Bianca threw her arms around Bo in a hug.

I lifted a brow as he got back into the car.

"What?" he asked.

"You two seem friendly," I commented.

"She's a client."

"Yeah, and you looked like you enjoy her company."

Bo's eyes met mine. "If you have a question, Kent, just ask."

Did I have questions?

Heck yes, I did.

Things I wanted to know: When did they meet? How old was Bianca? She looked older than Bo and me; that was for sure. How long had he been delivering flowers to her door? Why did she ask for him? Did he *like* that she asked for him? Did he like...her?

I tried to hold my tongue.

But then...

"Interesting how she asks for you specifically," I blurted.

Bo sighed. "I see Shin's been talking."

"Hmmm. Bianca's what, nineteen? Twenty?"

"I think she's 21 actually," he said.

Ah, so she was in college—or at least, college-aged. Maybe Bo liked older women.

"Pretty too," I said just to see what he'd say.

"She's not ugly," he replied.

What did that mean?

Blast Bo and his confusing responses.

"Do you...like her?" I asked hesitantly.

He shrugged. "She's a nice person."

Translation: He liked her.

Awesome.

My fake boyfriend had a regular customer, one who was beautiful beyond words and "nice." That didn't bother me at all. Nope.

"She seems nice." My mouth ran away with me,

and I added, "I'm not sure how Mrs. Lee would feel about that hug, though. A little unprofessional. Don't you think?"

Bo chuckled, and my eyes snapped to his.

"What was that laugh for?"

He shook his head and started the engine.

"Seriously, what?" I demanded.

Bo's gaze met mine.

"You're cute when you're jealous," he said.

"Jealous? Yeah, right."

"Cute when you lie, too."

I hmphed, knowing I couldn't deny it without sounding like a total fibber.

Why was I acting this way? I wondered. Bianca and Bo seemed to be close—but why should I care? Jealousy shouldn't have even entered the equation.

And yet, when I'd seen them together, when I'd seen him earlier with Meech, who I actually liked, it felt like a kick to the chest.

I tried not to examine the reason for that too closely.

18

Mrs. Lee didn't beat around the bush. The next time I stepped inside the flower shop, she was there, and it looked like she'd been waiting for me. With a scowl, she said, "You are seeing my grandson."

I didn't know what to say back.

"Well?"

"Did he say something?" I asked.

She put her hands on her hips. "Bo didn't tell me anything. I saw you at his game."

"Ah."

"You're very loud," she said.

I blushed. "Well...I'd never been to a game before, so it was the first time I saw him play in person. He was impressive."

Mrs. Lee lifted a brow. "My grandson's always impressive."

"Yes."

"He had his arm around you," she commented. "And he asked me to make extra kimchi for the Kent family. So? Are you with him?"

Bo came around the corner then with a sigh. "*Halmeoni*, I told you already," he said.

"You did?" I asked, wondering exactly what he'd revealed. She was his grandmother. They obviously had a special bond. I couldn't see him outright lying to her.

"We're together," he said simply.

Two words.

They were ambiguous and vague and yet...

My heart thrilled at hearing them.

I needed to get out of there before I did something stupid.

"Well, I'm off to the library," I announced which was unnecessary. Mrs. Lee knew my schedule. "See you guys later."

"Wait," Mrs. Lee said.

I was worried that she might ask more questions, but she merely gave me a flinty stare.

"Bo, you go with her."

He sidled up to my side with a nod.

"Bring these back for me," she continued, passing him a small stack of books as well as a note with scrawl that I recognized instantly. "My hip has been acting up again."

"Of course, *Halmeoni*," he murmured.

I tried not to show my surprise as Bo grasped the books and note, refusing to meet my eyes.

Mrs. Lee. She was the romance reader, not him.

Unless maybe Bo read the books too?

But no, I thought. He'd seemed lost when I'd referenced them in the past and even said himself that he hadn't read the few I'd mentioned.

Mrs. Lee patted his shoulder with a fond look. "You are a good grandson," she said.

Again, he nodded then began walking with me toward the door.

"Charlotte-Lottie-Lotte."

I turned to look over my shoulder. "Yes, Mrs. Lee?"

"A Night Out with Austen charity event," she said. "You're in charge?"

"Yes, ma'am."

"Will there be flowers?"

I nodded. "Oh yes, we'll have a few fake arrangements."

Mrs. Lee's face pinched as if she smelled something rotten.

"They're for the table centerpieces," I added.

"No," she said, "you need real flowers."

"Um, that would be nice. But we really can't afford to—"

"I will provide." She waved off my concerns. "*Mrs. Lee's Flower Shop* will be a sponsor."

My chest filled with warmth. "That would be

awesome! Thank you so much, Mrs. Lee."

"Hmph."

"Also, if you ever want to discuss romance novels, I love them too," I said. "I could give you a ton of new recs."

Mrs. Lee studied me with a thoughtful expression. After a moment, she said, "Contemporary?"

"Yes."

"Rom com?"

"Of course."

"Historical?"

"Always."

She lifted a brow. "Sweet and spicy?"

"Equal love for both," I said with a grin. "Though I never really look at that before I read a book. If the blurb hits me or I laugh within the first 10 pages, I'll read it."

Mrs. Lee sniffed. "I'll consider your offer."

"Awesome," I said, my lips lifting into a full-blown smile. "See you later and thank you so much again for sponsoring."

She nodded, and as we left, I could've sworn she mumbled, "Fake flowers? Not on my watch." The sun was setting as Bo and I walked to the library. I kept glancing at him then the books in his hand, couldn't help it. Bo was eyes ahead, alert—but obviously aware of my scrutiny. By the second or third time I looked at him, his scowl was etched so deep I thought his face would stay that way.

"So," I said casually, "those aren't your books."

"Never said they were," he grumbled.

"You check them out for your grandma."

Bo cut his eyes at me. "Yeah."

"Romance novels."

"Your point?"

"It's just interesting."

"What is?"

"You," I said.

His brow scrunched.

It was clear he didn't know what I meant and was waiting for more. Bo wanted an explanation—but I wanted him to ask for it. After five seconds, during which I bit my tongue, Bo caved.

"What's that supposed to mean?" he said finally.

"It means you're not nearly as broody as you pretend to be."

His answer was a scoff.

"Seriously, Stryker." I gestured to him and the books. "I never knew you were such a marshmallow."

"I'm not a...what'd you just call me?"

"Oh yeah, you are," I laughed as he gave me a look. "You're tough on the outside but soft on the inside.

Bo shook his head. "Never been called soft, Kent."

"Okay, well maybe more like a little ray of sun

wearing the clothes of a thunder cloud."

"Clouds don't wear clothes."

He sounded so serious laughter poured from my lips.

"What?"

"Do you have any idea how funny you are?" I said, wiping my eyes.

Bo sniffed, and I shook my head. Once we were on the other side of the street, we turned to face each other. Sounding reluctant, as if the words were pulled from his lips, he asked, "So, what exactly is a marshmallow?"

I smiled with delight. "A marshmallow is someone who acts all hard but secretly has a gooey center. An example might be a person who crosses the street just to pick up books for his grandmother, so she won't have to irritate her bad hip."

I shook my head.

"It's you, Bo. My boyfriend is a total marshmallow."

A slight grin tilted his lips.

"What are you smiling about?" I asked.

"I never smile, Kent," he said. "That's for do-gooders—like you—and oblivious people who don't see how awful the world is."

Despite his words, the ghost of a smile still lingered at the corners of his mouth.

It was equal parts gorgeous and unnerving.

"What?" I asked.

"You called me Bo," he said.

Heat crawled up my cheeks. "I did not."

"Yeah," he said, smile widening a bit more at my obvious discomfort. "You did. Called me your boyfriend too."

"Well," I stammered, "you must be hearing things."

"Don't think so."

When Bo just kept giving me that look, I changed the subject.

"You know, I'm still surprised about the book thing," I said. "Your grandma's so cool. I love how she reads books with and without heat."

"No idea what that means," he said.

I blinked. "Heat, Bo. Spice, smut, sexy times. That's what I meant."

His face flushed then. "Ah."

"You didn't know some of the books were like that?"

"Nope."

"The shirtless guys on the covers weren't a clue?"

"I didn't know," Bo gritted out.

I giggled but forced myself to pull it together as he shot me a dark glance. The idea of him checking out books for his grandma was sweet. But the fact that he was checking out naughty books for his grandma and didn't have a clue?

Priceless.

"It's understandable," I said with a shrug. "How

could you know unless you'd read them?"

"Yeah," he said, running a hand down the back of his neck. The motion stilled as his gaze landed back on mine. "But you read them, right?"

"Yeah. Honestly, I thought you were doing it to annoy me, picking these swoony romance titles," I said, thinking of all the times he'd come in, laid down a list, and made me accompany him to the proper shelves. "Either that or you enjoyed making me blush."

"Definitely the second one," he said.

His words caused a deeper blush to stain my cheeks, and Bo chuckled.

"Also, that wasn't what I meant."

I looked to him in question, and he lifted a brow.

"These books, you read them too," he repeated. "I remember you telling me some of them were your favorites."

"And I remember you saying you'd read them," I put in.

"Oh I'm going to," he said. "Just had to wait for *Halmeoni* to finish."

I gulped as a new expression appeared on his face, this one decidedly more wicked.

"Gotta see what all that blushing is about."

"That's not necessary."

"I think it is," he said.

"But your grandma gave you a new list," I

pointed out. "The old books have to be turned in soon."

"Yeah, but I read fast," he said.

"You do?"

He nodded. "When it's something I'm interested in—and I'm dying to know what you like."

My eyes widened as Bo coughed.

"In a book, I mean."

Breath leaving me in a whoosh, I nodded. Of course, that was what he meant.

"We still on for tomorrow?"

"If you want to come read to the animals at the shelter, I can't stop you," I said.

Bo nodded. "Wouldn't miss it."

As he turned toward the library entrance, I tugged on his sleeve. "Are you sure you don't want to return those?" I asked, gesturing to the books in his hand, hoping he'd change his mind.

"Nah," he said, "I've still got a couple more days until they're due."

And he read fast.

Bo would soon know exactly what I liked in a romance—some of which were very spicy.

Awesome.

Perfect.

Nothing wrong with that. I owned my reading habits like a champ.

"Well, then I hope you enjoy the books," I said, ever the good librarian's assistant.

"I'm sure I will," Bo said in that deep voice of his. A shiver ran down my spine.

"Are you cold? Let's go inside."

I didn't tell him then, but my goosebumps had nothing to do with the weather.

#

"Your boyfriend's good with animals," Viola commented.

We both watched as he continued reading *Clifford the Big Red Dog* to...well, a red dog. My cousin said her name was Princess Ana. I wasn't sure what kind of dog she was—neither was Viola—but whatever the breed, the furry hound was large. And shy. When we'd entered the shelter, she was skittish, curled up as far back in her cage as she could get. She'd eyed all of the story time volunteers nervously. But when Bo sat in front of her cage, opened the book, and started speaking in his low baritone, the dog seemed to relax more every second. I didn't blame her.

Bo's voice was smooth and decadent.

I could've listened to him read the back of a cereal box and been content.

Apparently so could Princess Ana.

"The kids like him too," Scarlett added. Most of the volunteers—besides Bo, Dare, Viola, and me—were from her mentorship program. "Did you see him showing them those karate moves earlier? One boy even asked if he was a superhero."

I smiled because yes, I had seen.

And it had been adorable watching Bo perform a move and then teaching the kids how to do it.

"Did you know he was like this?" Viola asked.

I shrugged. "Kind of. We've been neighbors forever."

"And she's had a crush on him forever," Scarlett put in.

"Shhh," I hissed, checking to make sure Bo didn't hear. We were standing in a far corner, and thankfully, he hadn't paused in his reading. "I have not."

"Have too," she said back then looked to Viola. "She's been crushing hard, even if she's never admitted it to herself or anyone else."

"Stop psychoanalyzing me, Scar."

"Stop being in denial, Lotte."

Viola laughed. "So, this is what it's like to have a sister. Sorry I missed out on that."

"Sometimes I wish I was an only child," I mumbled.

"Oh come on, you love me," Scarlett said.

"It's up for debate at this point."

"Getting back to Bo"—Scarlett lifted a brow—"don't you think they're awesome together, Viola?"

"Yeah." Viola gave me a questioning look. "But Lotte, I thought you said he was an uptight grouch."

"He is," I said and then sighed, "but apparently, he has hidden layers."

"You don't sound too thrilled about it," she said.

Viola was far too preceptive.

For that matter, so was my sister whose brows puckered. "Are you guys having trouble?" she asked.

"No, no," I said, shaking my head. "It's nothing like that. If anything, it's me. I'm the one with issues, not Bo."

"Want to talk about it?"

I took a deep breath. "Maybe."

Viola tilted her head, and we huddled in closer. "The way Dare talks about Bo—oh, I'm sorry, Iceman, his arch soccer foe"—she rolled her eyes—"I was expecting something else."

Me too, I thought.

Bo finished reading and silently closed the book. Princess Ana had come to the front of her cage a while ago. She was sitting there, just staring at Bo. As he slowly leaned forward, reaching out a tentative hand, the dog drew back into herself. But Bo didn't try to get any closer. He remained there patiently, hand outstretched.

"It's okay, girl," he murmured. "I won't hurt you."

After several moments, Princess Ana relaxed, sniffed Bo's hand, and even let him pet her, which he did with the utmost care.

I sighed, and I wasn't the only one.

When I looked back to my sister and cousin, Viola had a sheen of tears in her eyes.

"Are you okay?" I asked.

"Yeah," she said, quickly wiping her eyes, "it's just she hasn't approached anyone like that since she got here."

"Really?"

She nodded. "Most of these animals have been through a lot. It's a beautiful thing when they open up after they've been treated badly."

Dare came over and wrapped his arms around Viola from behind.

"What's up, ladies?" he said.

"Nothing," Viola said back. "What are you doing?"

He shrugged. "Taking a break. I missed you."

"But I talked to you like ten minutes ago."

"Too long," he said and dropped a kiss on her neck.

Viola smiled softly at him, and Dare grinned back.

"You guys are making me feel extra single," Scarlett said.

"Me, too," I agreed.

Viola frowned. "But you're with Bo, right?"

I forced a laugh and waved that off. "Oh yeah, of course, I am. It's just...you know how it is with couples. When you're around them, you feel kinda confused and alone. You know?"

She shook her head.

"Well, it's true."

Scarlett jumped in then to save me from my ramblings.

"Hey Vi, I wanted to talk to you about that new string piece we're performing," she said. "Can you come with me for a sec?"

"Sure," Viola said, and as my sister tugged her and Dare away, I shot her a grateful look.

In response, Scarlett mouthed, "What was that?"

"I don't know," I mouthed back.

There was only one explanation I could come up with. Faced with the very real relationship between Viola and Dare, the clear affection between them, I hadn't remembered my pretend arrangement with Bo. It was an honest mistake. Anyone would've made it.

Speaking of which, my fake boyfriend was coming this way.

I shook off all the odd thoughts and smiled at him. "Did you like story time? Princess Ana obviously loved you."

"Ah yeah," he said, "she's a sweet dog."

"Viola told me she hasn't let anyone pet her."

"Why not?"

"She thinks she might've experienced some hard times before getting to the shelter."

Bo's frown was fierce.

"It takes a long time to come back from

something like that," I said.

"What do you mean?"

I gave a shrug. "When you've been mistreated, especially if it's by someone you love, it's not always easy to trust again."

Bo studied my face. "Sounds like you know something about that."

I cleared my throat. "Nah, just guessing."

After a beat, he said, "See, this is why I hate people."

I looked up into his eyes, and his lips hitched up.

"Well, most people."

He means you, my heart whispered. He doesn't hate you, and you don't hate him, and you should both go off into the sunset and hold hands, make out, and not-hate each other until the end of time.

Sounded good to me.

But I knew that wasn't how this story would end.

"I'm reading one of the books you recommended," Bo said.

My eyes widened. "You are?"

"Yeah, about half-way through *The Kiss Quotient*."

"And?"

"You were right." His eyes danced with mirth. "There's a lot of heat."

I shrugged, trying to fend off my blush. "If you don't like it, you can always switch to a different book."

"Didn't say that," he said. "I'm liking it."

"Really?"

Bo crossed his arms. "You sound surprised."

I was.

The fact that Bo was reading a romance I'd recommended and enjoying it? As Jane Austen would say, I was all astonishment.

"You're not just pretending to like it for my sake, right, Flower Boy?"

"I read what I want, Kent. This has nothing to do with you."

Okay then.

For some reason that brought me down a little, but I tried not to let it show.

"Although," he added, "I wouldn't have even cracked the cover if it wasn't for you. So, I guess there's that."

My mood suddenly bounced back, and it felt like I'd experienced whiplash. Maybe it was from staying up too late. My mind had kept me awake with thoughts of the library charity event. Speaking of which...

"Hey, do you think Meech would be willing to do some artwork for A Night Out with Austen?" I asked. "It's for charity, so I wouldn't be able to pay her. But I would give her tons of props online and in our event program."

"I'll ask," he said, "but I'm sure she'll say yes.

Meech likes you, and she's a good egg."

A good egg that you're secretly in love with? I wondered.

"What else do you need?"

"What don't we need?" I laughed then pulled out the list that Casey, Natalia, and I came up with. "These are all the things yet to be done. We have to figure out how to keep spreading the word, get more donations—we've already surpassed last year's goal, thanks to a big bump we received because of our kissing video—"

Bo lifted a brow, and I coughed.

"—but we're shooting for more, so we can give more books this year. Anyway, we need to check in with the businesses who are donating and make sure everything will be ready. We need more volunteers to dress up as regency characters, preferably guys. We're always short on guys. We also need help moving the tables, chairs, flowers, props, stereo equipment...should I go on?"

Bo shook his head. "If you need me, I'm here."

"Yeah"—I nodded to his brace-less wrist—"and almost completely healed too. I'm glad you're getting better."

"Told you I heal fast."

"You did, and it's just in time for us to stop fake dating."

He frowned as I smiled brighter.

"Do you think we need to have a public break-up?"

"No."

"Just think, Stryker. After tomorrow, you'll be a free agent again," I said, stomach churning at the words. "Able to hook up with anyone."

Bo shook his head. "Already told you. There's only one person I want."

My pulse beat harder, but I ignored it.

"We should keep pretending for a while," he said suddenly.

"Why?" I asked.

He shrugged. "You're going to need help with the charity event."

I didn't know where he was going with this. "True...and?"

"Who better to ask than your fake boyfriend?"

Bo's almost smile told me he was joking. He had to be. Right?

"Funny, Stryker," I said. "I almost thought you were serious."

Bo mumbled under his breath, but I couldn't make it out.

"Sorry, I missed that," I said.

"You need a ride a home?"

I blinked.

"Scarlett said something about needing to stay behind and make sure all the kids get picked up. Since we live next door, I figured we're going to the same place. So?"

"Oh," I said, "then, yeah. Thanks, Stryker."

"No problem."

I said goodbye to my sister and Viola and then got into the car with him. The space was smaller than the flower shop van. It made me that much more aware of Bo's presence.

"So it's Stryker again," he commented.

I exhaled in relief—this was normal, comfortable. I knew how to talk to Bo like this. "Thought you weren't a fan of Flower Boy?"

"I'm not," he said. "But Bo sounded good when you said it."

I shook my head. "I actually came up with a new nickname."

"Do I want to hear this?"

"Probably not," I said. "But it's Marshmallow Bo."

Bo scowled then shook his head.

"What? It's awesome and accurate. Plus, it rhymes."

"I think your nicknames for me suck."

"You love them," I teased.

"I'm turning on the radio now, so you'll stop talking."

The drive was actually a fun one. We listened to music all the way back, taking turns on who chose the song. Mine were better, obviously, but Bo had good taste, too. As we pulled into his driveway, we got out of the car, and Bo turned to face me, looking over the hood.

"Wait here," he said. "I got something for you."

Before I could ask, Bo was already heading inside his house. He returned a moment later with two circular Tupperware containers in his hands.

"*Halmeoni*'s kimchi and pickled cabbage."

"Sweet," I said as he handed them to me, "I'll be sure to thank her later—and hey, thanks for asking her to make it."

Bo nodded. "Later, girlfriend."

"Bye, Marshmallow Bo."

After waiting until I was inside and shut the door, he walked back across our driveways, into his house, and my heart finally calmed.

The sparks in my chest hung around.

They were there when I had dinner with my dad and sister. They were there when I was practicing my violin in my room and when I went to sleep that night—only to dream about Bo.

And the sparks were there the next morning as I woke up, the thought that I'd see Bo today the first thing to cross my mind, bringing an unintentional smile to my lips.

Ugh, this was all because he wasn't just an idea anymore.

He was real.

The dark cloud and the sun, hard yet also soft.

And honestly? Though chocolate would always be my all-time favorite...

I was starting to think I might have a thing for marshmallows.

19

Five days passed.

During that time, I did (and didn't do) a lot.

I ate all the cabbage Bo gave me and refused to share more than a few bites with my family. Yes, it sounded kinda selfish. But Dad and Scarlett liked the kimchi better anyway. I let them duke it out over that dish and hoarded my pickled veggies (which included cabbage, carrots, cucumbers, and tiny red peppers for flavor) like a dragon hoards gold. Because that's what it was. Delicious, tasty, yummy, pickled gold.

I didn't have a public break-up with Bo.

Still wasn't sure if that was the right call.

But when I'd asked him again, Bo said there was no need. People could think what they wanted. That was all fine. The only downside was...I wasn't sure what we were now. Fake ex-boyfriend and girlfriend, almost-friends, next-door-neighbors with shared history? It got confusing if I thought about it too much. However, we weren't holding hands anymore (which I missed), but he was still sitting with us at lunch (so at least there was that).

Speaking of, I started making Bo extra of whatever I brought to lunch.

This typically involved baked goods.

The guy seriously needed to be introduced to more sweets.

Strangely though, instead of simply eating his own dessert, he liked to mooch off of my plate.

"But I brought you your own brownie," I'd said just the other day.

His response: "I like yours better."

Me: "They're exactly the same."

Bo: "Nah, yours is different."

Me: "How?"

Bo (frowning): "It just is, Kent. Can I have some?"

I'd sighed and gave him half—but only after he'd agreed to let me have half of one of his dishes. It was hardly fair; the only food he ever brought was healthy. However, a good bit of it was Korean, and I had to admit almost all of it tasted good; so, I guessed there was something to be said for adding the right seasonings.

I went to another one of Bo's games and

cheered my head off. Soccer, it turned out, was a lot of fun. So was yelling. Scarlett still seemed embarrassed by that, but whatever. Bo made awesome play after awesome play. I couldn't *not* yell for him. Plus, he didn't seem to mind at all if the small grins he shot my way were any indication.

Bo wasn't as frown-y anymore either.

Well, that wasn't right. He still frowned (a lot), but they weren't quite as sharp. I'd gotten him to laugh at least two more times. And in general, he seemed to be in better spirits.

I'd put it down to the dessert, but when I told Scarlett my theory, she'd rolled her eyes.

"Are you that blind?" she'd said this morning.

"What?" I'd said and then shook my head. "Anyway, it has to be the sweets. He didn't even get all snippy when I called him Marshmallow Bo. I think that's progress."

"You're so..."

"So what?"

"Is there a nice word for a person who's totally oblivious?"

"I don't know," I'd said. "I'll have to look it up later."

"Oh never mind," Scarlett had said, pretending to type it into her phone. "I've got it right here. The word is 'Charlotte.'"

"Hilarious, but I'm telling you, Scar. You should never skip dessert. It's a mood lifter."

One talk that I'd been dreading was the one I had with Mrs. Lee.

I'd handed in my verbal resignation yesterday.

Bo wasn't wearing his brace anymore. He had the full use of his hand again. You couldn't even tell he'd had a bruise on his cheek. All physical signs of the book slap had now disappeared. Plus, A Night Out with Austen was only a week-and-a-half away. I'd need to devote more time at the library in preparation for the event.

Mrs. Lee had sat there, stoically staring me down, as I explained all this.

"But I'll be right across the street if you need me," I'd hastily added. "And I brought you this."

She'd taken the romance novel I pushed across the counter without looking.

"Thank you, Charlotte-Lottie-Lotte," she'd said. "You have been a tolerable employee."

Tolerable? I'd take it.

"No, thank *you*, Mrs. Lee." I'd smiled while looking around. "I'm going to miss you guys and this place."

Mrs. Lee had clucked her tongue. "Miss us? You'll be back soon."

"I will."

"You and my Bo are together. You're his girl, so we will see you plenty." Her eyes had pinned me in place. "I'll let you know what I think about the book."

I didn't know whether it was a threat or a promise, but her scowl twitched ever so slightly, so I decided to take that as a good sign.

I did stress, wondering about Bo and my relationship.

I didn't correct Mrs. Lee when she'd called me his girl.

I did berate myself for not having done so.

But I didn't try to examine my reasoning, afraid of what I might discover.

Now, I was standing behind the library counter with Casey and Natalia, trying not to hyperventilate or freak out when I realized we hadn't gotten any donations in the past few days.

Natalia bit her lip. "Do you think the donation link is down?"

"No," I said while wringing my hands, "I checked it this morning, donated five bucks just to see, and it went through."

"Well, that's good."

It would've been better if other people were still donating too.

Casey gave a shrug. "Well, we just have to figure out how to keep driving people to the link. We've already sent out the invites."

I nodded. "We got our last boost when they went out. Ticket sales are good, but they could be better."

"Okay, so what made the biggest impact

donation-wise?"

Looking at my notes, I pulled out the graph I'd printed, reviewing our donation progress. There was no way to miss the largest spike—or the time during which it occurred.

"Hey," Natalia said, "isn't that when the video of you and Bo went viral?"

I nodded. "Yeah, but there's no sure way to prove cause and effect."

"Isn't there?" Casey said and brought up an app on her phone. "The video on Leif's account has over two million views, and this one on something called 'Romancing the Librarian'"—she held out her phone, and I nearly choked—"has almost seven million."

What the heck?

"Why are so many people watching?" I asked.

Natalia sighed. "Because everyone's looking for a distraction, and the world needs more love."

I blinked. "Well said."

"And," Casey added, "because they have like 100k followers—apparently people love librarians—and they paired it with the perfect song. It's by HERS, this new band that's going crazy right now."

"Hayden Davenport, the lead singer is so hot," Natalia agreed.

Casey shrugged. "I prefer Santino, but whatever."

Thinking about those numbers, that so many people had seen Bo and I kiss, made me feel a little dizzy.

"I think I need to sit down," I mumbled then did just that, knees giving out as I plopped into the chair behind the counter. "*Millions*...ugh."

"I love you, Lottie," Casey said. "You're like the only person who doesn't want to go viral in this attention-driven society."

Natalia and I looked to her, and she shrugged.

"What? It's true."

I shook my head. "Okay, back to the charity event. Any ideas on how to raise more funds?"

"I think it's obvious," Casey said.

"Me too," Natalia agreed, and they both looked to me with matching grins.

"No," I said immediately, hands held out as if I could stop them from saying what I knew was coming. "No way."

"Why not?"

"Because..."

As I trailed off, unable to concoct a good excuse—or at least not one I could say to the girls—Casey lifted a brow. "Lottie, do you want to donate more than ever this year to children who need books?" she asked.

"Well, yeah," I said.

"And do you want to feel like you've done everything you possibly could for the cause?"

"You know I do."

"Even if you may have to step out of your

comfort zone?"

I nodded resolutely.

"Then this is it." Casey lifted her shoulders. "I think you should kiss Bo again."

The words ran through me like wildfire.

"Film the smooch; be sure to mention the event, and we'll post it online. Everyone in favor?"

Both Casey and Natalia's hands shot up in the air. They waited, but eventually, I raised mine as well. They were staring at me with such hopeful expressions. What else could I do?

"It shouldn't be too hard," Natalia said with a laugh. "I mean, you and Bo must kiss all the time, right?"

"Hmmm," I said.

If by "all the time," she meant "just that one time," then yeah.

Casey frowned. "Everything going okay with you and Bo?"

Well, we technically ended our fake relationship—I think—which probably, most likely means Bo won't actually be down to kiss me again. But other than that, it's all good.

"Going okay," I repeated then stood. "I have to go."

My head was better, but I felt the need to escape. Lucky for me, I had the perfect excuse. Reaching beneath the counter, I pulled out the two containers aka my diversion.

"I've got to go return these to Bo."

"What's in there?" Natalia asked.

"Smells good," Casey commented.

I opened the containers and showed them the rice crispy treats. There were plenty, but I'd made them especially to thank Bo and Mrs. Lee for the kimchi and cabbage. After allowing my girls to take one each, I closed the lid.

"I'll be right back," I said and walked toward the door. "Hold down the fort."

"We will," Casey said, "and no rush."

"Tell Bo we said hi," Natalia said.

My hand was on the door when Casey added, "And don't forget to ask him about the kiss!"

With a nod, I left and quickly crossed the street. Why hadn't I objected? What was wrong with me? Yes, I'd do anything I could for Friends of the Library. I always dedicated myself one hundred percent. It was just...in the past, that hadn't included asking my fake boyfriend (ex-fake boyfriend?) to kiss me again.

But I would.

I just might not do it right this very second. Something like that took courage. I decided I'd have to work myself up to it then ask—and then, if he laughed in my face, possibly change my name, dye my hair, move across the world, and live in a hut on the edge of nowhere selling hair bows, playing the violin for tips, and reading romance aloud to keep myself company. Could be worse.

Shaking my head, I took a deep breath and entered the flower shop.

I was relieved when the only person I saw was Meech, sitting behind the register.

"Hey Meech," I said. "How's it going?"

Strangely, she looked just as relieved to see me.

"Lottie! Oh thank goodness," she said, standing up. "Mrs. Lee stepped out for a second; the guys are on break, and I'm supposed to be in charge until everyone gets back. But I have to pee *so* bad."

I bit back a smile.

"Can you watch the register?"

"Of course," I said and stepped behind the counter.

"Are you sure?" she asked, clearly doing the pee-pee dance. "It'll only be a few minutes, and no one ever comes in at this time anyway."

"Go, go," I said. "It's no problem. I just came to give Bo something. I've got nowhere to be."

"Bless you," she said then made a mad dash for the bathroom. She hollered, "And I'll do whatever art you want for the charity thing!"

"Thank you," I yelled back.

Chuckling to myself, I stood there, placed the containers on the counter and settled in to wait. How would Bo react to seeing me here? How would he react to what I had to ask him? How would I bear it if he turned me down?

The door to the shop chimed, breaking me out of my thoughts.

I smiled and said, "Welcome to *Mrs. Lee's Flower Shop*. What can I help you with?"

The customer looked to be in his mid-20s, male with a buzz cut, baggy t-shirt and jeans, tennis shoes that'd seen better days. His eyes were a little shifty, looking around the shop before they came back to me. I didn't like to judge based on appearance, though, so I just smiled brighter.

"There's a wide selection of flowers for any and all occasions," I said, trying again. "I'm Lottie. Was there something you need?"

"Yeah," he said, "there is."

Suddenly, he pulled out a handgun and leveled it at my chest.

"Give me all the cash in that register. Now."

I froze, unable to believe this was happening.

"You stupid or something?" he asked when I didn't move.

"No, I'm actually in the top 10 percent of my class," I said.

He gaped at me a moment then gestured with his gun. "Okay smartass, I'm only going to say this one more time. Open that register and give me the cash, or I'm going to shoot you right in your genius brain."

There was something seriously wrong with me. Either that, or I'd entered into some odd kind of fight or flight reflex that involved talking as much as possible in the hopes of discombobulating him so much he'd just leave. It was a decent plan. Plan B was to throw the rice crispy treats at his head, but I was pretty sure that'd just make him angry. And what a waste of good desserts.

Squaring my shoulders, I said, "Well, that was rude."

"What?"

"I said that was rude. I've been nothing but nice to you since you walked in, and here you are, calling me names. You don't even know me."

The robber blinked.

"I'm a good person. You might be too, who knows? You're not making a great first impression, but that doesn't mean you're unredeemable."

He squinted at me. "Girl, you know what this is, right? It's a stick-up. I'm robbing you right now."

"Yeah," I said, "I get that. But you should know it's bad karma."

Scratching the back of his neck with the gun, he tilted his head. "Say what?"

"Karma," I repeated. "It's real, and it's gets everybody sooner or later. Seven years bad luck for breaking a mirror. How much do you think this will get you?"

"I don't know," he muttered.

"Exactly. So, you seem okay—besides the whole holding me up at gunpoint thing. Why don't you just take some rice crispy treats out of this container, leave the way you came, and no one has karma following them around for the next seven years?"

I held my breath, hoping he might do the right thing, but the guy just grunted.

"Never believed in that stuff," he said with a mean smile. "I only believe in me."

"That's actually a healthy affirmation," I began, but he cut me off.

"Get the damn drawer open," he yelled.

I shook my head. "I can't. I don't know the code."

"Yeah, right."

"It's true," I said. "I don't even work here anymore."

"Listen, bitch—"

"There you go being rude again."

"—if you can't get me the cash—"

"You know, most people use cards now," I said.

"—I really will shoot you," he finished.

Before he could, the bell chimed once more announcing a new arrival.

It was Mrs. Lee.

She stood there in the doorway, assessing the situation.

"Who's this?" she asked, walking further into the shop.

"Get the hell out of here, old lady," he said dismissively.

"Charlotte-Lottie-Lotte, you okay?"

"I'm fine," I said quickly, "but you should go, Mrs. Lee."

"Why?" she said, as if this was all normal. "This is my shop."

"I know, but—"

"You own this place?" the robber said. "What a dump."

Mrs. Lee scowled. "What did you say?"

"I said it's a dump. Your stupid employee doesn't know when to shut her mouth, can't even work the cash register."

While his attention was elsewhere, I made a move to grab one of the containers. If I chucked it at him, at least it would give Mrs. Lee a running head start, time to get away. But the robber merely leveled his gun at me again.

"Ah ah, smartass. Don't even—"

I never got to find out how he would've finished that sentence.

It all happened in blur of motion. One second, Mrs. Lee was totally still. The next, she exploded into action, knocking the guy's arm down and away with the heel of her palm and taking his knee out with a kick. At the same time, Meech flew out of the bathroom and landed a kick to the guy's face that sent him spinning. Mrs. Lee punched him in the groin, and that was all she wrote. The robber fell to the ground with a crash.

While the robber was groaning in pain, Mrs. Lee got on top of him, pulled a book out of her purse, and proceeded to smack him over the head with it. Multiple times.

"You—"

Smack.

"—don't—"

Smack.

"—point—"

Smack.

"—guns—"

Smack.

"—at people."

Smack, smack, smack.

"And my shop isn't a dump." She sniffed, straightening once more. "You're the dump."

I was wide-eyed, looking from Mrs. Lee to Meech to the guy on the floor.

"How did you...what just...wow," I said finally. "That was freaking amazing."

Meech shrugged as if she hadn't just kicked major butt. "Would've been here sooner if I didn't drink all that dang bubble tea. I'm so sorry, Lottie."

"It's okay. You and Mrs. Lee totally kick ass."

"Thanks."

Mrs. Lee was still glaring down at the robber, but she nodded as well.

"I wish I could do that," I said.

The door chimed again, and Bo and Shin

stopped in the entrance, dumbstruck by the scene.

"What the hell happened here?" Bo asked. "*Halmeoni*, you okay?"

She scowled at him. "Why wouldn't I be? He's the one on the ground."

"But—"

"No buts, we're fine," she said.

"Who—Kent?" Bo noticed me then and was suddenly at my side. "What are you doing here? Are you alright?"

"Yeah," I said as he stood there, looking like he didn't know what to do with his hands. "I'm fine. I just came to give you these"—I gestured to the containers—"but instead, I got to see Mrs. Lee and Meech take down this punk. No big."

Though I was joking, inside I was starting to realize what'd just happened.

The trembling started in my stomach then moved out to the rest of me.

"I'm fine," I said again.

But Bo just sighed and pulled me into his arms with a curse.

"You're not," he said. "I'm sorry, Kent. I don't know what I would've done if you got hurt."

I relaxed into him, feeling the fear begin to dissipate.

"Hope you like rice crispies, Marshmallow Bo," I said.

He didn't laugh, just held me tighter.

"Hey, it's okay," I said softly, easing away from him even though I really didn't want to. "If I was like your grandma, I could've taken him no problem instead of trying to talk my way out of it."

Bo frowned. "You talked to him?"

I nodded. "I was trying to wear him down."

"Did it work?"

"More or less."

Mrs. Lee came over to us, looking from me to Bo.

"You take Charlotte-Lottie-Lotte to The Academy," she said. "She needs to learn."

"Yes, *Halmeoni*."

"You teach her."

"Was already planning on it."

With a nod, Mrs. Lee left, and I turned back to Bo with raised brows.

"What was that all about?" I asked.

"You're going to learn self-defense," he said.

"Oh really?"

"You said you wanted to be more like *Halmeoni*."

I nodded. "Yeah..."

"So, I'm going to teach you."

"I don't know."

"I do," he said, staring into my eyes. "You have to be safe. I need to know you're safe when I'm not there. Okay, Kent?"

What else could I say but yes?

20

Marshmallow Bo melted away once we got to The Academy aka the dojo. It was like there was no softness to him at all. He was all business.

"Faster, Kent," he said, forcing me to jog in place.

I couldn't respond—I was too focused on trying to breathe—but I was moving as fast as I could.

"Get those legs moving."

What the heck did he think I was doing? Knitting a sweater?

"Higher knees. You've got to be warm before we start."

"We haven't even started yet?" I gasped.

Bo's lips twitched. "Funny."

"Who's joking?"

"Keep going. Just two more minutes. I'll do it

with you."

I groaned.

Trying to distract myself, I took in my surroundings. The Academy was also owned by Mrs. Lee. According to Bo, it was her first entrepreneurial venture, and she'd made it a success. Judging by the number of students I saw kicking, punching, and doing multiple moves I didn't know the names of, Mrs. Lee had a good business going.

Blue mats covered the floors. Mirrors lined most of the walls, presumably so students could watch their reflection suffer. Several classes were going on at once in different parts of the room. The little kids looked like they were having fun. But ugh, sweat was already dripping down my back. Why was working out so hard?

For me, I mentally added.

Bo wasn't struggling.

In fact, when his alarm went off, he looked downright chipper.

"Okay, Kent, good job," he said.

I shook my head.

"Next, I want to see how you move," he said. "Give me four punches, alternating right to left, and a kick."

"I never learned how to do those properly," I said.

"That's okay."

Easy for him to say, I thought. Bo was a ninja

master.

When we'd walked into the building, loud cheers went up around the room. It was like the king had arrived. Everyone, faculty and students, knew Bo and clearly adored him. One little boy even came up, said, "Mr. Bo, watch this," and did a kick. Bo gave him high-five and said, "Nice one, Kwan. Keep working, and it'll get even better." The little kid grinned, said "Thanks, I will," and ran off to rejoin his class.

"I don't want to embarrass myself in front of all your adoring fans," I said.

He shot me a frown, but it didn't have any of its usual heat.

"Come on, Kent. No one knows anything when they're first starting out."

"Bet you were doing flying-round-house-dragon-haymaker kicks in the womb," I muttered.

"My mom says I was peaceful baby," he retorted.

Of course, he was.

With a sigh, I decided to get it over with. I punched, right, left, right, left, then kicked like I'd seen Bo do so many times during his morning workouts.

"Okay, now start with the left and kick your other leg."

I did what he said. The kids closest to our area giggled at my pitiful attempts, and I stuck my tongue out at them. They only laughed harder, and that made me smile.

"Alright, not bad." Bo nodded. "We can work with that. Next—"

I held up a hand. "I'm not doing pushups."

"But they build upper body strength," he argued.

"So does reshelving books five days a week," I said. "And you haven't ever seen my bedroom. My bookshelf is massive, and I reorganize at least twice a month."

"Is that an invitation?"

My eyes widened. "What? No."

"You sure? Kind of sounded like you wanted me to see your bedroom and check out your shelves."

"I...stop playing, Stryker," I said, noticing the small grin on his face. Jerk. "I just don't do pushups."

"Fine," he said, "then we'll table this discussion about when I get to see your room and skip the pushups. How'd you know that's what came next anyway?"

I shrugged, tugging on the ends of my t-shirt, hoping he couldn't see the truth in my guilty expression.

"Just a guess," I said.

Bo kept staring, almost as if a lightbulb had gone off in his mind, and then...

"Good guess," he mumbled. Shaking his head, he added, "Anyway, let's jump right into it. Self-defense. There are a lot of moves I can show you.

It'll make you work up a sweat, but it's worth it to know these things."

Tilting my head, I said, "Okay, but I want to make a deal."

Bo arched a brow.

"For every move I attempt, I get to ask a question."

"What?"

"One move gets me one question and a truthful, from-the-heart answer from you," I said. "It's called sweat equity."

Bo shook his head. "That makes no sense."

"Makes sense to me, Stryker." I smiled at him and pointed to my head. "I'm sweating. You're not. We need to make things equal somehow, and this is as good a way as any."

The drive over had been silent except for the music playing softly on the radio. We'd taken my car. Bo had seemed lost in his thoughts, and I was definitely in my own head. But there was so much more I wanted to know about him. Plus, if we were going to be working out, I desperately needed a distraction.

"So? Is it a deal?"

Bo stared at me.

I stared back.

Finally he said, "Yeah, but only after you complete a move *correctly*."

"Fine," I said while inside I was jumping up and

down in victory. "What's the first move?"

"Well, the first thing we need to do is correct your punches," he said. "My six-year-olds have better form than you."

"Ouch."

"Yeah, so stand with your feet apart." He watched as I got into position. "Raise your hands like this"—I mimicked his pose—"and make two fists. Nice, you didn't tuck your thumb."

I rolled my eyes. "I read, Bo, and watch TV. I know not to tuck my thumb; it could get broken that way."

"Maybe you should be teaching me then?" he snarked.

"Next lesson, please, sensei. I'm getting bored."

Bo frowned. "Tighten your core."

"Huh?"

"Your..." With a sigh, Bo came closer and splayed his hand across my stomach. It clenched in response. "Stay strong in your core, and use the energy from your legs to put power in your punch. Got it?"

What I got was a severe case of butterflies. They were fluttering around like crazy, originating from where Bo's hand touched, out into the rest of my body. And I had to admit it made me self-conscious, having him touch me there. A girl's stomach was not a place that typically inspired confidence. But dang if those butterflies didn't keep dancing around like a chorus line.

"Kent?" Bo said.

He was looking at me, expecting something. What did he say again?

"Oh yeah," I said as he finally stepped back. "I've got it."

"Then let's go. Right punch."

Centering myself, I did what he said, trying to get power from my core and legs.

"Good. Now, left."

I punched.

"Four in a row."

Right, left, right, left.

"Good job. Did you feel the difference?" he asked.

"Yeah," I said with a true smile. "It felt awesome."

Bo nodded.

"But not as awesome as it'll feel after you answer my questions."

"One move, one question, Kent," he said.

"Two arms, so two questions, Stryker," I retorted.

"Fine."

"And I actually did six correctly, so..."

"Don't push it."

I didn't. Thinking fast, I asked the first question that came to mind.

"Why flowers?" I said.

"Huh?"

"The flower shop." I rolled my eyes. "I get why you love it here. The martial arts, the being all tough, the sweating because for some crazy reason you seem to enjoy that." Bo coughed to cover a laugh, but I went on. "Besides your grandma, why do you work at the flower shop?"

Bo shrugged. "I guess because it relaxes me. As a kid, I had a lot of pent-up energy and nowhere to put it. I got picked on too by older kids. My parents signed me up for soccer and all the martial arts classes in the area. Those helped. But working with flowers is what really quiets my mind. Still does. They let me escape the world for a while. Plus, I like the smell."

I nodded. "I get that. Books are my escape."

Bo lifted his chin. "Escape from what?"

"Life," I said. Feeling the need to say more since he'd revealed so much, I added, "After my mom left us, things were...bad. My dad and sister dealt with it in their own way. The library became like my second home."

"Where is she now?" he asked.

"France, Spain, who knows? She and her new family move around all the time. She doesn't call us much."

"That sucks."

"Yeah, it does" I said. Mom left when I was five, and Scarlett was four. I tried not to think about it, having decided long ago not to let her—or anything else—get me down. "But books were there for me when I needed them. They helped me believe things could be good again."

"I'm glad you had that," Bo said.

"Me too. What's your favorite flower?" I asked.

"Cherry blossom," he said.

My smile widened. "Really? My shampoo smells like cherry blossoms."

"I know," he said quietly, almost to himself.

"You know," I repeated.

Those dark, intense eyes of his met mine. "Drives me crazy most days."

I didn't know what to say to that.

Bo had me repeat the punches, and he put on padded gloves, so I'd know what it felt like to actually hit something.

The next move he taught me was how to disarm an opponent. I recognized it as the same one Mrs. Lee performed on the robber today. I tried it a couple of times slowly with Bo giving me pointers.

"Keep your arms strong."

"Don't forget about your legs."

"Stay balanced."

I practiced several times—using the heel of my palm to knock his arm down and away then stepping into him and directing a kick to his knee. Then I did it some more before ever getting it up to Bo's standards.

"Well done," he said at last, and I nearly whooped in relief.

"Finally," I said, sweating and smiling like it was Christmas. "That means I get another question."

"It also means you can protect yourself," he pointed out.

"And I'm thankful, Flower Boy. I really am," I said sincerely. "Now, for my next question—"

Bo groaned.

"—why don't you have a girlfriend?"

He cocked his head. "You know the answer to that."

"Not really. You just said there's one girl whose attention you want, but that doesn't mean you can't date around. Seems like everyone does it."

"Never understood the point," he said. "Why settle for someone else if you know what you want?"

I swallowed.

"And I did have a girlfriend for a while," he said with a pointed look.

"Yeah, a pretend one," I said.

He narrowed his eyes.

"Just give me five more questions, and I promise I won't ask any more."

"Still don't get why we have to do this," he said.

"Because it's fun," I replied.

"Fine, Kent. Then I want to ask you questions too." Bo shrugged. "Fair is fair, right?"

He held out his hand, and we shook on it.

"Work now, talk later," he said.

"But—"

"We need to focus on these techniques."

"Can't we talk while we work?" I said.

Bo shook his head at that. "You're learning something new, Kent. I need your full attention."

He removed his sweatshirt then, revealing broad shoulders and a toned chest, covered only by a white cotton t-shirt. As he walked toward me, I could make out the faint outline of his abs. The material hugged his body like a lover. I found myself wishing I could do the same. And...

Whoa. Where the heck did that come from?

My gaze traveled up as Bo stopped in front of me.

His frown was there, but those eyes burned.

"Done staring?" he asked.

I crossed my arms. "I was just giving you my full attention."

"Trust me, I was enjoying it."

Before he could say more or I died of heatstroke considering my whole body had to be blushing at this point, I noticed the two people who'd just entered the room.

"Hey, isn't that your parents?" I asked.

"Yeah," Bo said, watching as they walked to the center of the mat hand-in-hand, "Mom doesn't teach as much as she used to because of her job, but they come in sometimes."

The classes had stopped to gather around, and I moved to join them.

"Must be hard finding time between movies," I said. "She's an actress, right?"

"Stuntwoman," he corrected. "But it's basically the same thing."

"Hey everyone," Mrs. Stryker said. She glanced around the group, eyes widening as they landed on me and Bo. Smiling, she whispered something to Mr. Stryker which made his lips kick up in a grin. He looked at us too and raised his chin in greeting. "We have some new faces which is always awesome to see."

She gave me a nod then continued.

"Most of you know me already. But if you don't, I'm Snow. My *Omma* founded The Academy years ago so anyone interested in martial arts had a place to call home. Tonight, I'm going to teach you a new skill, one you can use to fend off an attack, even if it's from a larger opponent."

Her smile brightened as she gestured to the man at her side.

"My husband Ash has graciously agreed to let me demonstrate on him."

He nodded, looking at her as if she was the sun, moon, and stars combined.

"Which basically means he's down to let me toss him around a bit," she added.

Laughs went up all around.

Then someone shouted, "You mean kick his ass!"

Snow shook her head, but Ash just smiled.

"That's right," he said with a shrug. "She is gonna kick my ass."

"Ash," she said.

"And I'm going to love every second of it."

More laughter filled the room as he kissed her temple.

I released a sigh.

"What was that?" Bo asked.

"Nothing. Just...I wish my parents were like that," I said.

He was silent a beat.

Then...

"They say they do this to help out," he said. "But honestly, it's more like foreplay."

I coughed a laugh. "Seriously?"

"Just watch."

I saw what he meant. The new skill was a flip which involved Ash wrapping his arm around Snow from behind, Snow using their combined weight to flip Ash over her shoulder, and his back hitting the mat with a crash. I winced. But Ash popped up a moment later, so she could do it all over again. Snow explained the mechanics of the movement. Ash assured the person who asked that he was okay. And the two of them were making heart eyes at each other the whole time.

"Want to try it?" Bo asked.

I nodded. "Sure. This won't hurt you, though, right?"

He shot me a look, as if offended I'd even suggest such a thing.

"Sorry," I said. "I know you'll be fine, even if I fail."

"You won't fail," he said, stepping closer and wrapping his arms around me.

My heart stuttered.

"I-I might," I said.

"You won't." Bo's voice caressed the shell of my ear, and I swallowed back a gasp. "Just concentrate."

On what? I thought.

The feel of Bo's chest pressed against my back.

His warmth surrounding me.

The sparks in my chest.

Taking a deep breath, I put my hands in the proper place, tensed my muscles in preparation, and...

"Good," Bo murmured.

Trying to keep my voice steady, I said, "If we're going to try this, you've got to stop doing that."

"Doing what?"

"Distracting me."

Because of our closeness, I felt as well as heard his deep laughter.

In response, I frowned, tightened my grip, and then flipped him before he could say anything else. It was an impulsive reaction. I definitely hadn't planned it—which was probably why, after executing the move to perfection, I went down right after Bo, landing ungracefully on top of his chest.

I looked up and saw that the frown was gone.

Shock was the only thing staring back at me. That and something else that as the moment wore on looked like...pride.

"You flipped me," he said.

"Yeah, sorry about that," I replied.

"Don't be. You—"

"Awesome throw, Charlotte!" Snow called from across the room. "Got it on the first try."

"She did. Nice job," Ash said next then added, "Good fall, son!"

Bo muttered under his breath.

"Hey," I said, smiling down at him, "don't feel bad, Flower Boy. It was beginner's luck. Besides, you're my teacher. You should be proud."

"I am," he said.

"Really?"

Bo nodded, studying my face.

"Want to try it again?" I asked.

"Yeah. Never thought I'd enjoy getting knocked around, but you proved me wrong."

The amount of joy I felt was totally inappropriate.

"Your smile's blinding me, Kent," he said.

I laughed at that, couldn't help it.

A guy who was passing by said, "Hey Bo, you

coming to *The Singing Fish* later?"

"Maybe," he said, "I rode here with Kent."

"That's cool. Just bring your girl too."

Bo looked to me. "You want to hang out after this?"

"Sure," I said, trying to sound calm when inside I was anything but. "If you don't think your friends will mind me tagging along."

"They won't." Jumping to his feet like it was nothing, Bo told the guy, "Yeah, we'll be there."

He turned to me as the guy left.

"You know, you don't have to go if you don't want to," he said.

"I know," I said then cracked my knuckles. "Now, stop stalling, Stryker. It's time for me to throw you around some more."

Bo lifted a brow.

"And then we'll go meet this fish, and I can ask you all the questions."

"The deal was five," he said.

"Thought we said unlimited?" I lied.

"Nice try." Bo got into position for the throw, placed his arms around me, then added, "Can't wait to have my hands on you again, huh?"

"You wish," I scoffed—and before I could overthink anything, I flipped him again.

Bo and I practiced several more times, and I couldn't deny it.

I loved this feeling. Throwing Bo to the mats

was more fun than it should've been. Then again, so was talking to him, being in his arms, and getting closer to him.

It was dangerous, this feeling, but I craved it more and more.

As Bo grinned up at me, my pulse pounded, and I knew I was in trouble.

I still had to ask him to kiss me again.

He could—likely would—say no.

And if that happened, I needed to be prepared, ready to brush it off, act as if my feelings for him were nothing.

Too bad my heart was already all in.

21

"Why do you frown so much?"

Bo lifted a brow. "You really want to waste one of your five questions on that?"

"Yeah," I said with a sniff. "I'm curious."

"That doesn't count as one of mine by the way."

"Fine. Asking for clarification won't count toward our totals."

I had to raise my voice to be heard over the music as well as the person onstage doing a decent if off-key rendition of *Love Story* by Taylor Swift. Apparently, *The Singing Fish* wasn't a fish at all, but a karaoke bar/diner open to teens and adults. Bo said students from The Academy came here after class all the time which made me jealous because it was literally one of the coolest places I'd ever been, and I hadn't even known it existed before tonight.

"Anyway," I said, "back to your favorite expression. I don't know if you realize this, Stryker, but you have resting frown face."

"That's not a thing," he said.

"Says the guy who made it famous—or should I say, infamous?"

In response, Bo frowned harder, and I pointed.

"See! There it is." Shifting forward in the booth, so I could stare him in the eye, I said, "Be honest, Flower Boy. You just want people to think you're a badass."

Bo leaned forward as well and rested his forearms on the table between us.

"I am a badass," he said seriously.

"So answer the question. Why do you frown so much?"

"Because the world is crap."

When he didn't go on, I said, "Seriously."

"There's not a lot to smile about, Kent," he said. "People suck."

"Okay, I'll give you that last part," I conceded. "*Sometimes*, people do suck, like when they burn books or say and do hateful things."

"Like bullying those who are weaker than them," Bo said.

"Or hurting animals."

"Or judging people based on their sex or the color of their skin."

"Or who they love," I added. After a moment, I

said, "Yeah, you're right. People really do suck."

"Yeah."

I shook my head. "But you're wrong too."

Bo waited for me to go on.

"There's so much to smile about, Stryker," I said. "Look at you? You're young and healthy. You've got breath in your lungs, two parents who love you, a kickass grandma who adores you, students at The Academy who obviously look up to you. You found your passion with soccer and martial arts, *and* you're good at both."

"Just good?" Bo said.

I rolled my eyes at the interruption.

This was important, and I was determined to make him see the light.

"You know you're amazing, okay?" I said.

He seemed satisfied with that.

"People at school made a bet to see who could hook up with you, for goodness sakes."

I couldn't be sure, but if the lighting was better in *The Singing Fish*, I bet Bo would've been sporting a blush.

"And now, you're here with me—after I successfully wiped the floor with you by the way—and I'm awesome," I added, pleasure coursing through me when his lips tip up. "So see? There's a lot to be thankful for."

"Alright, Kent," he said. "I get it. Things could definitely be worse."

I nodded.

"My turn. Why don't you believe in happily ever after?"

"I do," I said. "In books."

"Why not in real life?"

"I feel like that's two questions."

He narrowed his eyes, and I sighed.

"Alright fine"—I shrugged—"I guess it probably has something to do with all that stuff with my mom. After she left...I don't know. I saw my dad's grief. I saw how easy it was for her to leave us behind. If life was a romance novel, she would've come back for him, for us. It just made me stop believing in happy endings, you know?"

I gave another shrug.

"I think that's why people read books. Ninety-nine percent of the time, they're better than reality."

It was silent a moment, then...

"Careful, Kent," he said. "You're starting to sound pessimistic like me. I've seen your resting frown face. Not sure you can pull it off."

Bo's words brought back the light. I appreciated that more than he could ever know.

I smiled. "No worries, Stryker. I'm still an eternal optimist and a romantic."

"Just not one who wants to fall in love," he said.

"Not if I can help it," I said.

Though as I looked into Bo's eyes, something shifted inside my chest, and I wasn't sure I had any say in the matter.

"But if you did," he added, "if you found love, you wouldn't run away from it, right?"

"I hope not," I said slowly. "That was kind of a weird thing to say."

He shrugged. "Just curious."

Shaking myself, I said, "Do you like older or younger women?"

Bo looked surprised for a beat, but then he sat back, relaxing into the booth. "Not sure. I don't think age is a factor for me."

Well, that didn't help at all. I was trying to determine whether Meech or Bianca was Bo's mystery woman. His answer didn't eliminate either one of them which meant I'd just wasted one of my questions. Shoot.

He watched me with a thoughtful expression, and I started to grow twitchy, like he could read my thoughts.

"Shin and Meech are killing it up there," I said, wincing as Shin's voice pierced the air on a high note. Meech wasn't doing much better, though her dance moves seemed more natural. Shin was just jumping around. "Literally, I think they're trying to murder each other with their voices."

Bo nodded. "Yeah, they do this a lot. They call it battle karaoke."

I didn't recognize the K-Pop song, but I was pretty sure it had never been performed with so much enthusiasm.

"Why haven't you ever had a boyfriend?" Bo asked.

My eyes widened as I whipped back to him. "How do you know I've never had a boyfriend?"

"I pay attention."

What? Did that mean he paid attention to *me*? Crazy.

"Kent, question two is waiting for an answer."

"I had you," I said. "Didn't I?"

Something flared in his eyes but was gone in the next instant almost as if it had never been.

"That you did," he said so softly I almost missed it. "But that doesn't answer the question."

I exhaled long and loud. "Well, no one asked me out, which was okay since I was never really interested in anyone."

Besides you.

"And as you know, Stryker, everyone on my suitor list ran the other way," I said. "So there's that."

"I didn't run," he said.

I blinked. Bo was right. He hadn't, and now I was starting to wonder why?

"Favorite flower?" he asked.

I grinned. "That's an easy one. You."

"Me?" he repeated.

"Yeah, you're it, Flower Boy."

Bo rolled his eyes. "Thought I was Marshmallow Bo."

"You're both," I said happily.

Looking toward the stage, I clapped with the rest of the crowd. Shin and Meech had finished their song. It was a strong finish too. Meech was in a split, and Shin had spun twice and did something called a death drop—or he'd slipped by accident. The jury was still out on that one. As they left the stage, four guys entered. They had instruments, so I knew they were an actual band, not karaoke.

As Meech ran over to us, I smiled.

"You guys were awesome," I said, "especially the dance moves."

"Did you see Shin fall?" she asked. "I nearly peed myself."

Shin, who'd come up behind her, frowned and said, "I didn't fall, Meech. I did a double pirouette to the floor. It's an advanced skill, not that you'd know."

"Oh really?"

"Yeah, sorry to outperform you—again."

"Next time I'm picking the song."

"Already want a rematch, huh?"

They went back and forth a couple more times before I tugged on her sleeve.

"Who's that?" I asked, gesturing with my chin to the band, who looked like they were almost ready to play. The crowd at the front of the stage had grown, filling up the entire space. They looked energized, eager.

"Oh," Meech said, eyes bright, "that's HERS. They're incredible!"

"Yeah," Shin said, "they're blowing up right now. About to be on tour officially. They're performing tonight."

I nodded. "Yeah, I think my girls at the library might have mentioned them. I've never heard of HERS."

As the lead singer came up to adjust the microphone, I heard several squeals from the crowd. It was easy to see why.

"Whoa," I said. "Casey and Natalia were right. He's gorgeous."

Bo grunted. "I don't see it."

I threw him a look then turned back to the stage. "Come on, Stryker. He's got that whole carelessly handsome, rockstar vibe about him. I'm just saying he's objectively attractive."

"I'd like to objectify him," Meech put in. "I think most of the people in this bar would like to objectify Hayden Davenport. He's so hot."

I giggled, but Shin didn't laugh.

"I guess if you're into broody musicians," Shin said.

"Who isn't?" Meech asked. "But I heard he has a girlfriend. They say the good ones are always taken."

"That include girls too? Probably why you're still single," Shin quipped and received an elbow in the ribs from Bo and a glare from Meech.

One of the other band members with a guitar strapped across his front was hyping up the crowd, strutting his stuff across the stage. He was tall, dressed like Prince, and walked like Mick Jagger. The guy's star power was undeniable, and the crowd ate it up.

"Santino is such a babe. Ryker's on drums, and he's like a silent, sexy giant. Elliot's nerd hot. And then again, there's Hayden freaking Davenport." Meech sighed. "They've got the full package."

"Sounds like it," I said.

"I'm going for marshmallow fluff," Meech announced. "You guys want anything?"

"They have that here?"

"Yeah, on tap."

My eyes went wide. "Okay, it's official. This is the coolest place ever."

Meech laughed, and as we crossed to the packed bar, several people from The Academy called out to her. Their eyes, however, stayed fixed on me.

"Is it just me, or are people staring?" I asked.

"They're definitely staring," she confirmed.

"Why?"

"Because you're the first girl Bo's brought here."

I blinked. "That can't be true."

"Trust me, it is," she said, waving to get the bartender's attention. "Now that I think about it, you're also the first one he's personally escorted to

The Academy."

I looked at her face, trying to discern if there was any animosity in the statement. There didn't seem to be. But I wanted to be sure.

The man behind the bar came over and asked, "What would you ladies like?"

"Two marshmallow fluffs on tap, please," Meech said.

"You got it."

It took only moments for him to fill two small bowls, add spoons, then pass them over to us.

"Thanks," I said, and he nodded before leaving to help someone else.

Meech turned to me with a grin. "You're going to love this, Lottie."

"I bet," I said then added, "Hey, Meech?"

"Hmmm."

Running my spoon along the top of the fluff, I asked, "You don't mind that Bo brought me tonight. Do you?"

"No, why would I? You're his girlfriend."

I let out a sigh. "Oh good."

"You sound relieved. What's up?"

After taking a bite of marshmallow fluff, I nearly groaned in delight. It was sweet and smooth and oh-so-good. "Honestly?" I said. "I thought you guys might be into each other."

Meech nearly sprayed marshmallow everywhere. "Seriously?" she gasped. "Me and Bo?

You thought..."

I shrugged.

"No way," she said with a laugh. "I would never go there. Not even if you paid me."

"Why not?" I asked a tad defensively. "Stryker's a wonderful guy."

She nodded like that was a given. "Yeah, it's just I'm into someone else—not that it's ever going to happen," she mumbled.

Her gaze, I noticed, had moved back to our table—or to one person in particular. And it wasn't Bo.

"Shin?" I asked and smiled as she nodded. "I can totally see that."

Her eyes met mine, and they were filled with hope. "You can?"

"Oh yeah, he'd be crazy not to want you, Meech."

"Thanks, Lottie. I've been in love with him since we were kids." She sighed, gazing at Shin across the space as if he was the only one she could see. "I've dropped tons of clues, but when that didn't work, I just ended up arguing with him. Shin's such an idiot sometimes."

My smile only widened. She'd said idiot as if it was an endearment.

"So, it's a definite no to Bo then?" I repeated.

"Absolutely," she said then grimaced. "I mean, it's Bo. Even the thought grosses me out. Blech."

Someone behind me cleared their throat, and when I turned, my eyes widened as they landed on a familiar face.

"Mrs. Lee," I said, "I didn't see you there. How's it going?"

"Hmm. You should pay better attention to your surroundings, Charlotte-Lottie-Lotte," she said, and her eyes turned cold as they shifted to Meech. "So Mi-Cha, you think you're better than my grandson?"

Meech paled. "I didn't mean—"

"You called him gross."

"Yes," she said quickly, "but I was just trying to assure Lottie I don't harbor secret feelings for her man. You've gotta believe me, Mrs. Lee. I love Bo like a brother."

"Hmph."

I jumped in then. "It's true. We were just spilling the tea."

Mrs. Lee's face remained expressionless. "I see no tea in front of you, only unhealthy fluff."

"Oh no," I said, smiling, "it's just an expression."

The woman sitting on the other side of Mrs. Lee leaned forward then.

"I believe 'spill the tea' is code for gossip," she said then looked to me. "Isn't that right?"

"Yes, ma'am. Gossip, girl chat, that kind of thing."

Mrs. Lee frowned at her friend. "Then why didn't they just say that?"

"Kids today," the woman said with a sigh. "They have a code for everything."

I couldn't believe I hadn't noticed her before. True, she'd been half-hidden by Mrs. Lee, but this woman would've been hard to miss in any crowd. Her gray hair was styled to perfection. She wore a tiny mint green fascinator with a matching dress that must've been tailored because it hugged her curves like a glove. She'd paired that with high-heeled shoes which she had crossed at the ankle while she sat on her barstool. The woman commanded attention, in a different way than Mrs. Lee, but the effect was just as powerful.

"Remember the code name they gave me?" she asked.

As Mrs. Lee grinned, Meech and I exchanged a surprised look. Guess I wasn't the only one who hadn't seen anything besides a scowl from my former boss.

"I do," Mrs. Lee said. "I also remember you arguing with your service detail until they changed it to something you liked."

"A girl's got to have standards," she said. "There was no way I could be called the Pink Pearl. I needed something better. Like the Pink Mamba or the Spider, something catchy."

"Only you, Constance." Mrs. Lee shook her head then looked back to the two of us. "Mi-Cha."

"Yes, ma'am?" she said.

"I forgive you for saying those things about my Bo."

Meech seemed to breathe for the first time since Mrs. Lee's appearance.

"Charlotte-Lottie-Lotte, I have something to discuss with you."

"Okay," I said.

Meech gave me a supportive look then said, "I'll take your bowl back to the booth."

With a nod, she left, and I turned my attention back to Mrs. Lee. "I hope you're okay after what happened. I didn't really get a chance to talk to you at the shop before I left—not that you had any trouble dealing with that robber."

Mrs. Lee waved it off, but Constance sat forward.

"What's this about a robber?" she repeated.

"Nothing," Mrs. Lee said. "Some idiot tried to steal from us."

"Oh no! From your charming little flower shop? The nerve."

"Yes. He pointed a gun at Charlotte-Lottie-Lotte, but she distracted him until help came."

"She was the help," I said with a smile. "Mrs. Lee came in, and the guy didn't know what hit him."

Constance let out a tinkling laugh. "I bet he didn't. You've still got it, Seung, even after all these years."

"He definitely picked the wrong shop," I said.

Mrs. Lee shrugged, but her face looked more relaxed than I'd ever seen it. Her gaze settled on mine.

"I wanted to confirm something," she said. "Snow-Soon tells me you flipped Bo to the mat perfectly on the first try."

I nodded. "That's right."

"How did it feel?"

"Good," I said, "great, actually. I couldn't wait to do it again. He was a good sport about it too."

"Of course, Charlotte-Lottie-Lotte. He wants to make sure you're safe."

I blushed at that.

"You keep practicing," she said.

"I will," I promised.

She nodded then turned to Constance. "Are they ever going to play?"

"My grandson is the best," the other woman sniffed. "They're just making sure everything's ready. Trust me, they're worth the wait."

A girl who looked about my age joined us then, grinning from ear-to-ear.

"They had some trouble with the sound system, but everything's good now," she said. "I knew carrying a screwdriver in my purse would eventually come in handy."

"Thank goodness for you, Magnolia," Constance said, looking at her with clear affection. "How was Hayden when you left?"

"Nervous, but ready to rock, as always."

"Naturally." The older woman turned to me then with a grin. "This is my grandson's band."

"You must be so proud," I said. "I've heard wonderful things."

"Oh, I am."

Mrs. Lee grumbled, "Wish I could hear some music. That's what we came for."

"Oh, pipe down, Seung. They're about to start." She nodded to the girl. "This is Hayden's girlfriend Magnolia. Maggie, the scowling old lady is my dear friend Seung Lee."

"Nice to meet you," the girl said with a nod.

"You too." Mrs. Lee huffed, "And old, Constance? I'm still younger than you."

"Maybe in years, but not in spirit," the woman chimed.

Mrs. Lee's eyes lit on me next. "This is Bo's girlfriend, Charlotte-Lottie-Lotte."

"Cool name," Maggie said.

"Thanks"—I blushed—"I like yours too. Very unique."

As Mrs. Lee and Constance talked, the girl turned to me with a smile.

"Is this your first HERS show?" she asked.

"Yeah," I said. "I can't wait."

"See that guy up there? That's my boyfriend."

At that exact moment, Hayden spoke into the microphone, his voice carrying around the room.

"Hey Chariot," he said, grinning at the crowd. "Sorry for the wait. We had some technical difficulties, but we're good now."

The crowd cheered.

"You ready for us?"

The cheers grew.

"Glad to hear it. We are HERS."

"This is a good-looking crowd," the superstar guitarist put in, and someone yelled, "We love you, Santino!"

"Love you, too," he said with a wink.

Hayden just laughed. "Just so you know, he says that to everyone."

"I do," came the solemn reply, but it was ruined when he added, "but Hayden's just jealous 'cause I have so much love to give."

After the crowd quieted again, Hayden said, "So, this first song goes out to the girl in the elevator, Magnolia Wilhelmina Mills, the best girl in the world."

Beside me, I heard Magnolia sigh.

"I've asked him not to do that," she said, though her smile belied her words.

"She's here somewhere probably blushing like crazy. Or wishing I'd shut up. Hope you like this one, Chariot."

She shook her head as they started the song.

"That's so romantic," I said.

"That's Hayden," she said back with a smile. "So,

where's yours?"

I looked to her in confusion.

"Your boyfriend," she said. "Didn't Mrs. Lee say you're dating her grandson?"

"Oh yeah." I flushed then pointed to Bo. "That's him over there, the big grumpy one with the frown."

Maggie nodded. "He seems...nice?"

I released a laugh. "Oh, he is, total marshmallow."

"Cool."

As if he'd heard, Bo turned our way, locking gazes with me. His lips tipped up, and I felt my heart trip over itself in reaction.

"Very nice," she said again. "I can feel the connection between you from here."

"You can?"

"Definitely."

Maybe it was because she sounded so sure. Maybe it was because she was a stranger. But I needed some guidance, and Maggie was there, so I said, "Can I ask you a strange question?"

Magnolia shrugged. "Sure."

"When did you know it was real? With Hayden?"

She gave me a smile. "That's a tough one. We had an unconventional beginning, definitely a few bumps in the road."

What bumps? I wondered but didn't dare interrupt.

"Looking back on it...I think I knew all along," she said. "I think he did too. We just had to admit the truth to ourselves, you know?"

I nodded.

"Did that help at all?"

"I think so," I said. "Thanks, Magnolia."

"No problem, Charlotte. Enjoy the show."

She walked away, and after a deep breath, I returned to the booth. Bo looked up as I sat across from him. Looking around, I said, "Where did Meech and Shin go?"

"Meech dragged Shin out to dance," he said, studying my face. "You okay?"

"Hmmm," I said. "Your grandma's here."

"I know, saw her walk in with Constance Davenport about ten minutes after we got here."

I shook my head. "Always paying attention."

He shrugged.

"Want to dance with me, Stryker?"

"Is that one of your questions?" he said.

"Yeah."

"Then no."

"Why not?" I asked.

"Because I don't dance in public," he said. "Favorite book?"

"I...there's no way I can answer that," I said flustered both by his quick rejection and the impossible question. "I can give you like a top 15 books, maybe. But there's no way to narrow it down more than that. Plus, there's all the books I still have to read—"

"Okay, okay, I get it," he said with a chuckle. "You can't pick."

I nodded then said, "Thanks—but back to the dancing. You won't do it? Even for me?"

"Even for you."

With a sigh, I got to my feet. "Okay, I guess I'll just have to go find another partner."

Bo froze. "What?"

"Looks like they're starting a slow song, so that means we'll have to get close. Ah well, it's all good."

As I walked away, Bo was right on my heels.

"Thought you weren't coming?" I said as I turned to him.

He frowned. "Changed my mind."

Bo's hands went to my waist, and I bit back a gasp as he pulled me inexorably closer. My hands went to his shoulders. We swayed to the music, and a second later, I recognized the song. It was the same one that account had paired with our kiss—which only reminded me of what I had to ask Bo. Before that though, I had another question.

"Why be a bodyguard?" I asked.

"I want to protect people, and I'm good at noticing things," he said.

"Like what?"

"Like the guy who's been watching you since you and Meech went to the bar. Red and white t-shirt, glasses, kind of looks like Where's Waldo. Ten o'clock."

I shook my head. "You're crazy. No one's been watching me."

"He's been waiting to shoot his shot. Wasn't going to give him the chance."

"I don't understand you," I said.

"Don't you?"

Before I could answer, he said, "What's your first memory of me?"

I smiled. "You were fighting off these guys who'd cornered a dog on the sidewalk in front of our houses. I remember because you were so much smaller than them. You couldn't have been more than eight or nine? And they were teens, but they all ran away—and that was before your dad came out to yell at them." I looked up into his shocked expression. "That's when I knew you weren't as unfeeling and gruff as you pretend to be, Bo Stryker."

He exhaled, pulling me closer. "I…wasn't expecting that."

"I have a good memory," I said.

"Apparently."

"I'm going to ask my final question now."

Bo lifted a brow. "Go ahead."

It's no big deal, I assured myself. Just ask him.

"Well, we're trying to make one last push for donations for the library charity event," I said. "And

Casey and Natalia had this idea—it's kind of crazy, but I think it could help."

Bo waited.

"Remember that video of us?"

"How could I forget?" he said.

"It's okay if you say no. I want to make that clear."

"Just say it, Kent."

I took a deep breath and decided to let the chips fall where they may.

"Will you kiss me again?"

22

Ten seconds.

It took Bo ten whole seconds to answer.

I felt like I died a little more with each passing moment. But then he said...

"Yes."

Part of me thought I might've been hearing things, so I said, "Can you repeat that?"

"Yeah, Kent, I'll kiss you."

He leaned forward, and my breath hitched.

"Did you mean right now?"

I shook my head. "No um, not now."

"When and where?" he asked.

"I was thinking we could do it at the library over the weekend," I said still feeling breathless. "We need to record it."

"I've got work, but I'll come by after."

The song ended, and he took a step back, though his intense eyes stayed on me.

"Red t-shirt's still looking this way," he said. "Feels like I need to claim you or something, so he'll back off."

A laugh escaped my lips. "So, you did read some of the books I recommended. Also, that's not necessary. Mainly because one, this isn't a paranormal romance, and you're not my mate, Stryker. Two, I think this guy is a figment of your imagination."

"You're the one who made me read those books," he said.

"Technically, you had a choice."

"But you're the one who got me hooked."

I shrugged. "You're welcome?"

Bo shook his head.

"Even if the guy was real, I think our slow dance plus that scowl of yours got the message across," I said.

"Still," he murmured, "just in case."

Before I could respond, Bo's lips were pressed against my forehead, making my knees go weak and my eyelids flutter closed. His hands cradled my cheeks, strong yet gentle. If there was a sweeter kiss in all the world, I didn't know it. And I'd read tons of them.

Even after he pulled back, it took me a second to open my eyes.

"You good?" he asked.

"Y-yeah," I said, "I think I should get home though. My dad will worry."

"Okay, I'll walk you out and get a ride from Shin," he said.

My brow pinched. "Sure you don't want me to take you?"

"Yeah, I'm good," he said. "You?"

Besides all the hearts I saw floating around Bo's head after that kiss and my liquid-limbed state?

"I'm awesome," I said.

Bo made good on his promise and walked me to my car. He even waited for me to drive away before going back inside. All night, I thought about him. In my dreams, we danced to an endless playlist of songs, never getting tired of being in each other's arms.

#

Saturday morning, I was at the library, trying not to watch the door like a hawk.

"You're staring at the door again," Casey commented.

"No, I'm not," I mumbled, looking away. "And if I was, it's because Tuesday we're supposed to start loading in all the furniture for A Night Out with Austen. I was eyeing the door dimensions to make sure there wouldn't be a problem."

Natalia tapped her chin. "Hmm, I thought you did that weeks ago."

I had.

"And didn't you measure this morning when you got here?"

Yes again.

"Lottie, stop it with the lame excuses," Casey said. "Bo's on his way, and you can't wait to see him."

"And kiss him," Natalia added.

"And love on him."

"And record every sweet, sweet moment."

"It must be tough kissing your hot boyfriend for charity."

"But someone's gotta do it."

They high-fived, and I gave them my meanest glare.

"Friends don't tease friends," I said.

The girls laughed, and I gave a sniff.

"At least not about important stuff."

"They absolutely do," Casey retorted. "Teasing your friends is almost entirely what makes life worth living. Well that, and baked goods."

"And pizza," Natalia added.

Casey's eyes went liquid. "Ooh, pizza is the best."

I grinned. "If you guys are hungry, take a break. Bring me back something."

"Yeah, right," Natalia said. "And miss you and

Bo's kissfest? I don't think so."

"I am hungry," Casey added with a bounce of her brows, "for love. Starving for it actually."

The bell above the door chimed and in walked Bo.

He couldn't have known what we'd been talking about.

But his eyes went straight to mine.

"That look is everything," Casey whispered.

"I'm living for it" Natalia said back, and I shushed them both as Bo stepped up to the counter.

"Sorry, Kent," he said. "I tried to hurry, but work ran late. We had a lot of deliveries today."

I nodded. "Anyone I know?"

Bo gave a shrug. "There was one for Bianca Briggs."

"Again?"

"Yeah, came here as soon as I was done."

I tried to ignore the twinge in my chest.

"So, what were you thinking?"

I was thinking I want him. More than that, I wanted to let myself want him. And that was as thrilling as it was scary.

"For the video," he added.

Shaking myself, I said, "I think we should practice, try a few different things, see what works."

"Okay." Bo shrugged, removing his jacket, and turned back to me.

In my peripheral, I saw Casey and Natalia

fanning themselves. I rolled my eyes at their antics then faced Bo again. He gave them a nod.

"Casey, Natalia," he said in greeting.

"Hey Bo," Casey said while Natalia twinkled her fingers at him.

"You guys here to help?"

Casey's eyes lit up then. "Of course! If you need someone to record, I'll do it."

"I'll supervise," Natalia offered, and I bit back a laugh.

"How nice of you guys to volunteer your time," I said.

Bo lifted a brow, and I told them my idea.

"So, I came up with a script last night. It's short, sweet, and to the point. We promote A Night Out with Austen and...end with a kiss."

"Sounds good," Casey said, holding up her phone and giving me a thumbs up. "I'm ready when you are."

Going around the counter, I stepped in front of Bo and looked up.

"Ready?" I asked, feeling a bit breathless.

"Mm hm."

I turned to the camera, gave Casey a nod, and smiled.

"Hey bookworms!" I said. "Next Saturday, we're hosting the charity event of the season. And you're invited! If you love books, romance, and making a difference in the lives of children, join us for A

Night Out with Austen. Who knows? By the end of the night, you might just find your happily ever after."

With that, I turned to Bo and was struck by several emotions at once.

Yearning, nervousness, excitement, fear, confusion.

His piercing stare was on me, unaware of my inner turmoil.

A bit stiffly, I reached up, guided his face down to mine, delivered a quick peck to his lips then pulled back.

Even that, though, fed the spark inside me.

When I looked to Casey and Natalia, they wore matching frowns.

"How was that?" I asked.

"It was..." Natalia trailed off.

"You want the truth?" Casey said. When I nodded, she added, "Well, I think we should do a second take. Maybe shake off some of the awkward."

"Okay," I said, looking to Bo. "Are you alright with that?"

He nodded. "Yeah, I'm good."

So we tried again. I delivered the speech, leaned up to Bo, kissed him (even shorter this time), then looked back to Casey. She was whispering with Natalia about something. I couldn't hear them, but I knew we'd be doing a third take.

"Why don't we try it with Bo kissing you, Lottie?" Natalia suggested.

I nodded—but that take wasn't right either.

When Bo kissed me, I was so aware of the camera, so aware of Casey and Natalia watching us, even more aware of Bo's lips and the fact that I was enjoying this far too much. I jerked back, and Bo looked at me in surprise.

"Sorry," I said.

"No problem," he said.

Casey and Natalia started talking about trying different lighting or changing the location, but I knew it wouldn't do any good.

"I have an idea," Bo said. "If you want to try it."

I looked to him in surprise. "Sure. What should I do?"

"Say the lines then face me. I'll do the rest."

Casey raised her phone, gave me the cue, and I said my piece. When that was done, I turned and looked up at Bo. His eyes met mine, and his hands rose to cup my cheeks. As he leaned forward, I felt myself tense—but then he murmured, "Stay with me, Kent," and pressed his lips against my forehead.

It was just as sweet as the night before.

My eyes closed on a sigh.

Bo kissed the tip of my nose.

And then he laid a final kiss to my mouth.

I didn't want to let him go.

As Bo leaned back, I knew there was a slight

smile on my face, but I couldn't help it. I looked up—only to find his eyes already on mine. I didn't know how long we stood like that, five seconds, a minute, an hour.

But he held my stare until Casey said, "And cut!"

Feeling like I was coming out of a dream, I turned my head to see both my friends smiling.

"It was perfect."

Natalia nodded. "The best yet. Good idea, Bo."

"Thanks," he said.

"Okay, let's go with that," I said shakily. "I'm gonna get lost in the shelves for a bit. Thanks, guys."

Bo was silent as I walked away, but I could feel his eyes following me. Ducking into an aisle, winding through the shelves, I walked until I'd put a sufficient amount of distance between me and the guy I couldn't get out of my head. I leaned back against a shelf and closed my eyes.

Deep breaths, I thought. Just shake it off.

The problem was those kisses, even the awkward ones, still made me feel something.

A lot of things actually.

My heart was brimming, nearly overflowing with feelings, and I didn't know how to deal.

Sure, I was nervous in front of the camera. But I was more scared that I'd accidentally show Bo how much I want him, so I tried to hold back, praying he wouldn't notice. Then he stepped in and made everything better.

"You okay, Kent?"

Bo's deep voice.

I opened my eyes and watched him as he walked down the aisle.

"You left pretty fast."

"I just needed a second."

"Do you want me to leave?" he said, stopping in front of me.

With a sigh, I shook my head. "No, stay. I'm the problem, Stryker, not you."

"What do you mean?"

"I'm scared, okay?"

Bo's frown deepened. "Of what? Me?"

"Yes," I said then shook my head, "and no."

He looked almost as confused as I felt.

"Honestly, I'm scared that we might not have the same chemistry as before. Then the video will be terrible, and it won't drive donations like we need it to, and I'll let everyone down."

"That won't happen," he said.

I swallowed. "But I think I'm even more scared that we will have chemistry."

He tilted his head.

"I don't want these feelings, Stryker," I said.

Instead of giving me a look of horror or running in the opposite direction, Bo did the very last thing I expected.

He chuckled.

"Really?" I shot him a frown, but that only made

him laugh harder. "You're so serious all the time, and Mr. I-Never-Smile decides to laugh now? So inappropriate."

"Sorry," he said.

"You shouldn't laugh when someone confesses their feelings," I muttered. "Even if you don't return them."

"Who says I don't?"

My eyes shot to his as Bo came closer.

"Stop right there," I said, but he shook his head, not stopping until there was only an inch of space between us. "W-what are you doing?"

"What I wanted to do five minutes ago," he said, "minus the camera and audience."

I blinked.

"Your friends are nice but kind of nosy."

"They are not!" I said, though yes, they kind of were—so was I. But that was beside the point. "Casey and Natalia are wonderful."

"Hmmm."

Bo leaned forward, his gaze intent on my lips, but I placed my hands on his chest, trying not to swoon at the way his muscles felt against my palms.

I swallowed. "You're...what is happening right now?"

"I'm kissing my girlfriend," he murmured.

"You mean, fake girlfriend," I said automatically.

He slowly shook his head, staring into my eyes.

"Nothing fake about it," he said. "There never

was."

And then Bo kissed me.

He stole the breath from my lungs. His mouth moved with mine, gently crackling and sparking like embers in a bonfire. I clutched his t-shirt tight in my hands, tugging him closer, wanting to feel more of his warmth. He came willingly until his chest was pressed against me, one of his hands wrapped around my waist, leaving no space between us. But still, I wanted more. Trying to communicate this through the kiss, I moved my hands up to his shoulders, stood on my tiptoes and pressed my lips more firmly to his.

As if he'd read my mind, Bo broke the kiss only long enough to grumble, "Finally," then placed his hands on my waist and lifted.

My legs wrapped around him on instinct.

The kiss ignited.

One of Bo's hands moved to grip my thigh, making sure I didn't fall, leaving a trail of fire in its wake, the other burrowed into my hair, and as I sat perched atop one of the bookshelves, our lips never parted. I felt Bo's breath hitch as I deepened the kiss. I nipped his top lip, and a low growl sounded in the back of his throat. His kiss grew more heated then. And I loved it. I should've been concerned about knocking books to the ground—but right then, I was lost in the feeling. The absolute serenity of being in Bo's arms, having his lips caress my lips, wanting nothing more than to keep kissing him and kissing him and kissing him.

It was bliss.

It felt like we were the only two people in the world.

The kiss gentled. When I thought it was over, Bo kept giving me these little lingering kisses that made me want to laugh and cry at once. He finally set me back on my feet and leaned back, and for a moment, we just looked at each other.

I shook my head. "That was unexpected."

"Just showing you how I feel," he said.

When I gave him a questioning look, Bo sighed.

"You're not the only one struggling with feelings, Kent."

I couldn't believe my ears, but my heart remembered the kiss that'd happened only seconds ago. It was filled with hope.

"Does this mean you have feelings for me?"

"Yeah," he said, "I have for a while. It's pretty annoying."

"Annoying you is one of my favorite things," I said with a grin.

He shook his head, but the corners of his lips lifted.

"So is making you smile."

"Don't get used to it," he said back, but the smile remained.

Tilting my head, trying to get my heart back

under control, I said, "I'm glad you didn't kiss me like that before."

"Why?"

"Because this one was just for us."

Bo tucked my hair behind my ear, his eyes following the movement, as I shivered.

"Are we an 'us'?" he said softly.

"Only if you want to be."

A beat passed, and I held my breath.

"I do." Bo pushed his hands into his pockets and gave an adorable shrug of those big shoulders. "I want you, Kent."

"That's good, Stryker," I murmured. "Because I want you too."

Bo's smile was brighter than a thousand suns.

Just like that, my heart let him in without question. I lowered my shields. Perhaps, I should've been more cautious. But I'd read somewhere that kissing could addle your brain and affect your judgment. And Bo's kisses were better than good.

They were soul-stirring.

So, I kept on smiling, filled with joy and happiness.

And completely unaware of what was coming.

23

The first sign that something was off came when my sister and I were on our way to school.

"How are things with Bo?" she asked.

"They're good." A blush immediately swept up my cheeks, and I couldn't fight back a smile. "You're actually the first person I've told, but we're together now. For real."

"Oh my gosh!"

Scarlett squealed, dancing around in her seat.

"I knew it," she said. "I *knew* it! This is my I-told-you-so dance."

I shook my head. "You seriously need lessons, Scar. Those moves aren't even to the beat."

"They go perfectly with the music in my head," she retorted then turned to me with a smile. "How did it happen?"

I told her about inviting Bo to the library, recording the video, and then what happened in the stacks.

"He said he has feelings for me." I sighed. "And then he kissed me, and oh, Scar. It was beautiful."

The whole weekend had been a whirlwind. Bo and I texted and talked nonstop after the kiss, and I couldn't remember a time when I'd been happier.

"I knew he could do it," Scarlett said with a smile.

My brow furrowed. "What do you mean?"

"Ah, nothing."

She waved it off, but I was still curious. "No, really. You knew he could do what?"

"I just had a feeling Bo could make you happy if you'd let him," she said. "And obviously, he has."

"Yeah," I said. "That's true. How's your love life by the way? Anyone special I should know about?"

"Nope, I'm not looking for anything serious."

"Neither was I." I shook my head. "You know, Scar, the last time I even remember you mentioning a crush it was years ago. What was his name? Sam?"

Scarlett scoffed. "That's old news, ancient. I haven't thought of him in forever. Besides, I want to hear more about your adventures with Bo."

And so, I told her about how Bo came to my window on Sunday night. It was after we'd talked for hours on the phone. I told him I missed him already. He said he wished he could see me. I said me, too. And minutes after we hung up, the next thing I knew, there was a light tap against my windowpane.

"What are you doing here?" I'd said, throwing open the latch. "It's past midnight."

Bo had shrugged. "Wanted to tell you goodnight."

"Such a marshmallow."

"Your marshmallow," he'd replied.

And then of course, there was more kissing. I told Bo he better leave before my father caught him. He said okay but made me promise that next time I'd show him my bookshelves. Reliving those moments and relaying the story to Scarlett distracted me from the remark she'd made in the car.

However, when I met Bo at my locker, it happened again.

"Hey," I said, leaning up to press a kiss against his jaw.

"Hey," Bo said back. His dark eyes were on me and looked lit from the inside. "What was that for?"

I shrugged. "Just happy to see you, I guess."

In response, he laced our fingers together and brought them to his lips, dropping a kiss on our joined hands. Flutters erupted inside my chest. I shook my head in wonder.

"I can't even believe this is happening," I said. "To be honest, I've had feelings for you for a long time, Stryker."

"Trust me," he said, "I've had mine longer."

"Debatable."

"Do you want to compare notes, Kent?"

"No"—I laughed—"but I never thought we'd really be together. We're so different."

"And there's the tiny fact that you don't believe in happy endings," he replied.

"Yeah, and that."

"I wasn't sure it would happen for us either." He laid another kiss to my hand then added, "Remind me to thank your sister."

"For what?" I asked.

"For all her help."

"Scarlett helped you? With what?"

The bell rang, and he said, "We should get to class. Talk later?"

"Yeah, sure," I said, giving him a smile.

But I was still dying to know what he'd meant.

It wasn't until a couple hours later that I got the answer.

I was just coming out of the girl's bathroom when someone stepped in front of me.

Aspen Vanderbilt stood there with her arms crossed.

"Hey Aspen," I said. "Did you need something?"

"Yeah, I do," she replied. "I want my $20 back."

"What?"

"Oh, drop the act. I know what you and your

sister did."

I shook my head. "Sorry, I'm so confused right now. What are we talking about?"

Aspen released a long-suffering sigh then pinned me with an accusatory stare.

"The HUBS bet," she said. "The one about who could be the first to hook up with Bo Stryker. I knew it was rigged all along. Your sister started the bet, then she somehow got Bo on board, just so you and she could split the money."

It felt like I'd been slapped.

"Scarlett started the bet?" I asked just to make sure I'd understood her correctly.

"Yeah, like you didn't know," Aspen said.

"I didn't."

She looked at me for a long moment before giving a careless shrug. "You're either a better actress than I gave you credit for, or you're telling the truth. If it's the second, I truly feel sorry for you," she said then scowled. "But I still want my money back."

Without a word, almost as if on autopilot, I reached into my purse, pulled out a twenty and handed it to her.

"Thanks, Loser Lottie."

"I really didn't know," I repeated.

"Getting duped, not just by your boyfriend but your sister?" Aspen gave me a sympathetic look, and I honestly couldn't tell whether it was real or not.

"That's gotta hurt."

She was right.

It should've hurt. I should've been angry or sad or a combination of both. But I was still trying to process everything.

Scarlett's words from earlier replayed on a loop in my head.

I knew he could do it.

Then the conversation I'd had with Bo rang in my ears.

Remind me to thank your sister.

For what?

For all her help.

And finally Aspen's accusation.

Your sister started the bet.

Scarlett had also been the one to add Bo to my suitor list. She'd been in his corner from day one, and I'd never questioned it. But I was starting to do so now.

Still, the pieces weren't quite fitting together like they should.

I had to wait until my next class was finished, but after the bell rang, I went looking for answers. Only two people could give them to me. I just hoped I was wrong.

Scarlett glanced up when I approached her, and seeing the look on my face, she frowned.

"Hey Lotte," she said. "What—"

"Did you start the HUBS bet?" I said without

pause. When she didn't reply, I added, "Scarlett, seriously. Don't lie to me about this."

Looking defiant, she gave me a shrug. "So what if I did?"

"Why would you do something like that?" I threw up my hands. "And why didn't you tell me?"

Tugging on my arm, dragging us further down the hall and behind a bank of lockers, she said, "Honestly, Lotte? I thought I was doing you a favor."

"Yeah, right." I scoffed.

"Come on. You've been in love with Bo for years, but you were never going to tell him. I thought hearing about the bet might give you a jumpstart."

"And when it didn't, you thought you'd just 'help' Bo along," I said. "Is that right?"

She nodded. "I offered help here and there, yeah. It wasn't a big deal. I don't get why you're so upset about this."

"You should've told me, Scar," I said.

"You would've never given him a chance if I did."

"That wasn't your decision to make."

My sister shook her head. "I just wanted you to be happy, sis. And you are...aren't you?"

"I thought I was," I said, watching her expression dim. "Now, I'm just trying to sort out what I'm supposed to feel after finding out that my sister, my best friend, has been keeping things from me."

"I didn't—"

"See you after school," I said.

Walking away, I didn't look back even as she called my name. It felt like this was a dream happening to someone else. But when I got to my locker to switch out my books, Bo was there waiting for me. He was leaning up against the locker beside mine, and the sight of him usually brought a smile to my face. Today, though, I couldn't find it in me.

Bo noticed my mood immediately.

"What's wrong?" he asked.

The concern in his voice almost undid me, but I kept it together.

With a shrug, I said, "Nothing. I just got done talking to my sister."

His frown didn't relax. "Your voice sounds off."

"Sorry."

"Why won't you look at me?" he asked.

I took a deep breath then looked up and met his gaze. "Answer me one question, Stryker."

"Okay."

"Have you and my sister ever talked about me?" I said.

He nodded. "Yeah, we have."

"What exactly did she tell you?"

"She just gave me advice," he said slowly. "About relationships. I wasn't sure how to approach you, so I asked Scarlett, and she helped. Will you answer one of my questions now?"

There was a lump in my throat, and I didn't know why.

"Sure," I said.

"Why are you so upset?"

Because you didn't tell me. Because neither one of you thought to tell me any of this.

When he went to place a hand against my cheek, I pulled away, trying not to notice the hurt in his eyes.

"I just need some time to think," I said. "About everything."

Bo put his hand in his pocket, then said, "Does everything include us?"

"Yeah. I think, we should maybe take a break for now."

"I disagree."

"Noted," I said. "But I have to figure out how I feel about you and my sister going behind my back, Stryker."

"It wasn't like that," he said. "You've got to know it wasn't like that. I wanted to tell you a long time ago that I like you, that I...more than like you."

My heart wanted to jump into the palm of his hand and never come out.

But I held back, unsure of so many things at that moment.

"Scarlett just said I should be patient, not to move too fast, to let you set the pace."

I nodded. "She knows me, almost better than I

know myself."

"Don't be mad," he said. "She loves you."

Looking up, I found him staring at me. The late bell rang, but neither of us made a move to go.

"I'm not mad," I said, "at either of you. I just need time."

"Alright." Bo nodded, and as I turned to go, he added, "But you're not getting rid of me that easily, Kent."

I paused.

"I'm not giving up."

The truth was I didn't want him to. I didn't want to give him up either.

But I needed a break to figure out where we go from here.

#

"We're still short on male help," I said, looking down at the list. "The living regency statues were a good idea in theory. I posted it on the Chariot High student board, but no one signed up."

"Same with my school," Natalia said.

"So, you're saying no teenage boys volunteered to hang out at the library on a Saturday Night?" Casey rolled her eyes. "I'm shocked."

I shrugged. "I thought the promise of free food might entice them."

"Guess not," Natalia said.

"Yeah, but we'll still make it wonderful."

The girls nodded.

"Okay, the truck's outside," I said, rolling my shoulders to loosen them up. "We should start bringing stuff in. It might take a while."

"Yeah, like all day," Casey grumped.

"It'll go by fast."

"My nails are not going to thank me for this."

"Eh, we'll take turns working the desk."

Natalia offered to stay behind while Casey and I went out to the truck. The tables were heavy. It took two of us to carry one. There were six others as well as chairs, a chaise for ornamentation, faux white columns, and other little things. Casey and I set down the first table right inside the entrance, noticing a large crowd around the desk.

Of guys, I mentally added.

There was a large group of males standing around the library counter.

"Am I hallucinating?" I asked.

"If you are, I am too," Casey murmured.

"It's like the library's been infiltrated by a convention of male models."

"Or a SWAT team."

Natalia noticed us and smiled.

"Oh hey, girls," she said, gesturing to the assembly in front of her. "Looks like we got some sign-ups after all."

"But how?" I asked as two of the newcomers

separated from the group to take the table.

Casey laughed. "Who cares? My back is killing me, and we need all the muscle we can get."

"Where do you want this?" one of them said. I felt like I'd seen his face somewhere but couldn't quite place him.

"Oh," I said, "well, there's a storage room in back. We're keeping everything there until Saturday."

He nodded and off they went.

"Thank you," I called after them. To Casey, I said, "Someone must've sent out the Bat-Signal."

"Yeah, I'll give you one guess who," she said back.

"What do you—"

She nodded to the group, and out of all those faces, I saw Bo. He and Shin stepped forward.

"Hey," I said, shaking my head, "what are you guys doing here?"

"What's it look like, Lottie?" Shin said with a grin. "Heard you needed help, so we're here. Ready to sell our bodies for a good cause."

"Huh?"

Bo shook his head. "He means we're here to lift stuff and do anything else you need then get out of the way."

"Oh," I said, feeling flustered, "well, thanks."

"No problem," he said.

After Casey got everyone's attention, we began delegating responsibilities. Natalia held up the sign-up sheet for statues. Casey led the guys to the truck. And I stood there, answering any and all questions. There were 12 guys total. They were all strong and, like Bo said, willing to do whatever we asked. I couldn't believe it. I was still sorting through my feelings, but I wouldn't look a gift horse in the mouth.

After a few minutes, Bo came to stand beside me.

"So, where did you find them?" I asked.

"The Academy," he said. "They're students in the elite class."

I looked up in surprise.

"I called in a favor."

Swallowing, I shook my head. "How did you even know we needed help?"

"I listen to you, Kent." Bo gave me a look, and there was so much tenderness there, I had to look away. "I'll always listen to you. Always be there for you. I hope you know that."

As he walked away, Shin took his spot at my side.

"Looks like it's going to be an awesome event," Shin commented.

"Thanks, I hope so," I said.

"Don't thank me. This was all Bo."

"Really?"

Shin nodded. "He told us his girl needed help. Everyone jumped at the chance. Even though Bo's been there for everyone here, he never asks us for anything."

My heart warmed, and I tilted my head.

"When was that exactly?" I asked.

"Ah man, I'm not sure. Like a week ago?" he said. "We've known for a while."

Feeling suddenly overcome with emotion, I nodded. "That was nice of him. You know, to do this for the kids and the library."

"Ah Lottie, I think we both know who he's doing this for."

Shin gave my shoulder a pat then walked away.

The work went much quicker with more hands, and just as he'd said, Bo and the others left when it was done. I didn't even get a chance to say goodbye. I assumed that was his way of trying to respect my space.

"We're all set on living statues," Casey said, and Natalia added, "Under all that bluster, Bo is a sweetheart. You're so lucky, Lottie."

I knew she was right.

The tug in my chest begged me to go after him, tell him how I felt.

But he and my sister were keeping secrets from me. It was a matter of self-preservation. I didn't believe in real-life HEA—but I'd wanted to with Bo. I had to be more careful, had to make sure my heart wasn't in danger, even if it wanted nothing more than to be his.

I had to keep my guard up—right?

24

It was finally here.

A Night Out with Austen was in t-minus four hours and counting. I'd set an alarm on my phone, so I'd stay on track. I was putting the final alterations on my dress when there was a timid knock at my door.

"Come in," I said.

I heard the door open and that was followed by a sigh.

A familiar if forlorn sigh.

Still, I waited for her to speak first.

"Hey," Scarlett said, "I made a checklist for tonight, thought it might help."

I nodded without looking. "Thanks. You can place it on the bed."

Scarlett's footsteps came farther into the room

and stopped beside me. I was looking down, working on my dress, so I could see her shoes as she shifted from one foot to the other.

"Your dress looks nice," she murmured.

"Hmmm."

"Very Austen-esque."

"That's the point," I said brusquely. "If there's nothing else, I should really finish this and get ready."

Scarlett released a heavy sigh.

"Was there something else?"

She mumbled under her breath.

"What was that?" I asked.

"I'm sorry, Lotte," she said with a huff. "You were right, okay? I shouldn't have done any of it, the bet, giving advice to Bo—"

"Not telling me," I put in.

"Especially that part." She plopped down beside me on the bed and put a hand over mine, halting me mid-stitch. "I should've told you everything. I should've been upfront with you and not meddled in your love life, even if I had the best of intentions. I'm sorry. Please forgive me, sis. I won't ever do that again. Okay?"

Looking up, I gave her a bright smile and a shrug.

"Okay," I said.

Scarlett gave me a suspicious look. "That's it? Just like that, we're all good?"

With a roll of my eyes, I placed my hand on top of hers. "Did you want more drama? Because I can yell, stomp my foot, and throw a book at you as you leave."

"Like you'd ever throw a book," she said.

"You're right," I said. "I've only done that twice in my life, and both times I regretted it—even if the endings were horrible."

She tilted her head. "I thought you were mad at me."

"I was upset," I corrected, "but I could never stay mad at you, especially over a guy. You're my sister."

"But I messed up."

"Yeah, but you admitted it." I shook my head. "That's all I wanted."

"Really?"

I elbowed her side. "You know how I hate the dark night of the soul moment in a book."

Scarlett threw her arms around me, squeezing in a death grip of a hug.

"I love you," she said. "You know that, right?"

"Love you too," I gasped. "Now, don't kill me. I've got a charity event to run."

With a laugh, she sat back and stared at the material in my hands. "This dress really is beautiful."

I nodded. "It better be. I pricked my finger like a thousand times."

"Wish I had one," she said wistfully. "The only

nice dress I have is the one I wore to homecoming two years ago. Too small and definitely inappropriate for the time period."

"Scar, please," I said, reaching back and tugging her dress out with a flourish. "You didn't think I'd make one for myself and not you, did you?"

Her eyes widened as she held up the light blue material. "Again, I thought you were mad," she said.

"I was for about two seconds, but then I got over it."

"Ahhh"—she pulled me in for another hug then stood, the dress in hand—"you're the best."

I shrugged. "I think we already knew that."

"Also, Bo's going to love you in that dress," she added.

"Still pulling for him, huh?"

"I'm pulling for *you*. I always have been."

I smiled at that. "Thanks, sis."

"You are going to tell him, right?"

"Tell him what?" As she gave me a look, I sighed. "I was planning to confess to him tonight, if he'll hear me out."

"He will," she said. "Trust me, Bo feels the same way you do, maybe even more so."

"I hope that's true," I murmured.

"No worries, sis," she said. "Love always wins in the end."

She left, closing my door with a click, and I shook my head.

"Yeah, in books," I muttered.

There was another light knock, and then Scarlett stuck her head back inside.

"Ooh, also, Dad wants to talk with us downstairs," she said then added, "Don't forget your violin."

Once I was dressed and ready, I went downstairs to find my father. He was seated at the kitchen table, drinking a mug of coffee, and looked up when I entered.

"Charlotte," he said, "you look beautiful."

"Thanks, Dad," I said.

"Where'd you get that dress?"

"I made it."

"She made one for me too," Scarlett said as she came into the room and did a twirl. "My big sister is the best. Period."

"Scarlett, wow." Dad got to his feet and shook his head. "How did my girls grow up so fast?"

We just smiled at him.

"You know you can tell me anything," he said. "Right?"

"Of course," I said, and Scarlett nodded.

"You'll both be safe tonight."

"It's a library charity event, Dad," Scarlett said. "I think we'll be fine."

He gave a nod then looked to me. "Are you getting picked up? Any dates I need to meet?"

"No," I said with a chuckle. "Why would you say

that?"

"Ah, I don't know," he said. "Maybe because I happened to look out my window the other night and noticed Bo Stryker jogging back to his house. Looked like he was coming from your window, Charlotte."

Scarlett choked back a giggle then excused herself.

"It's not what you think, Dad," I said quickly. "He was just saying goodnight."

"After midnight?" he asked.

"Yeah..."

"Is he your boyfriend?"

I shrugged. "Honestly, at this point, I have no idea. We've gone from fake to real to I'm-not-sure-what-to-think so many times. But I hope he will be."

"Do I even want to know?" Dad asked. After a second, he sighed. "Listen, I'll probably never be okay with you or your sister dating. Maybe if you started when you're 30. But I see now, that might've been wishful thinking."

I thought he was joking, but he didn't smile.

"I just wish you would've told me."

I gave a shrug. "I'm telling you now."

"Guess if you have to date," he muttered, "you could do worse than the Stryker kid."

"Really?" I asked.

Dad gave a nod. "Yeah, he's alright. Good family, good kid as far as I can see, kind of grouchy.

He doesn't smile much, but I guess you do that enough for the both of you."

I laughed. "I've learned that he's part grouch, part marshmallow, so it's all good."

"No idea what that means," he said then pointed at me. "You'll tell me if he ever does anything to hurt you."

"Okay."

"And he's coming to dinner, so we can have the talk."

I opened my mouth, but Dad's look silenced me.

"No talk, no date," he said.

I nodded, and Scarlett suddenly reappeared. "Car's ready," she said.

"Alright then," he said, coming forward and pulling us into a hug. "Charlotte, I know you put a lot of work into this event. Scarlett, I've heard you practicing well into the night. I've got no doubt it'll be a success."

"Thanks, Dad," we murmured in unison.

"You two have fun and be safe."

"Hey Dad, about Bo," I said as I got to the door, "I'm pretty sure I'm in love with him, but I still don't know if he loves me back. So, you might not even get to have the talk. Just putting it out there."

Dad shook his head. "He'd have to be stupid to let you go, Charlotte. Bo's never struck me as the stupid type."

That sealed it. My dad was officially the best.

"I'll have my talking points ready."

#

Hours later, the charity event was in full swing. Mrs. Jenkins brought several of her friends from bridge club. They arrived in a real-life carriage and looked amazing, having gone all out with their regency garb. Everyone kept talking about the wonderful flower arrangements. Mrs. Lee was here somewhere, and I knew she had to be brimming with pride. Meech came through too. The floral picture wall she'd created was a huge hit. There was a line of people waiting to take pics in front of it. Shin was posted as one of the living statues, posing for all he was worth, eating up the attention. And I'd gone to find Casey and Natalia minutes ago to report that we'd surpassed our fundraising goal. We whooped and hollered, jumping around as much as you could in these dresses. But the group hug we'd shared was part celebration, part relief. We'd done it!

I felt lighter than air.

Like I could do anything.

Like I could be courageous and confess my love.

But that was five minutes ago.

Now, I was standing with my cousins, getting ready to play a few string pieces. Scarlett was giving us all a pep talk. But I couldn't really concentrate because of the two people who'd just walked in.

Bo and Bianca.

Arm-in-arm.

She looked happy, smiling up at him.

He looked...not unhappy.

Bo's frown was in place, but he seemed content.

And he was still touching her.

Maybe I shouldn't have taken so long to untangle my emotions. Maybe I had lost him. Maybe Bianca was the one all along, and I'd never had him in the first place.

Oh, my heart.

It felt like it was caving in on itself.

"Lotte." I looked up to see Viola staring down at me. "We're about to play. You ready?"

"Sure," I said, forcing a smile I didn't feel. "Let's do this."

Freya my other cousin leaned over then. "Awesome job with all this. Feels like we're in *Cinderella* or something."

"More like *Pride and Prejudice*," Aurora said with a sigh. "Something about the books really makes it come alive. Don't you think?"

"That's just because you dream of having your own library," Freya said back.

"Who doesn't?" Viola replied.

"Hey, isn't that your boyfriend?" Freya asked, gesturing to the crowd with her chin.

Sure enough, there was Dare, fully kitted out in

regency wear.

"Took an hour to convince him to put on the costume," Viola said with a sigh.

"Handsome," Scarlett said with a sniff, "but also a distraction. Let's get it together ladies. We're about to go on."

As the song ended, we moved to take our seats, and Viola sidled up next to me with her cello.

"Thought I saw Bo out there," she said with a grin. "He looks gorgeous tonight."

"Yeah," I said, swallowing as I spotted him and Bianca together by the food table. Bo really did look good in his suit. "Dashing, rugged, and totally unattainable."

Viola gave me a funny look, but before she could ask, we went into our first song.

As we began, the crowd listened politely. Then a few couples made their way onto the dance floor. One of them was Mrs. Lee and Shin. Meech, I noticed, was standing off to the side recording the whole thing. Then there was Bo and Bianca. If I'd thought I was dying before, that was nothing compared to now. It really was over. I knew it when she threw her head back, laughing at something he'd said, and my stomach clenched painfully.

We played three songs before we finished our set.

Bo danced with Bianca for two of them.

As the stereo system clicked on again, and music

streamed through the speakers, I stood and moved to go back into the stacks.

"Hey," Scarlett said, "we just killed it. Where are you going?"

"Nowhere," I said, "just away."

"Why?"

"Bo brought a date."

"What?"

"He's here with someone, Scar," I said with a shrug. "It's no big deal."

"The hell it's not," she said. "I don't care who he's with. I know he wants to be with you."

I shook my head, but she was insistent.

"Seriously, Lotte, go talk to him," she said.

"I will later," I said, fighting back the stupid tears clogging my throat. "Right now, I'm just going to go for a second."

Scarlett let me leave, and I didn't waste any time, winding through the shelves, trying my best to escape the vision playing on a loop in my head. Bo and Bianca really did look nice together. Why couldn't I just be happy for them?

I didn't know whether it was fate or bad luck.

Probably a bit of both.

But on the next aisle I turned down, I ran straight into Bo.

He glanced up, looking unsurprised to see me.

"What are you doing here?" I said. "I mean, hi. Thanks for coming."

Bo nodded.

"Bored with the party already?" I forced a laugh. "Guess I need to do a better job next time."

"I wasn't bored," he said. "Just looking for you."

"Why?"

"Why do you think?"

Gathering all my courage, I turned to face him with a smile. "I saw you with Bianca. I'm...really happy for you."

"You don't look happy," Bo said.

"Ah well, maybe it's the lighting."

"No, you look miserable, Kent. Like someone just tore out the pages of your favorite book and burned them."

He stepped forward.

"Tell me who did it," he said. "I'll make it better."

Shaking my head, I ran a hand through my hair. "No one did anything, Stryker. Honestly, I'm good."

"Then why are you hiding?"

"I'm not," I said.

"Yeah, you are," he said. "You always come here when you're down."

"Can you blame me? Some of the best romance authors are right here, G through H. Garwood, Hoang, Hibbert, Hazelwood—"

"Kent."

"—but of course, the L's are amazing too. Liv Lamoreaux, Julie Anne Long, L.J. Shen—which is technically an S, but whatever—"

"Stop."

"—and then there's YA romance authors like—"

"Charlotte," he said, placing a hand on my shoulder. The combination of him using my real name and touching my arm stunned me into silence. "It's not that I don't want to hear about all the authors you love. I do. I just want to talk to you about something else first. Okay?"

I nodded and stepped back, watching his hand fall to his side.

"I already know," I said sadly. "And it's fine."

"What's fine?"

"I know you're with Bianca."

He was frowning again, but that was normal, so I hurried on, desperate to get the words out before I did something stupid like cry or beg him to stay with me.

"She's the one you told me about, right?" I said. "The girl whose attention you've always wanted, the one you love. I knew it when I saw you two dancing. And I'm happy for you, really I am. She seems nice."

"She is," he said.

"And she obviously has good taste if she's into you."

I bit my lip to stop myself from saying more.

Bo stared at me then said, "She's also very much married."

"Married?" I repeated.

"Yeah, her husband's away a lot on business. That's mainly what we talk about."

I nodded in sympathy. "Oh, so you're pining after a married woman. That must be hard."

Bo scoffed. "Not as hard as talking to you sometimes."

I blinked.

"Kent, Bianca's not the one," he said, staring into my eyes intently. "It's you."

"What?" I breathed.

"It's always been you."

I shook my head unable to believe it.

"Ask me about my first memory of you," he said.

"Why?"

"Just ask."

"Okay," I said, "what was your first memory of me?"

"It was summer," he said. "The sun was setting. I'd been practicing outside my house, trying to get my round-house kick for hours. I was tired, and I got sloppy, fell to the ground, knocked my head on the cement, and scraped my knee. You came running out of your house a minute later, wearing overalls and a white t-shirt. Your hair was in these two little doughnuts on your head."

He smiled at the memory.

"I remember you kneeling down, holding up a hand, asking me how many fingers. I must've gotten it right because you ruled out a concussion. Then you touched my knee and bandaged me up. When I asked how you knew what you were doing, you said—"

"I read it in a book," I finished.

Bo nodded and took my hand. "I knew then."

"Knew what?"

"You were it for me, always have been."

"But...then why didn't you tell me?" I asked.

"I don't know if you've noticed," he said, "but I'm not the best with people. Or talking. Or smiling. All the things you do so easily."

Threading my fingers through his, I said, "I don't think you give yourself enough credit, Stryker. Look at all these people from The Academy who came to help. They did that for you. They obviously like you a lot."

"Are they the only ones?"

"No," I said, and he seemed to exhale in relief. "I more than like you, Stryker."

"Good to know."

"But I do have a confession to make."

He looked at me in question.

"Though this may make you want to run in the opposite direction," I said. "That day we met I'd been watching you practice from my window. That's how I knew when you fell."

"Ah," he said.

"And that's not the worst part." I blushed. "I...I've been watching since then. When you work out in the mornings, I wake up pretty much just to see you."

Bo's eyes were bright.

"So," I laughed, "now, that you know what a stalker I am, I'd understand if you want to take back everything you said. Even though..."

"Even though," he prompted.

"Even though I think I'm in love with you," I said softly. "I love how kind you are without even realizing it. I love how you're strong and gentle. I love how you challenge me. And I honestly think you have the sexiest frown I've ever seen."

I shrugged.

"I think I've loved you since the moment you frowned at me."

Bo chuckled then. "Good, because I have a confession too."

I lifted a brow.

"I knew you were watching," he said, stepping closer as my eyes widened. "I wanted you to. That's why I never took my workouts inside, even when the weather was awful."

My smile couldn't be contained. "Seriously?"

He nodded. "My mom and dad used to get so mad about it. They said I'd catch my death. But I didn't care. I needed some connection with you."

"Oh."

"I liked arguing with you too. It made my day."

He laid a kiss against my cheek, and I trembled.

"Since I'm confessing," he murmured, "guess I better get it all out."

"Probably for the best," I said.

"It's true that I went to the library to help my grandma," he said, "but I also went there for you."

My breath hitched.

"Every night, I watched to make sure you got to your car okay."

"You did?"

His lips tipped up ever so slightly. "Guess you're not the only one with secrets."

Lifting up to my toes, I tugged him closer until our foreheads touched.

"I love you," he said quietly.

His words made my heart take flight.

"I love you, too," I said.

And then we kissed. I'd read that ninety-nine percent of the time fiction was better than reality. That was probably true.

But that kiss was the exception.

Bo Stryker was better than fiction.

And I couldn't wait to live our happily-ever-after.

Epilogue

"Your dad hates me."

Bo's voice was serious, but I laughed.

"He doesn't hate you," I said. "You're just the first guy I brought home. This is a totally normal reaction."

"He's glaring at me like he hates me," he said.

Couldn't deny the truth in that statement.

Though we'd had a long talk before Bo arrived, it was almost as if my father couldn't help himself. I'd convinced him not to call in the Kent uncles. That would've been way over the top. But it seemed to make him even more determined.

My dad had been eyeing Bo throughout dinner. Scarlett thought it was hilarious, but Bo was sufficiently freaked out. Even when Bo knocked on the door and handed him the kimchi, even while my dad was wolfing down said kimchi like it was the best thing he'd ever tasted, Dad's glare hadn't wavered.

"It's just his way of looking out for me," I said.

"Least we have that in common," he mumbled.

"Why don't you just scowl back? You're good at that."

Bo looked at me like I was crazy. "And make him hate me more? No thanks, Kent. I want to be with you for a long time."

My heart stuttered.

"I want to be with you too," I replied.

"Still think he might take a swing before the night is over."

Patting his chest, I said, "Guess it's a good thing you're a black belt then."

Scarlett gave me a conspiratorial look then pulled Dad into the other room, saying something to him about discussing her college options for next year. I was grateful. Bo seemed like he needed a pep talk, and I was more than ready to give it to him.

I turned him so that we were facing each other and put my hands on either side of his face.

"Remember what I said about the talk?" I asked.

He nodded.

"It's going to be brutal, Stryker. But you can take it. Remember rule one?"

"Show no fear," he said.

"Rule two?"

"Leo Kent's bark is worse than his bite."

"That's right. My dad's a total marshmallow. You can do it."

Bo wrapped his hands around my waist. "I will do it. For you."

"That's the spirit."

He tilted his head. "Reminds me of another set of rules."

I smiled up at him. "Oh yeah?"

"The first one didn't last 24 hours."

"Yes, because you couldn't keep your hands to yourself."

"Hmmm." As his thumb caressed my side, I bit back a gasp. "Thought we agreed to be open on the physical intimacy."

We had.

"Rule two had an end date. It's been over a month, and we're still together."

"But some of that time we were faking," I put in.

Bo shook his head. "Told you already, Kent. Nothing fake about it."

I swallowed as his gaze held mine.

"And rule three..."

He paused. That was the rule about falling in love. I waited with bated breath to see what he'd say next.

"Well," he said, "I told you they were stupid."

"Whatever, Stryker. They're not—"

"I was already in love with you before we

started," he added, making my jaw drop. "Broke that rule a long time ago."

"You're the best boyfriend ever," I said.

"I know. Still nervous about your dad, though."

"You got this, Flower Boy."

"I meant to tell you, I think you're using that wrong," he said with his usual frown. "Flower boys are a real thing in Korea. They look nothing like me."

"It's not about looks," I said, giving him a wide smile. "And besides, you're gorgeous. You could totally be a member of a K-Pop band. Casey and Natalia agree."

He rolled his eyes. "Oh yeah?"

"We've discussed you at length. You could also be in ads for marshmallows," I said. "Marshmallow Bo would sell the heck out of those."

"You're ridiculous," he said.

"It's a good thing you love me," I said back.

"Yep."

"And I love you, frowns and all." I smiled. "Seriously though, you have so many awesome names: Flower Boy, Marshmallow Bo, Iceman, best boyfriend ever, Stryker, of course. Which do you prefer?"

He shook his head.

"You don't like any of them?" I asked.

"I don't care what you call me," he said. "I just want to be yours."

If my soul wasn't already his, it would've been after that. He'd said it with such conviction, such certainty. And I was melting as he pulled me closer.

"One question, Kent."

"Okay," I breathed, tugging him even closer. He paused with only a breath between us.

"Do you still not believe in happy endings?" he asked.

I looked into his eyes, searched deep inside myself, and found the answer.

"You made me believe again," I said.

Regardless of my dad being in the other room, I kissed Bo with all the love I had inside me, and he kissed me back with just as much feeling. I knew then I'd never doubt it again.

Happiness is a choice.

And I chose Bo.

He was my favorite flower, my marshmallow, my person. As a bookworm, I'd read tons of romance novels with countless happily-ever-afters. I would read a ton more.

And I knew our book would always be my favorite.

* * *

Acknowledgments

Charlotte/Lottie is a bookworm, and I relate to her on so many levels. If you're a book lover, I so hope you see a bit of yourself in her! And Bo...oh, I fell in love with him and his grumpy, swoony ways. I could picture him and Lottie so clearly, and they led me on a hilarious and romantic journey to their HEA. I love them so much, and I hope you did too!

Thank you to my mom and Aunt Colleen for everything—you're my first readers, #1 supporters, and two parts of my heart. Thank you to Aunt Pat, my best friend, the part of my heart that is missing and that I miss every single day. I love all of you so much. You're my favorite marshmallows.

To Stephanie Mooney for the beautiful ebook cover! You're amazing, and I'm so grateful for you.

To my wonderful ARC readers: You rock!!! I'm so thankful to you for your support and help with spreading the word about BOOKWORM! Seriously, I can't thank you enough!

To anyone who loved Snow & Ash from NINJA GIRL! I hope you loved seeing them again and enjoyed reading about their son!

To anyone who spotted all the character crossovers: Thank you so much for supporting my books! I loved, loved, loved writing those scenes, and I hope you loved reading them!

Thank you so much to the readers who leave a review, tell a friend about BOOKWORM, and help spread the word! As an introvert and indie, I appreciate you more than I can say! Thank you!!!

To librarians, you are awesome. Thank you for taking care of the books and helping readers find their favorite reads.

To libraries and books, thank you for existing and being a much-needed escape for so many.

To Bookworms: no matter what, keep reading what you love! Keep spreading the love of books!

And to YOU!!! Thank you so much for reading this book! Oh, I hope you loved Lottie & Bo as much as I loved writing them! This is book baby #13, the fastest full-length book I've written, and it was like a breath of fresh air. That's how I think love is sometimes. Like the best books, it fills you up, lifts the spirit, and steals your heart. I hope BOOKWORM made you laugh, swoon, and believe in happily-ever-after. Sometimes reality is better than fiction.

And I truly hope your life is full of family, friends, marshmallows, books, true love and HEA.

About the Author

Cookie O'Gorman writes stories filled with humor and heart for the nerd in all of us. Fiery first kisses, snappy dialogue, smart girls, swoonworthy boys, and unbreakable friendships are featured in each of her books.

Cookie is a hopeless romantic, a Harry Potter aficionado, and a supporter of all things dork. Chocolate, Chinese food, and Asian dramas are her kryptonite. Above all, she believes that real life has enough sorrow and despair—which is why she always tries to give her characters a happy ending. She is the author of *Adorkable*, *Ninja Girl*, *The Unbelievable, Inconceivable, Unforeseeable Truth About Ethan Wilder*, *The Good Girl's Guide to Being Bad*,

COOKIE O'GORMAN

Wallflower, *Cupcake*, *Fauxmance*, and *Bookworm*. She is also the author of NA sports romances, *The Best Mistake*, *The Perfect Play*, and *The Sweetest Game*.

Whether it's about her books or just to fan-girl, Cookie would love to hear from you!

Website: cookieogorman.com

Instagram: www.instagram.com/cookieogorman

Facebook: www.facebook.com/cookieogorman

For the latest news on Cookie's books, access to fun, free content and monthly giveaways, subscribe to *The Cookie Jar* Newsletter!

Printed in Dunstable, United Kingdom

66622006R00224